I0657819

Artemis Rex

Ultra Meridian Series: Book 2

Theo Mann

Invisible Publishing Company

Ultra Meridian Series

Contents

Chapter 1

The *Artemis Rex* screamed past Minius OLY4, caught the sun's gravity, and hurtled out of range into black space, but Reserve Wing Daggers hounded it all the way.

A punishing Howitzer barrage slammed the EM shields on the starboard side and sent the little Drifter tumbling wing over wing.

Bandit gunned the engines and jammed his stick hard to port to roll the *Artemis Rex* farther in that direction.

"Another four Stalwarts coming in fast!" Rodeo reported from tactical. "Are you sure you don't want to arm accessory cradles?"

"To hell with it!" Sheriff Mace Davenport called back. "Arm and return fire!"

"It's about damn time!" Rodeo activated the communications link on his console. He barked into it to the accessory Howitzer positions behind the cockpit. "Fire at will, boys! You have my permission to send those bastards back where they came from."

Cheers broke out from the ship's rear compartment as the Chorion Team laid into the Confederate Corps Reserve Wing with every gun blazing.

The incoming Stalwarts rocketed past the sun to hound the *Artemis Rex* far and away. Bandit couldn't drive the engines any harder. The Daggers streaked alongside and engaged with the gunners.

Bandit ripped his stick back to starboard. He slammed the throttle into reverse and the *Artemis Rex* spun sideways into a skid. The ship twirled backward and Bandit punched it for all he was worth. He bolted back toward the Confederacy that the crew just escaped.

"You're going the wrong way!" Davenport yelled.

"I know what way I'm going, Sir. Just sit tight and we'll teach these assholes a lesson they won't forget."

"Seven Nitrols moving to intercept from Macron Calypso!" Rodeo reported.

"Good," Bandit muttered his breath. "We'll hold a damn tea party for the whole Reserve Wing. That will make it more fun for all of us."

"We don't want to......" Davenport began.

Another blistering assault from the Daggers cut him off. They swatted the *Artemis Rex* to port only to drive the ship into the Stalwarts' guns. The Stalwarts couldn't keep up with the fast-moving Drifter, but with the Nitrols moving in, they didn't have to.

The *Artemis Rex* whizzed between them in a corkscrew dive, but the Daggers kept up all the way. The Drifter trembled from the accessory cradles slamming back and forth.

Reserve Wing ships attacked from all sides. Howitzer fire exploded all over the hull. A deadly halo of shots erupted from all the cradles at once, but it wasn't enough.

Bandit plunged for the same sun he used to slingshot himself away. "Where the hell are you going?" Davenport yelled over the noise. "You'll take us all the way back to Ultra Meridian if you keep this up."

Bandit didn't answer. He growled something under his breath and plunged the Drifter into the sun's gravitational field. Heat radiated through the hull and the boys in the rear stopped shooting.

Davenport made a quick check of his onboard systems, but he already saw it was no good. The Reserve Wing ships didn't enter the sun's orbit, but they didn't leave the Drifter alone. They flanked the ship outside the sun's halo, but they couldn't hit the *Artemis Rex* as long as it stayed inside the outer umbra.

The EM shields protected the Drifter from the heat, but Davenport and his friends couldn't stay in here forever.

A second later, Bandit ripped the ship out of the field, made a mad dash back the way he came, and the Reserve Wing pounced. Daggers and Nitrols surrounded the little ship in hundreds of shots.

The accessory guns vibrated the hull, but Davenport couldn't tell if the boys landed any shots in this mayhem.

He caught a fleeting glimpse of Ultra Meridian gliding past him and then Bandit hammered the throttle to the limit.

He steered directly back toward the sun, and this time, he didn't aim for an orbital trajectory.

"Go! Go! Go!" Rodeo roared from behind.

"No!" Davenport yelled.

Bandit didn't respond to either of them. He crushed his stick in both hands and beads of sweat stood out on the back of his neck. He crouched over his controls hardly moving a muscle. His shoulders strained with the effort of holding the ship on course.

"All accessory cradles withdraw!" Rodeo ordered. "Pull back inside!"

"No!" Davenport roared.

No one answered him. Bandit hunched his shoulders just a little more. A howling shriek trembled through the ship as the Daggers closed in. Their gunfire pounded the hull and an alarm shrieked from the EM shields.

Davenport glanced down to see the shields buckling under the effort of holding the ship intact. He almost said something else when Rodeo switched off the alarm.

A dangerous silence fell over the cockpit. The sun loomed huge and gleaming beyond the front window. Davenport gulped and almost looked away. He couldn't watch the sun growing bigger until it blocked out his whole view.

The Daggers veered into the starboard wing and jostled the *Artemis Rex* into the Nitrols on the other side. They bumped the ship back and forth bombarding it with gunfire.

Another alarm startled Davenport out of his trance, but Rodeo turned this one off before Davenport had a chance to read it.

Rodeo adjusted readings and instruments with lightning speed, but Davenport couldn't look away from the sun. It throbbed with light and heat. He squinted in the blinding intensity.

All at once, Bandit jerked upright and bellowed at full volume. "Now!"

All the accessory cradles exploded at the same moment. They spouted shots on both Reserve Wing flanks and the Reserve Wing attacked with murderous ferocity. They swerved inward unloading all their guns on the *Artemis Rex*.

The Drifter's hull crashed under the assault, but at that moment, Bandit flung himself back in his cradle. He hauled the stick back with all his strength. He wedged his heels against the console fighting the G force.

He forced the throttle all the way down and the *Artemis Rex* plowed upward in a brutal climb. He did it so fast that the Reserve Wing didn't have time to react.

The Reserve Wing ships plunged nose first into the sun while the *Artemis Rex* soared through the sun's orbit to rocket out the other side.

"Woo-hoo!" Rodeo cheered. "That's my boy! That's what I'm talking about!"

Laughter and whoops broke out in the accessory cradles, but Davenport couldn't breathe. He stared in stupid disbelief at the sun's light fading beyond the cockpit window. Black sky and twinkling stars took its place as the *Artemis Rex* raced away to safety.

The Stalwarts rotated to confront the ship when it got near them, but *Artemis Rex* was flying too fast to stop. The Stalwarts opened fire, but Bandit dodged between them and put on speed.

"Ha ha!" he burst out. "Too slow, suckers! Better luck next time!"

The Stalwarts fired their engines to pursue the Drifter, but in a second, the ship left them far behind, too.

Bandit collapsed back in his cradle. Sweat drenched his shirt and he passed his wrist across his forehead. "Phew! That was close."

"That one is definitely going in *Bandit's Greatest Hits*, boy!" Rodeo told him. "You're the man!"

Bandit let out weak laughter and glanced over his shoulder. He caught Davenport's eye and laughed again when Davenport blinked at him in dumb shock. Who the hell was this kid? Davenport had never seen anyone fly like that—not ever.

"Sacron Enigma coming up in fourteen hundred lightyears," Rodeo reported. "More Reserve Wing ships launching from Macron Calypso, but they're nowhere near close enough to intercept us."

"Where should we go, Sir?" Bandit turned back to his instruments. "This place is endless."

Davenport dragged his attention back to the present and searched the navigation chart in front of him. "We need somewhere to hide the Ithium cartridge and the chip. We need to find a way to make sure Admiral Joyce doesn't get his hands on them again."

"Sacron Enigma is a pretty big place," Rodeo pointed out. "The options are wide open."

"Get across the border and get us good and lost. We'll work out the fine points later."

Bandit gunned the *Artemis Rex* over the boundary and Davenport suffered a pang of disappointment when he bid the Confederacy goodbye. So many miles had passed under the bridge since he left Ultra Meridian and he couldn't see any way back.

He dedicated his life to the law and now he was on the run like any common criminal. Everyone in the world who cared if he lived or died was a known criminal or a fugitive just like he was. He would have arrested them all, but they were all he had left.

He watched the charts while Bandit did what he said. The *Artemis Rex* ventured farther and farther into unknown space until not much turned up on the charts at all. What would the crew find out here?

Davenport unbuckled from his harness and climbed out of his cradle. He went aft and found Dice, Fiddler, Beauty, and Emmet in the galley.

They sat in their safety seats and wore their own protective harnesses. The four friends passed food back and forth and chatted like they didn't know anything about the deadly battle that almost destroyed the ship—again.

Fiddler handed Beauty an open packet of small white chips. "Do you like cocoa-bears, Beauty? These ones are fresh. I've only had the stale ones. The fresh ones taste completely different."

He took the packet out of her hands and jammed the whole thing into his mouth, wrapper and all. A cloud of white powder billowed around his swollen cheeks when he tried to wedge his lips around the food.

"Hey!" Emmet roared. "I wanted some of those."

Beauty pulled the empty, saliva-drenched wrapper from his mouth and blinked his big eyes first at Emmett and then up at Davenport. White powder covered his face and made him look ghostly and skeletal.

He started chewing and more white dust puffed between his lips when he tried to close them around the wad of food.

Dice strained against his harness, pulled a glass bottle from a crate at his heel, hacked off the top with his other hand, and guzzled the contents. He put the empty bottle back in the crate and pulled out another to repeat the whole process.

"You might want to leave some of that for the boys," Davenport told him. "I think they'll want to celebrate once we land."

"Are we landing anytime soon?" Dice boomed.

"I have no idea."

"Then what they don't know won't hurt them." Dice lopped off another one and drained it in a few gulps.

"Slow down, hotshot," Fiddler told him. "We'll need you sober if we have to shoot anything."

"Hmmpff!" Dice grunted. "If we have to shoot anything, you won't want me sober. Trust me."

Davenport turned away and headed down the gangway to the crew quarters. He came to a compartment and stepped into the shadows.

A single small light gave him a dim view of the cabin and the still figure lying on the bunk. The stars whispered past the ship beyond the one tiny window.

Davenport eased over to the bed and looked down at Lyons's sleeping face. The starlight shone on her closed eyelids.

A panel next to her bed showed readings on her vital signs and everything read as normal. Davenport came down here to check on the injuries she sustained helping him escape from Pandora's Needle. She looked fine, but he couldn't bring himself to wake her up.

He started to turn away when another shudder rumbled through the ship. His eyes shot to the window and his heart stopped when another four ships rushed into view.

He didn't recognize them. They definitely didn't belong to the Reserve Wing. Of course they didn't. He was in the middle of Sacron Enigma. The Reserve Wing wouldn't come out this far.

The forwardmost ship rotated in front of his eyes and his stomach turned when he saw an alien in the cockpit. Davenport didn't even know what species it was, but he would have to be blind not to see the guns rotating to target the *Artemis Rex*.

He whirled away in time for another pounding assault to hit the *Artemis Rex* on the port side. The blow knocked him off his feet. He barely got his arms up to stop himself from pitching on top of Lyons.

She shot awake with a gasp and bolted upright staring in all directions. "What......? Where....?"

Davenport laid his hand on her arm. "Easy. Lie down. We're...."

"We're under attack!" She glanced out the window and her expression changed. "What the hell is *that*?"

"We're in Sacron Enigma. Stay here. I'll find out what's up."

"I can see what's up."

She tried to get out of bed, but Davenport stopped her. "You'll only make a mess of yourself and none of us wants to go through that again. Lie down and leave this to the experts." Another barrage shook the *Artemis Rex* and Davenport tore himself away. "Stay here."

He stepped out onto the gangway to find Breeze, Wolf, and Laub scrambling to get back into their accessory cradles. Breeze fell over himself and would have stopped the other two from getting their hands on their weapons, but Wolf hauled off and shoved the clumsy boy away with unusual ferocity.

Breeze crashed down on the gangway in front of Davenport while Wolf and Laub dove back into their cradles. The rest of the Chorion Team hadn't made it out of their cradles since the first battle. They manned the Howitzers while alien ships swerved back and forth outside the hull.

Davenport raced for the cockpit, but the impacts of enemy fire stopped him from getting to his cradle. "What the hell is going on?"

"You can see what's going on!" Rodeo yelled back. "We're under attack!"

"Who are they? Why are they attacking us?"

"How the hell should I know? Maybe we encroached on their territory. We don't know anything about these aliens. Sacron Enigma is unknown. That's what unknown means—it means we don't know anything about it."

Bandit hit the throttle again, but he only wound up soaring into another cloud of attackers. They buzzed around the *Artemis Rex* in droves.

"We don't even know if we're flying deeper into their territory!" Bandit cried.

"We can't let them shoot down the ship," Davenport told him. "They might destroy the Ithium."

"That would definitely keep it out of Admiral Joyce's hands, wouldn't it?"

"To hell with the Ithium!" Rodeo countered. "I'm more concerned about us!"

Bandit put on speed, but when the boys in the accessory cradles opened fire, the aliens struck with incredible force. They increased speed to a wild blur. They revolved around the *Artemis Rex* so fast the ship's instruments couldn't keep up with them.

Rodeo's sensitive fingers danced over the controls trying to track the aliens' movements. "Holy shit! What the hell are they doing?"

"Get us out of here, Bandit!" Davenport ordered.

"I can't! They're matching us move for move. We can't get away!"

Another blast punched the ship from behind and Davenport staggered. "They're overcoming our shields!" Rodeo reported. "They'll destroy the ship in a second!"

"Get out of here, Bandit!" Davenport bellowed.

Bandit shook his head in desperation and drove the throttle forward. He aimed the ship's nose toward a random planet to pull one of his feints, but at that moment, a crushing blow hit the ship hard from port.

"The engine is hit!" Rodeo reported. "We can't keep up this speed."

"Get us on the ground," Davenport ordered.

"What about the aliens?" Rodeo asked.

"We'll deal with that later. They might not be able to follow us down to the surface."

Rodeo sneered at him. "Please."

Davenport leaned over him and pointed at the chart. "That one has an oxygen atmosphere. Land the ship, Bandit. We won't be going anywhere without that engine anyway."

Chapter 2

Davenport returned to the galley to find the whole Chorion Team already there. Coon took one of the few remaining bottles out of the crate that Dice had almost completely demolished.

Coon gazed at the label and a fond smile spread over his face. "Rose Blossom 1700! I always liked this stuff."

"Whatever happened to Ekol Thaine not letting you boys drink on the job?" Emmet asked.

"This stuff doesn't affect Chorions." Coon twisted off the cap and sniffed at the opening. "Mmmm. I could drink this stuff all day."

"Not with Dice around, you couldn't." Fiddler unbuckled her harness. "What was all the shooting about? Are we over the line or what?"

"There's another group of aliens out there shooting at us." Alla picked up the empty Cocoa-bears wrapper and shook out the last crumbs. "Don't tell me you ate all the food."

"Beauty was hungry."

"He can't be hungry anymore," Dice rumbled. "He just ate."

"If he isn't hungry anymore, he can come help us fix the engine," Davenport replied. "All of you can come help out."

"'Help' and 'out' are two words that aren't part of my vocabulary," Dice growled.

"You just said them." Fiddler slapped a spanner into his hand. "You can hold the engine up while the rest of us weld them into place."

She and Emmett headed for the door, but Laub dodged into their path. He held up his burly arm in front of them. "You all stay here. We'll handle the repairs."

"Seriously," Fiddler countered. "We can help."

"No." Axel and Coon swiveled in to stand next to Laub. "You stay here. Seriously."

Bandit and Rodeo strolled in at that moment. "What's going on?"

"We need to repair the engine," Davenport replied. "We were just about to head out there to take a look."

"No," Rodeo returned. "You all stay here. We'll deal with the engine."

"What's your problem?" Dice thundered. "We can repair the engine as well as you can and Beauty can probably repair it a hell of a lot better."

"I don't care. This is our ship. You're just passengers." Rodeo jerked his thumb at his friends. "Let's go. The sooner we fix it, the sooner we can figure out what those aliens were doing."

"You better pull your head in, kid," Dice boomed. "Someone bigger than you might decide to squash that fat attitude of yours."

Rodeo turned around very slowly and his milky white eyes narrowed at nothing. His expression went ice cold and the rest of the Chorion Team sidestepped together on both sides of him.

Rodeo stiffened and a charge of tension went through the room. Davenport stepped in and stuck his arm between the Chorion Team and the other four.

"Okay, okay. Let's not turn this into a fight. We have enough trouble just surviving this place. You boys get your tools and go to work. We might be safe on this planet for now as long as those aliens don't come back."

"What the hell are you doing?" Dice roared. "They're just kids."

"Rodeo is right," Davenport replied. "It's their ship and they know how to work on it. If they need your help, they'll ask for it."

The Chorion Team inched toward the door, but not without plenty of backward glances toward the other four.

As soon as they left, Fiddler, Dice, and Emmett rounded on Davenport. "Don't tell me you expect us to step and fetch for a bunch of kids," Fiddler told him. "We have as much right to say what happens on this ship as they do."

"I don't even want to tell you how stupid that sounds," Davenport countered. "Now all of you arm up and go outside. We might need to defend the ship while the boys are working on it."

The others grumbled, but they finally did what he said. They got their weapons and stepped out onto the planet.

Laub, Axel, Coon, Breeze, and Bandit were already welding on the engine housing while Alla brought them supplies from inside. Wolf shadowed Davenport over to Rodeo's side.

The boy stood off to one side checking something on a handheld device. "What can you find out about this place?"

"You were right about the oxygen atmosphere."

Davenport snorted. "I figured that much since we're standing here talking about it. What else?"

Rodeo shrugged and lowered the device. He cocked his head and pricked up his ears to listen. "You can probably tell me more than I can tell you. This place doesn't look inhabited."

Davenport surveyed the surroundings. The ship sat on its landing gear in the middle of a towering forest hundreds of feet tall. Only the dimmest light made it to the ground and cast the surface in perpetual shadow.

The soil squished underfoot without actually oozing any water from the spongy moss. Clicks and buzzes came from high in the canopy, but no other life forms moved down here on the ground.

Dice, Fiddler, and Emmet migrated around the ship patrolling the surroundings with their XQs ready, but nothing came to attack the crew.

"We should hide the Ithium here," Rodeo suggested. "We should make it as difficult to find as possible. Maybe the Admiral's people will never find it and then the Ithium will be safe."

Davenport grimaced at the surroundings. "How would *we* find it again? We would have to stand guard over the Ithium to make sure no one else got it."

Rodeo inclined his head the other way. He turned his unseeing eyes toward Davenport without actually looking at him. "How exactly did you plan to stop the Admiral from getting the Ithium? What did you plan to do with it once you got it?"

"I didn't really get that far in my planning. I was more concerned with stopping him from getting it back. I wasn't even doing that at first. I just wanted to stay alive."

"You maybe want to think about it now. Even if we found a way to take it back to the Confederacy, there's nowhere safe you can turn it in. Even if you found someone trustworthy to take it off your hands, the admiral would only go after them next."

Davenport chuckled and squeezed the boy's shoulder. "That's what I keep you around for, boy. You always know how to cheer me up."

"Think about it. You could have handed the Ithium to Sheriff Healey. He would have taken it back to Pandora's Needle—if he took it at all—but the Admiral would only track him down. That Ithium isn't safe anywhere."

"Then it isn't here, either. We might as well keep it on board."

Just then, a shout went up from Laud and Axel on top of the engine housing. Laub pushed back his welding mask, scanned the ground, and spotted Rodeo and Davenport talking.

"We got damage to the ion reverter," Axel called out. "This is gonna take a while."

"Wouldn't you know it?" Dice growled. He stalked around the *Artemis Rex's* other side and stumbled. He supported himself against the hull for a second.

Coon laughed at him. "Take it easy on the Rose Blossom next time, big guy."

Dice growled something under his breath, heaved himself to his feet, and staggered on. He lurched around the other side of the ship, doubled over, and hurled into the undergrowth.

The boys burst out laughing and Dice's enraged bellows answered them from behind the ship.

Fiddler planted herself by the hatch and balanced her XQ on her hip. She cast flinty gazes out at the forest.

Beauty came to the hatch entrance and peered out. His large ears swiveled toward the forest, but he didn't venture to the ground.

Alla passed him on his way back outside. Alla sweated under the burden of a large carton of steel fins and Beauty dodged out of his path with a frightened squeak.

Rodeo raised his device again and frowned at it. "That's weird."

Davenport turned to ask him what he meant when a tempest wind shook the treetops. Everyone looked up to see three spaceships pivot overhead. They shone lights into the trees, but the high canopy hid the *Artemis Rex*.

Bandit dove off the engine housing. "Get to the cockpit, boy! We have to mask our presence."

Rodeo shoved his device into Davenport's hands. Rodeo and Bandit bolted up the ramp and disappeared inside. Beauty sprang out of their way. He kept looking into the trees and then behind him to the ship's interior.

Davenport glanced at the thing Rodeo had been working on. The screen on its surface was totally black. That didn't do Davenport much good, so he followed the boys inside.

Thumps and sizzling sounds from a welding torch echoed through the ship on his way to the cockpit. "Were those the same aliens that shot at us?"

"These ships have Reserve Wing identity profiles," Rodeo replied. '

"The Reserve Wing! They can't be all the way out here."

"They don't belong to the Reserve Wing. They have Reserve Wing profiles, but these ships belong to another group. They're mercenaries."

"I'll take care of them." Bandit activated the accessory cradles.

He swiveled the guns upward to fire, but Rodeo stopped him. "Don't. We're masked. They can't see us."

"Yeah, but...."

"If you fire on them, you'll be showing them exactly where we are." Rodeo jerked his thumb at Davenport. "You better go outside and tell the others not to fire, either."

Davenport did as Rodeo said and just in time. Dice and Fiddler had been aiming their XQs at the mercenaries, too.

Rodeo came back. "What are they hanging around for?" Davenport asked.

"They probably followed us. We can expect a lot of that out here. We're new which makes us a target."

Everyone kept the strangers in view while the boys finished welding the ship. Laub and Axel hopped down and started putting their stuff away.

"Is the *Artemis Rex* ready to fly?" Rodeo asked.

"Not entirely. We still have to repair the ion reverter."

"How long will that take?"

"As long as it takes."

The two boys headed inside and Rodeo turned back to Davenport. "We might as well get comfortable here for a while."

Davenport jutted his chin at the device in Rodeo's hand. "What are you doing with that?"

"I was checking the area for life forms."

"Did you find any?"

"That's the weird thing." Rodeo squinted at the blank, black screen. "There aren't any to find."

"That's impossible." Davenport pointed up at the canopy. "We can see and hear them moving around up there right now. They have to be there."

"That's what I'm saying. They don't show up on here."

"What is that thing, anyway? Is that one of your inventions?"

Rodeo started to answer when a strong gust of wind kicked the treetops into a flurry. They thrashed and tossed in the engine wash as the same mercenary craft veered over the area.

Dice and Fiddler pivoted their guns upward, but the ship was already wheeling away. In a second, it disappeared out of sight. "Good riddance," Davenport muttered.

"If it isn't them, it will be someone else." Rodeo lowered his device to his side. "This thing is useless here. There must be something in the atmosphere that stops it from working."

"Either that or something in the lifeforms stops you from detecting them." Davenport turned to Wolf. The boy had stood silent through the whole conversation, but Davenport never doubted Wolf had been listening to everything. He never missed anything. "Can you pick up anything out there? Can you sense any life forms out there that we don't know about?"

The boy flared his nostrils to sniff the air. He cocked his head from side to side and his small, black eyes flashed with menace when he scanned the dim trees. He bared his pointed teeth and snarled into the shadows.

"I knew it!" Rodeo hissed. "There *is* something out there!"

"Why isn't it threatening us?" Davenport asked. "If it's just watching, it might not be dangerous."

Rodeo snorted. "Everything out here is dangerous in one way or the other. I'm going to see what's taking the boys so long."

He vanished inside the ship. Wolf didn't move. He and Davenport gazed out into the woods. The area appeared deserted, but that was obviously a trick.

Something was out there. Wolf kept bristling at nothing and even Davenport felt it. Someone was watching them, so why didn't they attack?

Wolf growled again. Davenport couldn't stand around looking at trees for the rest of his life.

He went over to Fiddler. Dice and Emmett had given up searching the area for something that wasn't there. Emmett approached Fiddler from the other side and Dice was already sitting down on the hatch ramp.

"What's the story?" Fiddler asked. "How long do we have to hang around here before we can go......?" She trailed off.

"Go where?" Dice boomed. "There's nowhere to go. We're in Sacron Enigma, for Christ's sake. It's the end of the line. It's the ass end of nothing."

"Stay on your toes." Davenport waved toward the trees. "There's something out there."

"There's nothing out there," Dice countered. "This whole planet is a dead zone."

"It definitely isn't that."

Fiddler peered into the trees. "I don't see anything. Did Rodeo pick something up?"

"No, but...."

Wolf cut Davenport off by whipping around backward and letting out an even more vicious snarl. He bared his teeth and all the fur on his back and shoulders stood on end.

"There's nothing out there!" Dice rumbled. "You're jumping at shadows."

"I doubt that." Davenport's hand flew to his sidearm and he pivoted to stand next to Wolf. He aimed his weapon at the forest. "I'm telling you something is out there."

Fiddler and Emmet leveled their XQs toward the spot Wolf was looking at, but they still didn't see anything.

"What's out there, boy?" Davenport whispered to Wolf.

The boy kept hissing and spitting at the undergrowth. His nostrils flared and his eyes narrowed to slits. He jerked an inch to his right and then back to his left.

"Give it up!" Dice propped his XQ against his knee. "There's nothing there."

Laub, Alla, and Axel came out of the ship carrying some more gear and supplies. Their chipper voices cut the tension. "And then I said to him, 'Dipper? I don't even know her!'"

All three exploded in laughter until Axel stopped on the ramp and stared at Fiddler and Davenport. "Is something wrong?"

"These four are hallucinating," Dice muttered. "It turns out Rose Blossom affects Chorions after all."

"Wolf doesn't hallucinate." Axel set his stuff down and crossed to Wolf's side. "What is it, boy?"

"Something's out there," Davenport repeated.

Axel spun around. "Arm up! We got company!"

The instant the words left his mouth, a fountain of rockets erupted from the trees exactly where Wolf had been facing.

The shots separated into five comets blasting through the clearing. One of them exploded right in front of Wolf and Davenport. Wolf collapsed at Davenport's feet and Davenport sprang forward to straddle Wolf's fallen body.

Davenport swept his sidearm back and forth across the trees, but he still couldn't see anything. He couldn't tell who was firing at him, so he couldn't shoot back.

Another rocket corkscrewed for the open hatch and detonated on the hull directly over Dice's head. He roared in fury, vaulted to his feet, snatched his XQ, and stormed over to join the others.

He, Emmett, and Fiddler stalked forward and started unloading on the spot. They didn't make it more than a few yards before more rockets sprayed from all over.

They exploded in the dirt around the crew's feet, against the *Artemis Rex*, and in the air overhead. Davenport heard the others yelling. Another rocket twisted out of a different part of the forest over by the ship's nose and slammed Fiddler in the back.

She hit the dirt and Emmett pounced on her yelling for her to get up. Dice bellowed louder than ever. He sidestepped and positioned himself over Fiddler.

Dice jerked his mighty XQ in all directions firing into the trees. He pounded the area with shots, but nothing stopped the rockets.

Davenport couldn't wait a second longer. He seized Wolf's wrist and dragged the unconscious boy over to Fiddler. Davenport snatched Fiddler's XQ and turned back-to-back with Dice.

They bombarded the surrounding forest. Davenport tried to target the places the rockets came from, but he still couldn't see anyone. Every time he and Dice smashed the undergrowth where the rockets came from, the shots seemed to move somewhere else.

Another burst of explosions scorched from a different location to Dice's right. He rotated that way, and as soon as he turned his back on Davenport, a rocket launched from the original spot.

The rocket smashed Dice in the face and he buckled like a ton of bricks. His giant horned head slammed against the ramp and he flopped to the ground.

The next instant, armed men swarmed out of the bushes by the dozen. Davenport took a split second to realize they were all human and they all carried Confederate-issue XQs. They could only be the mercenaries who tracked the crew here in the first place.

Chapter 3

D avenport pressed a piece of cloth to Wolf's head. The boy let out a blood-curdling yowl and jerked away. He bared his teeth and snarled at Davenport in murderous fury and slapped Davenport's hand away.

Davenport sighed and held out the rag to him. "Here. You do it, but you have to stop the bleeding. It's getting all over your face."

"This is just great," Dice growled under his breath. "Whose brilliant idea was this, anyway?"

"Which part?" Fiddler asked from his other side.

"Let me see if I can put the puzzle pieces together," Dice went on. "Lyons, Beauty, and I were flying through space minding our own business when Porkchop McLawdog here decided to break into our ship, steal our cargo, and drag us off to Terminus Anathema for no good reason. Four weeks later, here we are trapped in a cage as prisoners to some lunatic fringe elements that want to eviscerate us and devour our internal organs in some mystic rite of cosmic unification."

Fiddler laughed, but she was the only one who did.

Davenport didn't answer at all. Their situation was no laughing matter. He rotated over to Wolf's side and propped his back and shoulders against the wall. From here, he could see every miserable detail of the mammoth problem facing the *Artemis Rex* crew.

Dice, Beauty, Davenport, Fiddler, Emmett, and the eight boys sat crammed into a tiny cage that definitely wasn't big enough for them all. It was barely big enough for Dice by himself. The rest had to sandwich in shoulder to shoulder just to find places to sit.

Beauty, Alla, and Rodeo were the only ones without injuries. The mercenaries who stormed the *Artemis Rex* insisted on beating everyone into submission even after they surrendered.

The mercenaries only spared Beauty, Alla, and Rodeo because they were inside the ship at the time. The mercenaries overwhelmed the *Artemis Rex* with numbers. Those three never even raised a weapon in their own defense.

Davenport didn't get a chance to check on Lyons before the mercenaries dragged everyone off to their own ship.

He *did* see the mercenaries check the Drifter to see if anyone else was on board, but they didn't bring Lyons out when they captured the crew. Was Lyons dead? Why else would they just ignore her and leave her behind?

At least she wasn't trapped here with a bunch of surly, bleeding aliens with more attitude than sense.

The ship clanged outside their cage. "This cage is constructed into the cargo hold wall." Rodeo turned his ear toward the hull behind Davenport. "I'm guessing they do this kind of thing a lot."

"How did they know about us?" Fiddler asked. "I could understand aliens trying to drive us out of their territory, but these guys are all human."

"Their ships have Reserve Wing profiles," Bandit pointed out. "They can only have come from one place."

"I think we're about to find out," Davenport breathed. "Here they come."

A bunch of burly, tattooed, scruffy characters stomped across the cargo hold toward the cage. All the mercenaries carried giant weapons and many sported thick beards in states of filth and neglect. No way could these men belong to the Reserve Wing, no matter what they were flying.

They stationed themselves in a ring around the cage and one of them stepped forward. He wasn't the biggest. In fact, he was the smallest by size and his XQ couldn't have been more than a 65.

He jutted his chin at Davenport and the man's eyes dipped to Davenport's star. "Who the hell are you?"

"Who the hell are *you*, jackass?" Dice rumbled. "You better let us out of here before I shove that XQ where the sun don't shine."

"What the hell are you doing way out here?" The guy nodded at Davenport's star again. "That don't mean shit out here."

"It might not mean anything to you, but it means something to me," Davenport replied. "Your tats don't mean shit to me, but you don't hear me telling you to take them off."

Davenport didn't mean it as a joke, but Dice let out a loud, booming laugh. He blared in the guy's face so loudly that everyone jumped, including some of the mercenaries.

Davenport winced at the sound, but Dice's laughter unsettled the mercenaries so much that Davenport let it slide.

"Who the hell are you?" Davenport demanded. "What are you doing flying Reserve Wing ships in Sacron Enigma? Did you steal these ships?"

"Steal them! We bought and paid for them.... just like we'll get paid for dragging your sorry ass back to Admiral Joyce."

Davenport stiffened. "So you're working for him? Is that it?"

"That's right." The guy leveled his XQ straight at Davenport. "We'll get paid and you'll go straight to hell."

"So you already know who I am," Davenport began. "That means we can all stop pretending and you don't have to ask me anymore why I'm here or why I'm wearing this star. Now tell me who *you* are."

"I'm Boss Creed and these...." He nodded to the men flanking him. "These are the Mad Men."

Fiddler gasped and Dice muttered, "Shit!"

Davenport stiffened and Wolf growled low under his breath again.

"That's right, you pieces of shit. Maybe now you'll show a little respect." Creed raised his XQ to aim at the ceiling. "Anyway, none of that matters 'cuz we're taking you back to the Confederacy just as soon as we get word on where to rendezvous with the Admiral."

Davenport frowned, but he didn't say anything. He had been bracing himself for some kind of interrogation scene, but before he could open his mouth, Creed and the others stalked away.

A few went to work in the cargo hold where the prisoners could see them. Others left for the Nitrol's other decks. Davenport waited for them to come back, but they didn't. They all just ignored the prisoners after that.

"What the hell just happened?" Laub asked.

"We got captured by the Mad Men," Axel replied. "We're screwed."

"Why didn't he ask about the Ithium?" Fiddler asked.

"Maybe they don't know about it," Rodeo suggested. "I can see Admiral Joyce hiring the Mad Men to track us into Sacron Enigma and bring us back to him without actually telling them why he wanted us."

"Admiral Joyce won't be happy if the Mad Men take us back to the Confederacy without the Ithium and the chip," Bandit remarked.

"I doubt he'll care," Davenport replied. "If the Mad Men turn us over to him without the stuff, he'll just send them back out here to search the *Artemis Rex*."

"Which means we have to get the stuff off the ship as soon as possible," Rodeo agreed. "We need to stash it somewhere he won't find it."

"Where's that?" Coon asked.

"Hey, chickens!" Dice boomed. "In case you hadn't realized, we're locked in this shit-ass cage with no way to get out."

"Why don't you show us all how tough you are and bend the bars to get us out of here?" Fiddler suggested.

Dice grunted something and turned to the bars. "I might be able to...."

A bunch of the boys had to squash themselves into a corner just to get out of his way. Dice didn't notice them scrambling to sit on top of each other. Breeze accidentally stepped on Wolf's foot and Wolf let out another blood-chilling screech before shoving Breeze off.

Dice scowled at the bars for a second and then gripped them in his meaty fists. He flexed his enormous back to pull the bars apart. He heaved and snarled and groaned, but they didn't budge.

"God damn it!" he roared and shot to his feet.

The boys fell over each other crowding to the other side of the cage. More had to sit on top of each other and Wolf and Coon both ended up sitting on Davenport's lap.

Dice heaved to his feet and jammed his powerful shoulders hard against the cage roof. The metal creaked and the whole cage rocked and banged against the anchor bolts.

"You're doing it!" Rodeo called. "Just a little more and you'll break it out."

Davenport didn't see Dice making any headway, but Davenport didn't argue. Rodeo's encouragement spurred Dice to even greater feats of rage.

He bent his knees and smashed his shoulders upward into the ceiling. Tearing sounds echoed through the hold and the nearest Mad Men turned around to look.

Dice widened his stance and stepped on Coon's leg. The boy shrieked in pain until Davenport hauled him the rest of the way out of danger, but nowhere was safe. Dice lost all awareness of everyone around him in his single-minded determination to break the cage in half.

One of the anchor bolts stripped out of the back wall. The noise escalated to a deafening pitch mingled with Dice's furious bellows.

Two of the Mad Men picked up their XQs and came over. One of the biggest guys leveled his weapon at Dice through the bars. "Stop that! Sit down before I open fire!"

Dice either didn't hear or pretended not to. He kept smashing his giant body upward into the cage ceiling. He banged huge dents in the metal and finally managed to bend several of the bars. Two more anchor bolts tore out and the cage tilted violently.

Davenport shrank even farther into the corner. He plastered his body on top of Fiddler and the boys in some vain attempt to protect them from Dice's madness. Dice seemed to be growing bigger by the second. Davenport didn't see how the cage could possibly hold him.

The two guys standing outside became more agitated. The bigger one stuck his XQ straight through the bars and jammed the barrel into Dice's face. "I said stop that! Sit down now if you don't want to eat some of this!"

Dice gave another withering roar and slammed his weight hard to the side. The front bars clanged against the XQ and knocked it out of the guy's hands. His fingers jerked against the trigger and the gun went off in Dice's face.

The blast smashed into his skull and his whole giant body toppled sideways. He gave one last thunderous bellow and keeled over on top of the whole crew. His bulk tore the cage the rest of the way off the wall and it crashed onto its side with the prisoners all in a heap.

Yells and shrieks came from underneath Davenport. Dice's body crushed the breath from Davenport's lungs, but he couldn't move to heave Dice off.

More Mad Men came running. They surrounded the cage trying to tip it up, but they couldn't move it with so many people inside, especially with Dice sprawled on top of everyone else.

The Mad Men went through a confused discussion about what to do until Creed came back. He took one look at the mess, threw up his hands, and stormed off somewhere else muttering curses under his breath.

The other Mad Men exchanged glances. Then some of them shrugged and went back to what they were doing. The big guy who shot Dice pried his XQ from between the bars, checked it, and left.

"What the hell are they doing?" Coon gasped from under Dice's weight.

"What the hell *aren't* they doing?" Rodeo muttered. "They don't care what condition we're in as long as they hand us over to the Admiral."

"Can't……anyone……move……Dice?" Fiddler panted. She tried to push his enormous body off her tiny one, but she couldn't budge him.

"Let's all try together," Davenport suggested. "Emmett……"

Emmett grunted, dragged his arm out from under Wolf and Laub, and added his pathetic efforts to the job of moving Dice.

Emmett, Fiddler, Davenport, and all the boys who could get to Dice tried at the same time. They still couldn't move him.

"Does he have to be so damn big?" Bandit gasped.

Bodies kept wriggling underneath Davenport. He didn't want to think about who was doing what or what body parts anyone was touching.

"Can anyone see if he's even still alive?" Coon asked.

Davenport slipped his fingers around Dice's neck to check his pulse, but at that moment, Dice gave another bone-shaking roar and heaved off the stack of bodies. A bunch of people yelped and groaned as Dice rolled off them.

He rotated downward, toppled off the stack, and crashed down in a sitting position in his original place. His weight thumped on the cage floor and it tipped up to slam down where it was before.

It tottered without the anchor bolts holding it. All the other prisoners spilled across the floor and tumbled around Dice in a jumbled mess.

Davenport landed next to Dice with Wolf and Coon on either side of him. The others rearranged themselves and sat up straight when another crash made Davenport look behind him.

He almost didn't believe his eyes when the cage door flipped outward and hit the hull behind it. Breeze rolled across the floor and went through one of his ridiculous muddles trying to unwind his tangled limbs. Axel and Laub both fell partially through the door with their legs still inside the cage.

Breeze glanced around, spotted the Mad Men, and froze for a second. The Mad Men completely ignored the noise and went on with their work.

Breeze looked back at his friends and noticed everyone staring at him. "I meant to do that."

Chapter 4

Davenport dove for Breeze and dragged him, Axel, and Laub back inside the cage. "Get in here!" Davenport tossed the three boys willy-nilly on top of the others. He grabbed the door and swung it shut.

Davenport pulled it closed just as one of the Mad Men glanced over. The guy didn't notice that the door was ever open.

"How did you do that?" Davenport whispered.

"It wasn't hard," Breeze replied. "The lock wasn't as strong as it looked."

"We have to get out of here. We need to get to the *Artemis Rex* before these chumps decide to take us back to the Confederacy." Davenport turned to Dice. "Are you okay?"

Dice only grunted. He looked in surprisingly good shape considering he just took an XQ shot to the face. He wasn't even bleeding, but he did seem dazed.

He glared through the bars at the Mad Men across the hold and he smoldered in murderous fury. Davenport reminded himself for perhaps the thousandth time never to get into a situation where Dice would look at *him* like that.

Davenport waved his hand in front of Dice's eyes, but Dice didn't even blink. "What's wrong with him?" Fiddler whispered. "Is he gone?"

Dice burst to life and spun around before Davenport could answer. "Davenport!"

"Yeah, buddy," Davenport whispered. "I'm here. Is anybody home?"

"You see that thing those assholes are working on?" Dice gazed straight into Davenport's eyes. He didn't look away once.

"Uh...." Davenport glanced out into the hold. The two Mad Men were working on what looked like a giant cube. Davenport forced himself to bring his gaze back inside the cage so the Mad Men wouldn't see him gaping at the thing. "Yeah. I see it."

"It's a hyperdrive compartment. They plan to use that to send you back to the Confederacy."

"That's ridiculous," Fiddler countered. "That thing is way too small to transport all of us. We can barely fit in this cage and that cube is much smaller."

"That's because they don't plan to transport all of us," Rodeo pointed out. "They only want Davenport."

"What about the rest of us?" Emmett asked. "Will they leave us out here in Sacron Enigma."

"You wish," Rodeo replied. "They'll kill us all now that they have what they want."

"They won't kill anyone because we're getting out of here." Davenport turned back to Dice. "What do you know about that thing?"

"Who cares about the thing?" Bandit asked. "Are we getting out of here or not?"

"You bet." Rodeo turned his head the other way. He scanned the back wall. "We're still in the forest and the cage door is open."

"Great," Coon replied. "We just have to get across the hold without the Mad Men shooting our asses off on the way."

"We HAD to get caught by the Mad Men," Dice grumbled. "Of all the groups that could have captured us, it had to be them."

"Of course Joyce hired *them*," Bandit added. "They're notorious."

"Infamous is more like it," Davenport replied.

"Can we not split hairs about how bad the Mad Men are?" Fiddler asked. "We all know they're dangerous and, as it turns out, they're all armed and we aren't."

"I have a better idea than getting across the hold," Axel replied. "We overpower them, take their ship, and use it to defend ourselves while we get the *Artemis Rex* off the ground."

"If we had this, we wouldn't need the *Artemis Rex*," Emmett replied.

Bandit sneered at him. "You can keep this piece of shit if you want it. I'm not going anywhere in anything besides the *Artemis Rex*."

"You'll never fly in anything again as long as you live, will you?" Rodeo gripped the back of Bandit's neck in a comforting shake. "Don't worry, boy. We'll get her going again."

Bandit blinked rapidly and sniffed. "Thanks."

"So what's the plan?" Alla asked.

"We're sending you out to pilfer their food supplies," Coon replied. "Just kidding. You don't need extra food."

"*I* could go out there."

All eyes turned to Breeze and Davenport's heart lifted. "Now there's an idea!"

Breeze perked up. "Send me out there, Sir. I can do this."

Davenport burst into a grin and some of the other boys laughed. "Don't do anything you didn't mean to, boy."

Breeze smirked once and shifted his ass across the cage floor. He positioned himself closer to the door—the one he just broke open. "You all be ready to move as soon as you see an opening."

"How will we know when that is?" Fiddler asked.

"When the Mad Men have their backs to you."

"What about you?" Davenport asked. "We can't leave you behind."

"Don't worry about me. I can get myself out of anything."

"He really can," Axel replied, "especially anything he got himself into."

Davenport glanced over at the Mad Men, too. They were still hard at work on the cube, whatever the hell it was. "Okay, if you're sure...."

Breeze reacted so fast Davenport didn't have time to answer. Breeze pitched over backward so violently that Davenport jumped out of his skin. He never would have believed Breeze did it on purpose.

Breeze burst through the cage door, let out a piercing scream, flung his arms over his face, and writhed on the floor with the door standing wide open.

Wolf exploded out of the cage just as fast. Davenport could never figure out afterward how Wolf knew what Breeze was going to do or when, but no one had a chance to think about that now.

Wolf pounced on Breeze, tackled him flat to the floor, and started swinging his fists in devastating punches.

Breeze shrieked to raise the roof. Wolf snarled and growled and hissed and spat. Every hair stood up on his hackles. Anyone would think he really was trying to kill Breeze, but that couldn't be right. They were friends. Weren't they?

Everyone else in the cage sat frozen in shock. Davenport never thought once about getting out of the cage. He couldn't stop staring at the two boys locked in a death struggle.

The Mad Men noticed, of course. They stormed over to the struggling pair and hauled them apart.

The biggest one who shot Dice grabbed Breeze and jerked him to his feet. The other one seized Wolf, but he had a lot more trouble restraining the boy. Wolf kept trying to fight his way out of the guy's grip so he could attack Breeze again.

When Wolf couldn't get to Breeze, he turned his wrath on the Mad Man holding him. The guy had to hold Wolf at arm's length and vent all his strength to stop Wolf from clawing his eyes out.

Davenport's brain switched gears. Was this the moment Breeze meant?

The ruckus built to an epic pitch. Both Mad Men tried to bellow over the noise of Wolf's spine-chilling yowls and Breeze's plaintive explanations of innocence.

The noise attracted the attention of every other Mad Man on board. Creed and his flunkies came back from different parts of the ship. They tried to yell above the din to ask what the hell was going on.

Movement caught the corner of Davenport's eye. He glanced over to see Rodeo, Bandit, and Coon all inching closer to the cage door. The Mad Men were all so occupied with the scuffle to notice that the door still stood wide open.

Creed and the others gathered around Wolf and Breeze. Wolf kicked up an even more threatening struggle. The one guy holding him couldn't restrain him anymore, so two others grabbed Wolf's arms which drove him ballistic.

Creed and another guy concentrated on Breeze. They had to bellow to make themselves heard. Even then, their voices combined with Wolf's screeches and the pained roars of the guys trying to hold him blocked out all other sound.

Rodeo tapped Davenport's elbow and motioned Davenport nearer to the door. Here it came.

Breeze gesticulated wildly trying to communicate with Creed and the others. The Mad Men closed in a tighter group. Some of them tried to talk to each other about what to do about whatever it was Breeze was saying. They all stood dangerously close to the cube.

For the second time, Davenport couldn't figure out how Breeze did it. One minute, he stood up straight talking like any normal boy. No one would ever have suspected he could be anything but pure as the driven snow.

The next instant, he buckled to the floor and went into one of his maniacal flailing fits trying to straighten his limbs. He "accidentally" kicked one of the bigger Mad Men and that guy went down, too.

The man Breeze kicked really did go into a jumble of arms and legs while he tried to untangle himself from Breeze. Somewhere in the confusion, the guy's giant XQ went off.

The shot smashed one of Wolf's captors in the ankle and a third man hit the floor. The other guy lost his grip on Wolf and the whole cargo hold erupted in chaos.

Wolf exploded in pure animal rage and flew at the man holding him. Wolf slashed the guy across the face and the dude screamed clutching his eyes. Breeze seized the XQ and now no one could mistake his movements for swift, sure, and deliberate.

He wheeled the gun up and blasted Creed square in the chest. Then Breeze pivoted onto his side, all trace of confusion gone. He aimed straight into the back wall and smashed a hole in the ship right next to the open cage door.

"Go!" Rodeo bellowed. "Go!"

He shoved the rest of the boys out followed by Fiddler, Emmett, and Davenport. The boys dove into the darkness outside and took off running.

Davenport hesitated and turned back. Breeze and Wolf were still tied up fighting the Mad Men on their own. Dice remained locked in the cage with no way out. He couldn't fit through the tiny door.

The instant the XQ went off, Dice rocketed to his feet. Getting shot must have triggered something in him because he straightened his legs and punched his head and shoulders straight through the cage ceiling. The cage disintegrated with some of the bars still dangling from his massive limbs.

He let out a tremendous roar that rocked the whole ship. The surviving Mad Men whirled around to face him and many grabbed for their weapons.

"Come on!" Davenport waved Breeze toward the hole. "Let's go! Wolf! Come on!"

Wolf crouched over one of his fallen attackers. Blood covered Wolf's face and Davenport realized with a lurch that the blood wasn't Wolf's.

Davenport shoved that thought out of his head and motioned Wolf away again. Breeze scrambled to his feet and tried without success to lift the massive XQ he'd just been shooting. He couldn't get it off the floor.

"Leave it!" Davenport yelled over Dice's enraged bellows. "Come on! Get out now!"

Dice shook off the rest of the cage and stormed across the hold. Four Mad Men remained and two had the nerve to aim their weapons at him.

He stretched his giant muscular arms to both sides and thundered to High Heaven. One of the Mad Men fired and missed him. The shot pounded into the ceiling and drove Dice into an even more bloodthirsty frenzy.

He charged with sections of cage still flapping from his horns and shoulders. The Mad Men bolted, but Dice was too far gone to care. He charged after them leaving Breeze and Wolf alone among the bodies.

"Come on, Wolf!" Davenport urged. "Leave it, Breeze!"

Breeze gave the gun one last heave and fell over himself again. The XQ went off, and this time, the shot zinged across the cargo hold and smashed straight into the cockpit.

The whole front end of the ship detonated. jostled the floor underfoot, and Breeze keeled over. Wolf sprang to his side, seized Breeze by the shirt, and wrestled him to his feet.

The two boys sprinted for the hole and Davenport pushed them through into the darkness. Now he just had to deal with Dice.

Dice's furious bellows echoed from across the hold. He had cornered the last surviving Mad Men in some hole. His giant body blocked Davenport from seeing exactly where they were or what Dice was doing to them.

Dice couldn't get into whatever space they were occupying. He kept lunging for the opening, smashing his huge shoulders against the sides, and crashing while he tried to grab them.

The force of his blows jostled the ship back and forth until the whole vessel groaned and banged with the impact.

Davenport hesitated to go over there, but he couldn't leave Dice here, especially if he was injured. Davenport could only assume he was. Why else would Dice become so enraged?

Davenport approached him and Dice gave another ferocious lunge for the opening. He smashed into it, thrust his head into the gap, and the hull shuddered from his bellows.

"Hey!" Davenport grabbed Dice's elbow. "Hey! We're getting out of here!"

Dice ripped his horns out of the hole and rounded on Davenport trembling all over with fury. He thundered in Davenport's face, shot out one giant hand to seize Davenport by the jacket, and almost yanked him off his feet.

Dice's fist closed on Davenport's star and the points stabbed Dice in the palm and fingers. Dice's eyes darted to the thing that pricked him. He finished bellowing in Davenport's face and then Dice's countenance cleared.

He frowned down at Davenport still gripping a fistful of Davenport's lapel in one massive hand.

"Hey—buddy!" Davenport called up at him. "We're leaving! You don't want to mess with them anymore."

Dice blinked. Davenport dared to take his eyes off Dice long enough to look into the hole.

The Mad Men had blasted another ragged breach in the side of their ship and bolted. There was nothing there to see but a clear hole leading out into the forest.

Dice glanced into the space where he'd been roaring and he relaxed when he realized his quarry was gone. He let go of Davenport's collar and his arms dropped to his sides.

Davenport noticed for the first time that a crust of dried blood had formed around the rim of one of Dice's nostrils. Davenport couldn't do anything about that right now. He couldn't think of any way to help whatever was wrong with Dice until they got back to the *Artemis Rex.*

Davenport touched Dice's shoulder once. "You okay? Did they hurt you?"

Dice shrugged and looked away. He kept blinking like he was having trouble clearing his mind. Taking an XQ shot to the head must have hurt him more than anyone realized. He might be a beast, but he had a brain he never hesitated to use under normal circumstances.

These weren't normal circumstances. Davenport touched his arm again. "Come on, man. Let's get the hell out of here."

Dice followed him over to the hole, but Davenport saw before they got there that Dice wouldn't be able to fit through it.

Davenport glanced around for the dozenth time, but it was Dice himself who went over to the hold hatch. He opened it to reveal the forest spread around the ship.

The forest had grown darker while the crew was inside. The canopy blocked Davenport from seeing the sky, but the area looked like night was falling.

Davenport accompanied Dice outside and the others came rushing around the ship to meet them. "What happened? Where are the other Mad Men?"

"They took off. Let's beat it back to the *Artemis Rex.*" Davenport peered into the shadows. "Where is it?"

Wolf gave a low growl and headed off into the trees. Rodeo and the other Chorions started to follow him. "Hey!" Fiddler called. "Where are you going?"

"Wolf will lead us back to the ship," Rodeo replied over his shoulder. "It's this way."

Davenport fell in line with the boys. Fiddler, Beauty, and Emmett took longer, but Dice started forward right away.

Davenport studied him on the side while they walked. "You okay? Talk to me."

"I'm okay." He passed his hand across his eyes. "I don't know what happened back there. I guess.... I kinda lost it for a minute."

"You got shot in the head. Of course you lost it. Anyone would."

Dice raised his big, horned head and frowned at Davenport for a second. The light was coming back into his fierce, beady eyes. He was turning back into the man Davenport knew.

He looked away without saying anything and Davenport let the matter drop. He squinted toward the head of the line.

Wolf paused every few paces, sniffed the air to the left and the right, and then darted forward a few more yards before doing the same thing.

Rodeo, Bandit, and Laub followed Wolf at a distance to give him plenty of space. They left him completely on his own.

Davenport kept wondering at the Chorion Team's mysterious abilities. After what he just witnessed in the Mad Men's hold, he was starting to completely reevaluate his opinion of Breeze.

Davenport believed through his whole association with the Chorions that Breeze was a loveable idiot with no control over his own limbs. Now Davenport knew better.

Breeze's "accidents" were really his secret superpower just like Rodeo's senses, Bandit's flying skill, and Laub's great strength. Breeze really could do whatever he wanted. He accomplished magnificent feats with these ridiculous displays of clumsiness. It was pure genius hidden behind a mask of incompetence.

Now Davenport understood why Ekol Thaine kept Breeze on the most trusted hit team in all of Ekol's service. Davenport also understood why the rest of the Chorions put up with Breeze's antics.

So far, every "accident" Breeze ever had turned out to benefit their crew—all except for the moronic incidents of Breeze knocking things over and making a mess with the food supplies in Ekol's warehouse.

Breeze did that for effect. He did it to entertain his teammates....and also to make an impression on Davenport. Of course. It all made sense now. How did Breeze get the cage door open in the first place? Davenport couldn't figure it out.

Then there was Wolf. Davenport marveled at Wolf's abilities, too. Even as he did so, Davenport realized that he had no real clue what Wolf's abilities were.

How did he communicate with Breeze to distract the Mad Men?

How did Wolf know that Breeze would fall out the door when he did?

How did they decide beforehand that Wolf would attack Breeze and pretend to beat him up?

Wolf reacted in a split second—just as fast as Breeze did. Wolf never spoke. Even if he could, none of the crew heard Breeze and Wolf discussing their maneuver beforehand. They just did it.

Davenport couldn't imagine a more genius maneuver to get both of them outside the cage without the Mad Men suspecting anything.

It put both boys in a perfect position to do the enemy maximum damage. The Mad Men never realized what was happening until it was too late. The whole performance boggled Davenport's mind.

Fiddler caught up with him. "How far are we from the *Artemis Rex*?"

"No idea."

She grimaced at the Chorions at the front of their column. "Don't you think we should....?"

Davenport prepared himself to tell her exactly what he thought they should do and how far he was prepared to trust the Chorions to get the crew out of this mess.

He never got a chance before a deafening shriek of engine noise exploded out of the trees. Four ships rocketed into the air and searchlights wheeled through the forest.

The pursuit converged on the retreating fugitives and gunfire stuttered from turrets mounted on the vessels' undersides.

Davenport lunged forward herding everyone away. "Scatter! Get away into the woods! Don't give them a target!"

Chapter 5

The *Prometheus Vox* floated down to land outside the Ultra Meridian jail. Confederate Marshall Lawrence Healey climbed down from his cockpit and strode over to the building.

Healey cast a disgusted look at dozens of massive Stalwarts, lightning-fast Nitrols, and powerful Dagger-class attack vessels covering the plane all around the jail. Ultra Meridian hadn't been this busy in centuries—maybe even millennia.

Healey paused outside the dusty structure. He knew from the Confederate Corps database that the jail had recently been destroyed by Reserve Wing fire. It had only been rebuilt in the last few weeks.

No one would ever believe the jail hadn't been standing here for decades. The wind and sand had already scoured it to a dull, weathered grey. All the crisp edges and corners had been worn off. One piece of roofing steel had ripped up from its position.

It flapped in the wind and made a hollow, mournful sound that fit with the desolate, lifeless wastes surrounding the outpost.

At least twenty people crowded the jail so Healey couldn't get in. A bunch of Reserve Wing officers stood around listening to excited talk coming from inside.

Healey peeked between their shoulders. A tall, middle-aged officer in an immaculate uniform stood behind the sheriff's desk—the abandoned sheriff's desk.

Healey knew more than he ever wanted to know about Ultra Meridian from his fateful interview with Sheriff Mace Davenport, the man who by rights should be manning this outpost.

Davenport was the only sheriff with the integrity to man Ultra Meridian. He was the only sheriff Healey had ever met with the balls to stand guard over the Confederacy's most remote outpost.

This whole disaster started because Davenport was doing his job. He was the one who found the Ithium cartridge on board the smugglers' vessel *Echo Omicron* and the rest was history.

Now that rotten scumbag Admiral Killian Joyce stood where Davenport should be. The sight made Healey sick to his stomach.

Joyce was the one who destroyed the Ultra Meridian jail to steal the Ithium back from Davenport. Joyce was the one who tried to kill Davenport more than once to stop Davenport from turning the Ithium over to the authorities the way he was supposed to.

That was Davenport all over the place. He did his job and he never let anyone or anything stop him from doing it.

Davenport was still doing his job now by going on the run to stop the Ithium from falling back into Joyce's hands. Davenport sacrificed himself to keep the galaxy safe.

That was the kind of man Healey called a true-blue lawman. That was Davenport. He was a lawman down to the bone.

Standing here preparing himself to report to Admiral Joyce made Healey sick, too, but Healey had no choice.

No, that was all wrong. Healey *did* have a choice. That was why he was here. He was here to help Davenport. That was the least Healey could do.

He had to keep reminding him again and again why the hell he was here about to meet with this shithead admiral.

Healey was here to help Davenport. Healey was here to make sure Davenport stayed free. Healey was here to make sure Admiral Joyce never got his hands on the Ithium or Davenport or any of Davenport's friends ever again.

That was why Healey was here, but he still had to keep reminding himself. If he stopped reminding himself even for an instant, he might do something really bad to rid the galaxy of Killian Joyce's miserable, evil, rotten existence.

Now Admiral Joyce had the nerve to stand behind Davenport's desk—as if Joyce was some kind of pillar of law and order like Davenport was. What a joke.

Joyce towered over a tiny girl who had to crane her neck to look up at him. She wore a beaten brown leather jacket, boots, and pants with a leather gun belt slung around her narrow, bony hips.

Ammo cartridges studded her belt and she wore her two sidearms desert style for a quick draw. She reminded Healey of a miniature version of Davenport—which she was.

A colorless bandana knotted behind her neck and a pair of goggles perched on top of her forehead. Two rings of white skin surrounded her bright brown eyes.

Thick dust covered every inch of her from the top of her mask hood to the soles of her boots. It made her look like an animal with big rings around her eyes.

An air of mockery and disdain hung over the Reserve Wing officers watching her face off against the admiral.

The officers kept chuckling and snorting in contempt as they listened to Joyce interview this girl. None of these men understood an Ultra Meridian desert rat when they met one, especially not the admiral.

"I asked you before and I won't ask again," Joyce snapped. "Tell me your name now or you'll be on a one-way transport to Terminus Anathema."

"I already told you. My name is Flack."

The officers hanging around the jail entrance snickered again, which only seemed to enrage the admiral even more. "That isn't a name. We need to look you up on the Confederate database."

"That is my name and I already told you I didn't do anything wrong. You can't hold me. Ultra Meridian is a Confederate outpost. You can't send me anywhere without a full trial and you have no evidence that I ever did the things you say."

"So now you're an expert on Confederate law?" the admiral fumed.

"You're damn right I am. You're threatening me without cause, so it sounds like I know a hell of a lot more about Confederate law than you do."

She dipped her eyes suggestively to his spotless uniform and he lost his composure completely. "You're nobody! You're the trash of the universe. No one cares if you live or die. I could send you to Terminus Anathema and no one would ever even notice you were gone."

"You think so? Try it and see what happens."

Admiral Joyce stiffened, threw back his shoulders, and drew in a long, steadying breath. Healey had to bite back a grin. Flack didn't look ridiculous or worthless to him. Healey savored watching someone run rings around this jackass.

"We scanned the hills beyond the Khuntan Reserve," Admiral Joyce went on. "We have evidence that you and your friends fired on Reserve Wing ships. You were defending the *Blood Calliope* so Sheriff Davenport and his friends could get on board."

"You're full of shit," Flack countered. "You don't have any evidence that I was ever anywhere near the Khuntan Reserve. We wouldn't be standing here having this pleasant conversation if you did. You're making that shit up to intimidate me."

Joyce narrowed his eyes at her and his cheeks blotched between red and white as he struggled to restrain his mounting rage. "You know you were there. My pilots saw you stationed in the caves."

"I don't know what you're talking about and you can't prove I was. Now, unless you have some other more concrete evidence, I'm out of here."

"You were helping Davenport search for something on board the *Blood Calliope*. Tell me where he went and things will go a lot easier for you."

Now it was Flack's turn to snort. "I have no idea what you're talking about. I've never heard of the *Blood Calliope* and I haven't set foot in the Khuntan Reserve in years....and while we're at it, I hate Sheriff Davenport. He's been a barnacle on this planet and I'm glad he's gone. I hope the Confederacy never posts another sheriff out here because that asshole has been a thorn in our sides for years."

Healey actually had to turn away to stop himself from laughing in pure delight at her performance. The hills flanking the Khuntan Reserve contained heavy traces of iron ore, Culpex, and other elements. They made the hills impenetrable to scans, especially scans from space.

The Reserve Wing pilots that attacked Davenport and his crew to stop them from getting to the *Blood Calliope*—the same pilots that Flack and her Armageddon Core fired on to cover Davenport's mission—none of those pilots could have recognized the Armageddon Core shooters. The girls had been covered from head to foot in their desert protective gear at the time.

Admiral Joyce and the Reserve Wing pilots might have seen the Armageddon Core firing on the attackers, but he would never be able to prove it.

Flack was right. For all his rank and influence, she really did know more about Confederate law than he did.

She also knew more about Ultra Meridian than he could ever learn in his lifetime. That made all the difference.

Now he had no choice but to suck on it. She leveled him with a straight, unwavering gaze that weighed him, measured him, and found him wanting in the extreme.

She sniffed at him and stalked out of the jail. She had to shoulder her way through the assembled officers. They all towered over her and some tried to block her path, but she completely ignored them.

She raised her head as she approached the door, lifted her arms, and pulled her goggles and mask down to cover her face. She became completely unrecognizable just like every other desert rat at Ultra Meridian.

Just before she passed Healey, her sharp brown eyes caught his and registered the faintest hint of acknowledgment. The next instant, she slammed her shoulder into his, knocked him out of her way, and stormed out of the jail.

She crossed to a Skimmer parked among several Vagrant-class runabouts with Reserve Wing insignia all over them. Flack slung her leg over the seat, fired the engines, and burned out of sight with a column of dust rising behind her.

"That little bitch won't help us," Admiral Joyce snarled after the noise died down. He turned back to Davenport's desk. "We have no choice but to take drastic action."

"What do you have in mind?" one ship's captain asked. "We can't follow him into Sacron Enigma—if he really did go that way."

"You don't worry about that. I have my own ways of getting Davenport back. You men are all dismissed. Take your ships back into orbit and get back to your rostered positions. Leave Davenport to me."

Most of them said, "Yes, Sir," and left. None of them paid Healey any attention as they passed him on the way back to their ships.

A second later, they all started their engines and ships launched off the planet by the dozen. They kicked up one hell of a dust cloud. Healey squinted and held his breath to protect his lungs and eyes. He really wished now that he had a mask and goggles like Flack's.

"Come on in, Marshall," Admiral Joyce called through the door.

Healey cringed. Now he had to face the music. Admiral Joyce claimed he had pilot testimony and scans from space that the Armageddon Core fired on the Reserve Wing ships that went after Davenport.

If the admiral was telling the truth, he would have pilot testimony and scans from space showing the *Prometheus Vox* doing exactly the same thing.

Healey didn't have any hills to hide behind, either. He flew right out into the open and fired on Reserve Wing vessels. He drove them away from the *Blood Calliope* to make sure Davenport completed his mission.

Then, when it was all over, Healey went down on the ground to talk to Davenport before Healey let Davenport get away. He did all that when Admiral Joyce himself tasked Healey with apprehending Davenport and bringing back the Ithium and the computer chip that went with it.

Healey stepped into the jail, but he didn't shrink before the admiral. Healey actually almost hoped the admiral found out the truth. Then Healey wouldn't have to pretend to help with this illegal manhunt.

He was doing this for Davenport. He was doing this to make sure Davenport stayed at large and to keep the Ithium out of Admiral Joyce's hands. Healey was doing this to save the galaxy from this corrupt officer's evil plan.

Healey straightened up and faced Joyce across Davenport's desk. Healey didn't care who stood behind it. This would always be Davenport's desk.

Healey made a decision then and there. He would use whatever influence he still had in the Confederacy. He would make damn sure no other sheriff besides Davenport ever took this post. No one else alive deserved to call himself the Sheriff of Ultra Meridian.

Chapter 6

Admiral Joyce didn't notice Healey facing him with the air of a man facing the firing squad. Admiral Joyce worked over several detachable control consoles laid out on the desk. He didn't even look up when Healey entered.

"Our reports indicate that Davenport and his crew have crossed into Sacron Enigma. We've dispatched the Mad Men to bring them in and...."

Healey sucked his breath between his teeth. "The Mad Men! Are you out of your mind?"

Admiral Joyce waved that away and still didn't look up. "We needed someone who could go over the line and get the job done. The Mad Men came very highly recommended...."

"Highly recommended—by whom? They're one of the most notorious mercenary groups in the whole Confederacy."

"Like I said, we needed someone who could cross the line into Sacron Enigma. The Reserve Wing couldn't do it and it turns out that the Mad Men really did catch up with Davenport. They sent a signal of his location."

"Where is he, then? If the Mad Men have him, they're as likely to kill him as they are to bring him back alive."

"The Mad Men know they won't get paid if they don't bring him back alive, but that doesn't matter. He's landed on a certain planet—a planet without a name. It's listed in the database as HTWV-983." The admiral grimaced. "It's one of few in all of Sacron Enigma that actually has a number."

"Well?" Healey prompted. "If the Mad Men are getting paid to bring him in alive, why haven't they? Why are we even talking about this?"

Admiral Joyce winced again. "They sent a signal that they had him....and we haven't heard from them since. We've lost contact with the Mad Men who were on the ground. We don't know yet what happened...."

The admiral trailed off as though his unspoken words could somehow explain what was happening on some unknown planet in the vast remote reaches of Sacron Enigma.

Healey could pretty well imagine what was going on over there if the admiral had lost contact with the Mad Men. Something told Healey things were going to get sticky on HTWV-983.

"So what do you want me to do? Do you want me to go over there and find them?" Healey couldn't think of an order he would rather receive right now. If he went over to Sacron Enigma, he would make sure no one ever found Davenport ever again.

"You're too valuable. I understand you want to finish the job by bringing Davenport to justice, but we can't risk sending you across the line."

Healey stared at the admiral hardly daring to believe what he was hearing. The admiral still thought Healey was trying to capture Davenport the way Admiral Joyce ordered him to. The admiral really thought Healey was on his side. Did Admiral Joyce have evidence of Healey's treachery or not?

Admiral Joyce went back to tapping on his consoles. "I'm sending the Cannibals out to intercept the Mad Men—if there's anything to intercept. They'll find the Mad Men, or if the Mad Men are gone or out of action, the Cannibals will pick up Davenport and bring him back."

Healey gaped at the admiral too stunned to speak. The Cannibals. Healey's blood ran cold at the name.

The Cannibals didn't earn their name for nothing. The Mad Men might be violent, ruthless, and unprincipled marauders. They would take any job, no matter how brutal. They would do anything for money and they didn't care who got hurt in the process.

The Mad Men had been known to kill people they'd been paid to bring back alive. They'd been known to torture, maim, and dispose even of their own clients. The Mad Men might do anything simply because they were bored and needed some way to entertain themselves.

The Cannibals were in a class all by themselves. They weren't even mercenaries. They were.... well, cannibals. They recruited from every species, including human. They rarely accepted pay for anything.

Anyone who dared to deal with the Cannibals simply informed the Cannibals of the target's existence. Then the would-be client stood well back out of the way while the Cannibals rampaged across the galaxy destroying everything in their path.

In the best possible scenario, the target died in the mayhem, but plenty of clients and innocent bystanders often met their end in the ensuing disaster. The Cannibals had been known to raze whole planets simply because someone told them someone was on that planet that the original client wanted to find.

Admiral Joyce couldn't really be serious about sending the Cannibals after Davenport's crew. The admiral couldn't seriously believe the Cannibals would bring Davenport back alive. That was not possible, but here stood the admiral tapping away at his consoles like this was just another day at the office.

If the Cannibals found Davenport, the Cannibals might release the Ithium without even knowing it. They didn't have the brainpower to understand what Ithium was, much less the dangers involved.

"You're dismissed, Marshall," the admiral breezed. "You can go back to Pandora's Needle. We'll bring in Davenport and any of his friends that survive the assault. Then I'll let you know when I'm ready for you to take the next step."

Healey blinked at him and then shook himself. He heard what Admiral Joyce didn't say.

This charade Healey had been playing with Joyce always revolved around the plausible deniability that Healey didn't know about the Ithium.

Healey claimed to think Davenport was crazy. Healey went along with the fiction that Davenport hallucinated everything about a secret Reserve Wing cabal who wanted to steal the Ithium and release it somewhere inside Confederate space.

This fiction seemed to soothe Admiral Joyce's pathetic arrogance. He usually smirked at Healey. The admiral thought Healey was too stupid to grasp the wider implications of this mission.

Admiral Joyce didn't know that Davenport had already Healey everything at the Pandora's Needle jail. That moment changed Healey's life and now he was up to his neck in this. No true lawman could listen to Davenport's story and not accept responsibility for stopping the plot.

Admiral Joyce looked up from his consoles. "Is anything wrong, Marshall? You heard what I said. Go back to the Needle and I'll contact you when I know anything."

"Yes, Sir."

Healey turned on his heel and strode out of the jail. The dust had died down and only two ships remained parked on the plane—the *Prometheus Vox* and a big Stalwart whose nameplate Healey couldn't read with his eyes squinted against the stinging sand.

He didn't want to read it. He wanted to get the hell out of here, but he had no intention of waiting around until Admiral Joyce needed him.

He picked up the pace approaching the *Prometheus Vox* and pivoted around it to climb into the cockpit. He passed behind the ship....and stopped in his tracks.

The ship blocked the wind and he opened his eyes when he found Flack perched on his landing strut.

She had pulled her mask up, but she still had her goggles on. She was too smart and seasoned in the ways of Ultra Meridian to take them off.

She peered at him through the lenses. "Well, Sheriff? What did he say?"

Healey didn't bother to correct her about his new promotion. He let out a shaky sigh and cast a flinty gaze across the plane. He saw so many things all over the galaxy. He saw interconnected plans and schemes weaving in and out of each other.

"He said he's sending the Cannibals after Davenport and his crew."

She stiffened and stared at him. Of course she knew who the Cannibals were.

She swung off the landing strut and straightened up in front of him, but she didn't even come up to his chin. "What are we going to do about it? We have to stop them. We can't let Joyce get away with this."

"*You* aren't doing anything. You're out of this. You've done enough."

"To hell with that! Fiddler is on the *Artemis Rex*. We won't leave her in the Cannibals' path. What do you take us for?"

"What do you think you and your friends are going to do against the Cannibals? Stay here. You can keep an eye on things going on inside the Confederacy......"

"Hell, no! You're the lawman. You're the one who's supposed to be stopping these assholes, and if you won't, that means we have to."

He had to smile at her. "I *am* doing something about it. That's what I'm saying. I can do more than you can. Stay here."

She scowled at him from behind her goggles. "Why should I?"

"Because the third component is somewhere on this planet. You and your friends are in a much better position to find it and get it back than I am. You can blend in."

"What are *you* going to do?" She furrowed her brow even more. "How are you going to stop the Cannibals?"

"I think I might know some people who can help me with that."

"Fine." She rotated around him so she stood beyond him. "You go do that and leave us out of it."

He had to smile at her spunky attitude. These girls were really some of the best people he had ever met—right next to Davenport and his crew. "Thank you, Flack. I really appreciate your help."

"We aren't helping at all thanks to you."

"You already did. You helped Davenport when he went to the *Blood Calliope*. That's what I'm thanking you for—not for helping me."

She narrowed her eyes at him in suspicion and then shrugged. "You're welcome, Sheriff. Let us know if you want us to roll out the big guns again."

She turned on her heel, pulled down her mask, and walked off into the hills beyond Ultra Meridian. In a few seconds, the wind, sand, and dusty landscape swallowed her. Her drab clothes made her blend perfectly with the surroundings. No one would ever know she was there.

Healey watched her go with regret. He really wished he could take her and her friends with him. They were one of the best crews he'd ever worked with, but taking them off this planet would probably ruin them. They belonged here.

Chapter 7

Marshall Healey landed the *Prometheus Vox* on the jail roof at Pandora's Needle. This jail building couldn't be more different from the Ultra Meridian jail.

The jail occupied a tall building in the middle of the Pandora's Needle recreation satellite. The Sheriffs' Service needed a huge force of deputies to patrol all the illegal activity going on here.

Healey strode downstairs to his office and ten deputies mobbed him all talking at once. They bombarded him with questions about where he'd been.

They all wanted to know what was going on with the prisoners who blew up the holding cell and escaped. His deputies all wanted to know whether it was true that Admiral Joyce really promoted Healey to the rank of Confederate Marshall.

Healey only made a passing effort to answer them. He had much more pressing matters on his mind.

He looked up a few addresses, put his chief deputy in charge, and left again without explaining where he was going. Time was short. He had to act before the Cannibals made it out to Sacron Enigma.

He descended to the street and set off through the metropolis. Gambling dens, drug houses, brothels, watering holes, restaurants, and luxury hotels lined every street, but Healey ignored them all.

He walked for miles across town. Whores called out to him from street corners and a few drug dealers even had the nerve to greet him. Everyone who did any kind of business on the Needle knew Healey only too well.

He finally found a broken-down store selling second-hand clothes, out-of-date sweets, and even a few Xids that the proprietor said were well trained—which Healey took to mean they were still wild enough to literally bite off the hand that fed them.

Healey went through the store. The proprietor and his clerk barely glanced at him. He ducked into the back room and climbed down a dark, dingy staircase to the basement.

He opened another door and entered a vast underground hall stretching as far as the eye could see.

A thriving black market raged here selling everything too horrible to be traded on the surface. Illegal alien pets, drugs so dangerous they had been known to cause death at the very first experimental use, prostitutes from species with razor-sharp fangs studding every orifice—Pandora's Needle had it all and not in a nice way.

The trade going on upstairs—the trade the Confederate Corps could publicly acknowledge—none of it held a candle to this.

Healey could walk at his leisure here. No one had to worry about Healey busting anyone here because Healey *couldn't* bust anyone here.

Healey wasn't even a sheriff here, let alone a marshall. He would get his throat slit if he even thought about trying to enforce the law here. The law was beyond unenforceable here. Law didn't exist here.

He strolled between the stalls witnessing horrors, perversions, and displays too outrageous to even talk about upstairs. Most Confederate personnel preferred to pretend things like this didn't happen anywhere, let alone on a Confederate satellite.

Healey paused to watch an Okrot wrestling match. The two aliens slashed each other with their fangs, pinned each other, bit off chunks of each other's flesh, gouged out each other's eyes, and bled all over each other.

Spectators stood around cheering, betting on the outcome, and even hitting each other in their frenzy over the scene.

Healey was just getting ready to wander off somewhere else when someone attacked him from behind. He tried to struggle, but powerful arms pinned his elbows to his side so firmly that he couldn't move.

He tried to spin around to see who it was, but in a split second, someone jerked a black cloth bag over Healey's head. He couldn't see.

Strong hands bound his wrists and ankles before he could fight back. His kidnappers tackled him to the floor. They even landed a few blows before they completely subdued him.

Healey's heart hammered against his ribs. He kept turning his head from one side to the other, but the bag stopped him from seeing anything.

Many hands picked him up off the floor and started carrying him. He should have seen this coming. He *did* see it coming. Wasn't this why he came down to this underground market in the first place?

He heard aliens speaking in strange languages. Healey tried to listen to what they were saying, but the noise from the market drowned out the words.

A door slammed and silence descended. The aliens stopped talking. They knew exactly what they were doing. They knew better than to say anything incriminating in front of him—or to say anything at all in front of him.

They carried him for a long way. They pointed his head downward and his body jostled with their steps. They must be descending more stairs deeper inside the satellite.

Healey had never been down this far before and he started to panic. What if he really got out of his depth here? None of his deputies knew where he was. They wouldn't be able to come after him even if they did know.

None of that mattered. If Healey got into trouble here, he would be dead long before his deputies or anyone else found out about it.

Davenport. He was doing this for Davenport. He was doing this to help Davenport. Healey was doing this to make sure Davenport and the Ithium stayed out of Admiral Joyce's hands.

Chapter 8

Healey's abductors dropped him on a hard stone floor and then kicked him a few times. He jerked against the restraints trying to hear anything around him.

People whispered not far away. The sound echoed off stone walls and cold dread sank into Healey's heart. He asked for this and he got it. Now he really started to fear for his life.

If he didn't get out of here, Davenport would die for certain. Once Admiral Joyce got Healey, Davenport, and Davenport's crew out of the way, nothing would stop him from retrieving the Ithium, the chip, and the mysterious third component—whatever that was.

Of course that must be why Joyce set up shop at Ultra Meridian. He must still be looking for the third component .... unless he thought Davenport already had it.

Healey's mind went back to Flack and the Armageddon Core. They would keep an eye on things at Ultra Meridian. If the third component was there to find, they would find it.

Healey put that on his list of things he had to do to stop Joyce from destroying the galaxy. First, though, Healey had to get away from his captors—the same people he came here to find.

"Sheriff......" a deep gruff voice rumbled in the darkness.

Healey froze. He knew that voice. "Kalvov?"

"What are you doing here? You have no business here."

"I need to see Mexia."

"Mexia does not see scum-sucking lawmen like you." The voice dropped so low it vibrated through the floor into Healey's chest. "Mexia is an important dignitary who eats Confederate scumbags like you for breakfast. In fact, I think she might be hungry.... right.... now......."

More rough hands grabbed Healey and wrestled him off the floor. He exploded in panic. "No!...... Kalvov.... NO! I can explain! Don't......"

He twisted and yanked against the restraints holding him, but the aliens didn't let him go. They started carrying him somewhere again and then he felt himself going down even more stairs.

His heart threatened to explode out of his ribs. They were taking him to Mexia. Kalvov didn't say she ate Confederate scumbags like him for breakfast just for effect. He meant it literally.... which meant Kalvov really intended to feed Healey to Mexia.... right.... now.

Healey burst into a fresh convulsion of struggling. He kept calling out, and before he knew it, his voice spiked into a scream. "Kalvov...NO! You can't do this! You're making a big mistake! I can explain! KALVOV!!!"

No one answered him. The aliens carrying him punched him a few more times to stop him from fighting back.

A door slammed and then someone yanked the hood off his head. He screamed involuntarily when he saw where he was.

His captors from upstairs held Healey's bound body parallel to the floor. His head pointed at a massive alien that took up nearly half of the enormous room.

The boneless body billowed over the floor and even jammed into the corners. The thing had no eyes or face that Healey could see.

A giant mouth lined with several rows of teeth widened before Healey's eyes. A great, groaning yawn rumbled out of it as the creature prepared to swallow Healey in one gulp.

He struggled with all his might. The bonds holding him cut into his wrists. He was starting to lose sensation in his fingers, but that hardly mattered now.

His captors carried him closer to the thing and a long, speckled tongue uncoiled from deep in the creature's throat. The tongue looped through the air toward Healey's face.

"Mexia....!" He scrambled in his brain for the right thing to say and finally yelled out, "*Druhuzuno Udeohiri Nozegantu*!!"

Everyone present froze except for the creature. Healey ducked his head and shut his eyes to hide from the death about to swallow him down the creature's gullet.

The thing only groaned again and its tongue made a slobbering, swishing sound winding back into its mouth.

The people holding Healey dropped him hard on the floor. He grunted in pain when he slammed down hard on his shoulder.

The same booming voice rumbled from somewhere Healey couldn't see. "What do you want, Sheriff?"

"The Cannibals.... a Confederate admiral has released the Cannibals.... They're on their way to Sacron Enigma......"

"Our people have nothing to do with Sacron Enigma," Kalvov interrupted. "You are wasting our time and your own."

"Davenport...." Healey choked out. "Davenport is in danger...."

Dead silence answered him. Even the aliens who manhandled Healey down here held their breath and didn't move.

"Davenport sent you?" Kalvov boomed.

Healey swallowed hard. "Davenport is trapped in Sacron Enigma. I'm trying to help him. The Reserve Wing is calling on the Cannibals to go after him...."

"You have said enough, Sheriff," Kalvov snapped. "Be silent."

Healey cringed and tucked his head again. He couldn't look at Mexia without panicking. He didn't want to look at anything. He hadn't come this close to losing his life in a long time and he didn't want to repeat the experience—ever.

Mexia groaned again. "Davenport is our business," Kalvov rumbled. "You will not interfere with our business again."

"No...." Healey croaked. "I won't. I promise."

Lightning quick, someone jerked the bag back over Healey's head. The aliens picked him up and started carrying him back upstairs.

Healey's chest hurt from his heart beating so hard. He couldn't breathe, but at least he was moving away from Mexia.

No one spoke until they took him all the way back upstairs to the market. Healey's captors stood him on his feet, cut the ties holding his wrists and ankles, and finally ripped the hood off his head so he could see where he was.

The fights, bargains, and spectacles went on as before. Healey looked around him, but the aliens who captured him blended seamlessly into the crowd.

None of the stallholders or patrons looked sideways at Healey. He had no idea which of these people captured him and took him downstairs.

He rubbed the blood back into his hands and forced himself to stay calm, but at that moment, a grizzled old Drade stepped out of the mob.

"Remember your promise, Sheriff. Davenport is our business. You stay out of it."

Healey nodded, but the creature was already disappearing into the throng of jumbled aliens flooding the market.

Healey cast one last glance around the chamber and stumbled back the way he came. He went upstairs, and in a second, he was back on the streets of Pandora's Needle.

People called out to him. Prostitutes and drug dealers grinned at him. None of these people had a clue what just happened to him.

He swallowed down the sting of bile in his throat. He just saw Mexia and he was still alive. Everything around him looked so different, so out of place, so.... alien.

He was the one who was out of place. He shouldn't still be walking around. Was he a ghost? Maybe this was the afterlife...but no, people were still looking at him. They were still talking to him and calling him Sheriff.

Any second now, the world would right itself on its axis and go back to the way it was before.... the way it was before he looked down Mexia's throat and thought he was going there.

He staggered down the street hardly daring to think at all. He lurched up the stairs to his office and collapsed into his chair. Davenport. Davenport needed help.

Healey had to think. He had to do.... something. Then again, didn't Mexia just warn him to leave the whole Davenport situation alone? *Davenport is our business. You stay out of it.*

His office door opened and his chief deputy entered. Healey heard the man talking to him, but Healey's brain didn't register what the words meant. Mexia. Davenport. Joyce. The Cannibals.

He fumbled under his desk and pulled out a bottle of Zombie QP10. The bottle was still three-quarters full. It had been sitting under his desk since his first days as a deputy. He had only drunk from this bottle a handful of times in his whole career.

The glass almost fell out of his trembling fingers. He had to concentrate hard not to spill the drink when he poured it into the glass.

His deputy eased a few steps closer. "You okay, Sheriff? Is something wrong?"

Healey gasped for breath and brought the glass to his mouth with shaking hands. He was starting to lose it.

He tossed back the drink and slammed the glass down on his desk fighting to breathe. The Cannibals. Did Healey just make a giant mistake by asking Mexia for help? He might have released something a thousand times worse than the Cannibals. What did he really know about Mexia at all?

"Sheriff?" his deputy asked.

Healey inhaled one more shaky lungful of air and started to say something when an alarm went off on his desk.

He turned to it and his stomach dropped into his boots all over again. His deputy swiveled around the desk and looked at the screen over Healey's shoulder. "Holy shit! What the hell are they doing?"

Healey stared in horror as hundreds of ships launched from hidden locations all over Pandora's Needle. They came from below street level and not one of them transmitted a recognizable identity profile to the Confederate database. Technically, none of these ships should even exist.

They rocketed into the sky faster than thought and vanished into the stars. They left a terrible chill over Healey's heart, but he couldn't stand around feeling sorry for himself.

He shoved the bottle and glass back into their hiding place and attacked his controls in a frenzy. He searched every ship on the general allotment until he found some random freighter destined for Sacron Enigma.

"What are you doing?" his deputy asked.

Healey shot out of his chair and barged over to the weapons locker embedded in his office wall.

He ripped it open and started loading every weapon he could lay his hands on. "I need you to take over for me, Jason. I'm leaving the Needle for a while and I don't know when I'll be back."

"Uh...okay, Sheriff," the deputy said. "No problem."

"If you have any problems, you can contact Admiral Joyce on Atlas Arcane. I'm on a job for him, so he'll understand. He should provide you with any resources you need."

"What are you doing, Sheriff? What do all those ships leaving the Needle mean?"

"I wouldn't like to speculate. Just understand that this is way bigger than anything going on here on the Needle. All these pissant criminals don't mean anything compared to this."

"Okay, Sheriff. I'll handle things here. You don't have to worry about that."

"Good man." Healey pointed to the console. "I'm tracking that freighter. I'll set a trace on it so you can record its course. It's on its way to Sacron Enigma...."

The deputy gasped. "You can't go to Sacron Enigma! That's out of the question."

"Hopefully, I won't have to. That's why I have to leave now." Healey clapped the deputy on the back once and stormed out of the jail. He hustled back up to the roof and loaded into the *Prometheus Vox*.

He located the freighter in question and tagged it with a tracking signal. It was scheduled to launch in a few minutes. Healey fidgeted while he waited for it to get clearance to leave the Needle.

It finally launched and took off on the trail of all Mexia's people. Healey launched a second later and set out on the same course to track them down.

Chapter 9

Davenport ducked behind a tree and pulled Wolf, Breeze, and Alla in behind him. He searched the dark sky for the ships that pursued the *Artemis Rex* crew into the forest, but they didn't come back.

He gasped in a breathless whisper. "I think we lost them."

"There were four of them," Alla panted back. "They went over there. They must be tracking down the others.... which means they'll be coming after us next."

"They won't come after us because they won't be able to find us." Davenport squinted up at the canopy one more time. The forest was getting really dark now. "We'll stay lost until we know they're gone."

"Lost?" Alla glanced over his shoulder into the shadowy undergrowth.

His shoulders turned and Davenport caught a glimpse behind Breeze. Beauty squatted a dozen yards away from their hiding place. He didn't come forward to join them.

Davenport would have called out if anyone else had been standing off and avoiding hiding or staying with the group. Davenport would have gone over there and insisted that the person come over and hide with the rest.

Something in Beauty's posture told Davenport not to go over there. Beauty sat with his back to the four friends.

He gazed out over a wide swamp between the trees. Starlight glistened on the water. Davenport thought he might have some idea what Beauty was looking at.... or what he *wasn't* looking at.

Hidden whispers drifted over the water's surface except that they didn't make any noise. Davenport couldn't explain what it was because he didn't hear anything. The water seemed to swallow all sound and all trace of any living thing.

Wolf sensed that mysterious presence hovering around the *Artemis Rex*. Now it hung over the swamp. It almost explained why Rodeo didn't pick up any life forms out there even when Wolf smelled that they were there.

Something like a breath or maybe an invisible force drifted over the swamp. It made the whole forest seem alive. It watched the strangers who trespassed on its territory, but nothing moved out there.

Beauty stared out at it the same way Wolf stared into the trees when he sensed the Mad Men closing in on the *Artemis Rex*.

Beauty didn't sniff or turn his head. He crouched perfectly motionless. Davenport ached to question Beauty about what was out there, but the same unseen force stopped Davenport from interrupting Beauty's silence.

Davenport turned to Wolf and discovered the boy staring at Beauty, too. Wolf's small, drilling eyes fixed on Beauty's back. The little alien hunched with his wide, flapping ears trained out at the swamp. Beauty didn't notice his friends watching him.

"Where should we go to get more lost?" Breeze whispered.

"We can't go *that* way." Davenport nodded toward the swamp. It vanished into the woods with no end in sight. "We'll just have to stick to the dry land."

He peered around the enormous tree trunk that gave the party some concealment. He wasn't expecting to see anything particularly helpful on this deserted planet, but when he did, he spotted a wink of light. It flickered like flames.

"Something's over there," he whispered. "It looks like people with a fire."

He stood up to walk in that direction, but Alla caught his arm to pull him back. "What if they're hostile? What if they're working with the Mad Men or something?"

"I'm not going to show myself. I'm just going to see what they're doing. I'll stay hidden. You can stay here if you want to."

"But.... how will we find each other again?" Breeze checked behind him and Davenport saw with a sudden pang of alarm that Beauty was gone.

Davenport scanned the swamp Beauty had been looking at. It remained as smooth and glassy as before. Not a single ripple marred its surface so Beauty couldn't have gone into the water.

Davenport glanced right and left, but he didn't see Beauty anywhere. Davenport didn't want to go out into the dark to search for him. Then he really would get lost. He would never find the boys or the *Artemis Rex* again.

He straightened up. "If you feel that way, why don't you come with me? You're coming, aren't you, Wolf?"

Wolf got to his feet and moved into his usual place at Davenport's elbow. Good old Wolf. Davenport could always count on that boy.

Alla cast sidelong glances in both directions and fell in behind Davenport. Breeze brought up the rear and Davenport eased one cautious step at a time toward the firelight. He slowed his pace more and more the closer he got.

He was right. It was firelight, and as he drew nearer in the shadows, he saw several fires burning around a large village. Low, slouching houses had been constructed entirely of logs and branches from the forest.

The creatures sitting around the fires didn't come up to Davenport's waist. They shuffled bent over with long arms dragging almost to their knees.

They reminded Davenport of Beauty. Davenport automatically looked behind him to see if Beauty had reappeared, but he was still gone.

These aliens didn't have the large ears and they were smaller and less skeletal than Beauty. They also lacked his nimble agility.

These creatures moved slowly. Their overlarge heads hung low in front of their hunched shoulders. They barely raised their large feet when they trundled along the ground.

"Mud-dwellers!" Breeze murmured. "Disgusting!"

"Why do you call them that?" Davenport asked.

"That's what they are. Look at them!"

Davenport couldn't argue with the name. The aliens squatted around their fires and ate out of clay pots full of what looked like soil.

Everything they did hugged the ground. They didn't hesitate to use their oversized hands as secondary limbs for pushing themselves along the ground, either.

Davenport and the boys hid behind a tree and watched. The mud-dwellers pulled long, worm-like wrigglers from the soil pots and drop the worms into their mouths.

"Ick!" Alla groaned. "Is that all they eat?"

"Not quite. Look."

Another creature pulled a squirming centipede from one of his pots. The mud-dweller tilted back his head, opened his mouth, and dropped the thing down his own gullet.

Wolf snarled under his breath. "Damn it!" Alla whimpered. "I was hoping they would have something to eat."

"Be careful what you wish for." Davenport bumped Wolf. "Let's get out of here and see if we can find the *Artemis*......"

He froze when the aliens started talking. He couldn't hear everything they said, but he definitely heard one of them say the word, *Ithium*.

"They know about the Ithium," he hissed. "How is that possible?"

"Could the Mad Men have contacted them?" Breeze asked.

"I don't know, but I'm going to get closer and see if I can hear what they're saying." Davenport hunkered lower and stepped out from behind the tree.

He took a few steps forward. The aliens' voices became clearer and his heart skipped a beat when he heard the word, *Ithium,* more than once.

He spotted another large tree right at the edge of the village. He could hide there and listen in on their conversation.

He sidestepped toward it and bent down when a loud splash startled him from behind. It sounded incredibly loud in the oppressive silence.

Davenport, Wolf, and Alla spun around fast. Davenport froze when he saw Breeze up to his eyeballs in a giant puddle right behind where the friends had just been hiding.

Breeze lay on his back.... or at least it looked like that from where Davenport stood. Breeze flailed his arms and legs wildly. Davenport couldn't see very much through the fountain of droplets spraying in all directions.

Breeze raised his head above the churning froth kicked up by his own ridiculous antics. He gawped for a mouthful of air and went down again even though the puddle barely looked deep enough to cover him when he was lying down.

He rolled and tossed and spluttered in such an exaggerated display of drowning that Davenport actually feared Breeze might be in danger.

That fear evaporated when Breeze rotated onto his back. He kept floundering and opening and closing his mouth like a stranded fish. Davenport could plainly see the kid lying on the ground just a few inches below the water's surface.

Davenport stormed over to him and yanked Breeze out of the water. He shook Breeze and set him on his feet. "Be quiet! You'll...."

Davenport broke off and stiffened when a different bunch of mud-dwellers approaching from behind.

He braced himself to fight them. He even let go of Breeze to grab for his sidearm, but it wasn't there. The Mad Men had disarmed the crew.

Wolf growled again and advanced to Davenport's side. Wolf planted himself at Davenport's elbow and Wolf squared up to fight the mud-dwellers, too.

A second later, Davenport realized the mud-dwellers weren't coming to threaten him and his boys.

The mud-dwellers advanced from deeper in the swamp. They must have been out there all along, but they didn't surround the trio in anything like a threatening attitude.

They couldn't exactly threaten Davenport when they barely came up to his waist. Their waddling gait wasn't fast enough or nimble enough to do much of anything.

They raised their hands to Davenport and murmured in an almost trance-like hum. He cringed from them, only to realize with another jolt of horror that the mud-dwellers from the village were coming out into the forest to do exactly the same thing.

They surrounded Davenport and the three boys. The mud-dwellers crowded way too close, and when they got to the party, the aliens raised their hands to actually touch the four friends.

Davenport tried to shrink away from their groping hands, but he only ran into more mud-dwellers blocking his path everywhere he turned.

The mud-dwellers stroked his jacket, touched his star and his arms in awed reverence, and they started to sway in dreamy enchantment.

They caressed Wolf's fur and even tried to thread their fingers into it. Wolf gave a vicious shriek and slapped their hands away. He even knocked a few mud-dwellers over, but they didn't seem to care or even to notice.

They didn't stop touching him, Davenport, Alla, and Breeze. The mud-dwellers crowded around humming in that worshipful undertone.

"Um.... what the hell is going on?" Breeze yelped. "What do they want?"

"I don't know," Davenport called back. "I just...."

"The Ithium!" the mud-dwellers chanted. "They brought the Ithium! They brought the Ithium back to us!"

Their voices rose and fell on all sides as one alien after another took up the refrain. They chanted in a dazed murmur from beyond the grave.

"They brought the Ithium back to us! The prophecy has been fulfilled!"

"The what?" Davenport called back. "What prophecy? I didn't...."

"All hail!" The mud-dwellers raised their arms and hands above their heads. They swayed and waved in exaltation. "All hail—the Bringer of the Ithium!"

Wolf let out another shriek, but this one sounded more indignant than angry. "What the holy hell are they talking about?" Alla squealed.

"The Ithium!" The mud-dwellers' voices started to rise to a frenzy of calls and almost to cheers. "The Bringer of the Ithium has come at last!"

"Can we get the hell out of here now?" Breeze yelled.

Davenport started to step forward, but the mud-dwellers pushed him backward. The creatures behind parted to let him through. They started propelling him and the boys toward the village.

"Maybe we should go along with them," Davenport called back.

"Are you crazy?" Alla squeaked. "They think we have the Ithium!"

The mud-dwellers erupted in even louder, more frantic cheers. "The Ithium! The Ithium! The Bringer of the Ithium!"

Davenport couldn't bring himself to tell these people that he didn't have the Ithium cartridge on his actual person. He was too grateful that they weren't outright attacking him the way everyone else was.

He backed toward the village, and when he got near enough, he pulled Wolf along with him.

Wolf still tried to fend the mud-dwellers off. He snarled at them every time they touched him, but none of his efforts put them off. If anything, they got more enthusiastic by the minute.

More mud-dwellers arrived when the three friends entered the village. The aliens came out of houses and even out of the woods. Davenport never would have suspected so many of them could be living here.

They surrounded him in a throng, all hailing the Bringer of the Ithium. "How do they know about the Ithium?" Breeze called over.

Davenport started to answer when Breeze collapsed. He tripped over his own feet and hit the dirt among the startled mud-dwellers, but his usual explosion of windmill arms and legs still didn't stop them.

They crowded around him even more, hoisted him to his feet, and immediately started touching him all over while they murmured in rapt adoration.

The mud-dwellers clustered even tighter around the friends. Their awed caresses became increasingly insistent. They packed in so tightly that Breeze fell over again, but the mud-dwellers barely noticed.

Davenport didn't want to think about how they knew about the Ithium. He didn't really care. They might not be trying to kill him, but now he had to add these creatures to the growing list of people who wanted to get the Ithium away from him.

They might be worshiping him now, but that wouldn't last. He had no idea what abilities or resources they would bring out to get the Ithium if he tried to stop them.

They pushed him and the boys over to the fire. Breeze turned around and extended his hands to the flames to warm himself. Murky water dripped from his hair and clothes. His antics were bound to cause the group problems if Breeze got too cold.

Breeze turning around seemed to act as some kind of signal to the mud-dwellers. They burst into a fresh wave of activity.

Half of them got busy clearing their clay pots and other stuff from the area. The rest continued their reverential groveling around the four visitors.

"Please tell me they aren't going to feed us out of *those*." Alla shot a disgusted look at the pots, but the mud-dwellers didn't try to take anything out of them.

They scurried here and there removing all the pots from the ground near the fires. Then they started setting up spits, impaling some kind of monstrous arthropods to turn on the crossbars, and bringing out empty pots to heat over the coals.

They started boiling water drawn from the swamp. They added things to the brew. None of it looked any more appetizing than the worms and crawlers the mud-dwellers had been eating before.

Alla gulped hard at the sight and Davenport shuddered as the mud-dwellers got more and more excited over their preparations. This must be their idea of a celebratory feast.

That meant he, Breeze, Alla, and Wolf would have no choice but to eat the villagers' food. The mud-dwellers might turn hostile if their new heroes didn't appreciate the ceremony conducted in their honor.

The mud-dwellers' adoration seemed to be escalating into a full-scale ritual. Some of the aliens brought out long tree fronds decorated with colored shells and strings of hand-carved beads.

They raised more of these strings toward Davenport and tried to drape them around him while other mud-dwellers waved their fronds in grand style.

They surrounded Davenport in particular and chanted louder. "Deliver us, oh Bringer of the Ithium! Deliver us from the horrors within!"

"What horrors?" Breeze called over.

Davenport had had enough. He raised both hands and tried to yell over the noise. "Listen! I don't have the Ithium, okay? I didn't come to deliver you from anything."

No one listened. The frond-waving and chanting built to a chorus. Sing-song voices rose and fell in a confused hubbub. The mud-dwellers circled Davenport in an uncoordinated dance of waving arms and jangling beads.

Davenport took a deep breath and hollered one last time. "I don't have the Ithium! It isn't here!"

No one responded and he sighed. He tried. If they didn't believe him, he had no choice but to go along with this and see what happened.

Chapter 10

The mud-dwellers jostled Davenport and the boys over to the fires. Davenport couldn't exactly tell when the ritual ended. The mud-dwellers just kind of came to a stopping point. They put their fronds away and stopped swaying and chanting about the Ithium.

They drew the four friends nearer to the spits and boiling cauldrons of whatever these aliens were cooking. The creatures on the spits bubbled and spat hissing juice into the flames.

Davenport didn't want to think about anything being cooked in water from the swamp, but it was looking more and more likely that he was about to find out.

The mud-dwellers crouched down and started working over their food. They slid one of the arthropods off the spit onto a flat rock. One of the mud-dwellers raised another large stone high above his head and started hacking murderously at the roasted thing.

Juice and spattered broken exoskeleton flew in all directions. Davenport jumped out of the line of fire, but no one noticed.

The mud-dweller kept decimating the arthropod with brutal strikes until he pulverized the thing to a sodden pulp.

His companions scooped portions of the mess into wooden bowls, dolloped ladlefuls of the soup on top, and offered it up to the guests with as much submissive reverence as anyone could wish.

Wolf wrinkled his nose and growled more ferociously than ever. One of the mud-dwellers tried to waft the bowl under his nose and he smacked it away with a furious roar.

The bowl went flying and sprayed the food all over the surrounding mud-dwellers, but that only seemed to encourage them.

They placed some of the mashed arthropod on a flat wooden slab and held that out to Wolf, too. He lunged for them and would have slashed them to pieces, but Davenport and Alla hauled Wolf back.

That seemed to finally convince the mud-dwellers to leave Wolf alone, but that only left the other three for the mud-dwellers to take care of instead.

The villagers had better luck with Breeze. They held out both the bowl and the plate of mashed insect to him and he took them both. He sniffed at the soup once and then took a huge gulp.

He swallowed whatever was in it in one mouthful. "It's really...pretty good...." he mumbled between licking his lips. "It's really not that bad."

Then he picked up three finger-loads of the arthropod meat, opened his mouth, and dropped it in just like the mud-dwellers did.

Davenport watched closely to see if Breeze actually chewed the stuff or let it touch his tongue, but Breeze did everything too quickly. Davenport couldn't believe he was actually thinking this, but Breeze did it all expertly—so expertly that Davenport didn't see what Breeze did.

"Oh, Good Lord!" Alla whimpered. "Get me out of here! I'm gonna be sick!"

Breeze's performance delighted the mud-dwellers no end. They twittered to each other in high-pitched squeaks of excitement and delight. Some of them even bounced up and down in front of Breeze. They shoved fresh loads of food into his hands and he ate them just as eagerly. The food couldn't be that bad.

Next came Davenport's turn. He didn't want to touch the stuff, but diplomacy trumped all.

The soup looked like the lesser of two evils, so he took a bowl. He smelled it. It smelled a whole lot like the swamp looked.

He summoned all his courage and took a sip. It tasted like swamp water, too, but the mud-dwellers' reaction bolstered his resolve to get this over with.

They became even more thrilled that he was eating their food than they were by Breeze. They swirled around him in a vortex of swaying, murmuring, touching, and shuffling.

He took another two swallows of the water, but he stopped short of eating the arthropod meat at the bottom.

He passed the bowl back to the first hands available and tried to find someone in the crowd that he could smile at. "It was delicious, but I've had enough. Thank you."

A deafening crash interrupted him. He glanced over to see Breeze kicking and struggling on the ground. The mud-dwellers tried simultaneously to get out of his way and to help him at the same time.

His wild flailing bowled them sideways and several went flying. Without warning, one of his legs floundered at a strange angle and upset the stew cauldron. It toppled into the coals and the deluge drowned the fire instantly.

The soup washed the remaining arthropod mash off its rock and the whole mess streamed into the mud. It formed a river around the mud-dwellers' feet. At least a dozen of them stepped in it and squashed the meat in their flurry to jump clear.

More mud-dwellers swarmed in trying to save Breeze from himself, but they only got hit in the process. Breeze landed several telling blows that left the little aliens bloody and howling.

Breeze's grunts and moans of distress produced an electric effect on the mud-dwellers. They just could not stop themselves from trying to save him from the terrible fate afflicting him no matter the danger.

The mud-dwellers didn't have any success in getting him on his feet until Davenport and Wolf both waded into the mix. They picked up Breeze and jostled him to his feet.

Davenport didn't have time to tell Breeze off before the mud-dwellers moved in again. They started chanting, "The Ithium! The Ithium! All hail the Bringer of the Ithium!"

They pushed and prodded the friends away from the fires. Wolf flew into another violent rage until Davenport pulled him closer and held him back.

"What do they want now, Sir?" Alla asked.

Davenport glanced behind Alla to where the mud-dwellers were pushing him. "It looks like they want us to go to that house over there."

Sure enough, the mud-dwellers propelled the friends to what looked like the largest house in the village, but it still wasn't more than a hovel. The thatched roof came right down to the ground and the structure had no floor besides the bare ground.

The mud-dwellers kept murmuring and chanting, but their intention couldn't be plainer. "They want us to go inside."

"What for?" Alla asked.

"It's nighttime," Davenport pointed out. "Maybe they want us to stay here."

Breeze looked around at the many upturned faces glowing with awe and wonderment. "Aren't they going to try to get the Ithium from us?"

"It doesn't look like it. Come on."

Davenport pulled Wolf under the roof. The fires outside gave the only light and the glow barely made it into the hut.

There was nothing in the hut but plain, hard dirt. The mud-dwellers must sleep right on the ground. They had no furniture at all.

A second later, three mud-dwellers came in carrying branches and bundles of brush. They arranged everything into four piles and spread woven mats over everything. Then they gestured to these piles with so much bowing, scraping, and murmuring that Davenport understood.

He stretched out on one of the piles. The branches sprung underneath him and made something like a passable bed.

"Come on, boys. Lie down and at least pretend to sleep." Davenport almost broke off when he remembered that these mud-dwellers could speak English. They could understand everything he said. Then he gave up. He was so far beyond caring that none of this seemed to matter anymore. "Come on. Lie down. Don't insult them by refusing their hospitality."

Breeze went over to one of the piles and pushed down on the mat to test the spring action. Davenport held his breath for the next disaster, but it never came.

Breeze's expression relaxed into his usual benign smile and he and Alla both laid down, too. Wolf growled under his breath, shot the last bed a hateful glare, and curled into a ball on the bare dirt next to Davenport's bed.

That must have satisfied the mud-dwellers because they started to drift away. They returned to their fires and Davenport closed his eyes. The villagers murmured and even sang out there in the night, but their voices didn't disturb the guests.

Alla's voice drifted out of the darkness. "How long do we have to stay here, Sir?"

"I'm not sure. If they want the Idhium, staying here might be the best course. If we leave, we might end up leading them back to the *Artemis Rex* and we don't want to do that."

"How do you think they knew we were carrying it?"

"I have no idea, but it sure does make me suspicious. Do you remember how they came up behind us when Breeze fell in that puddle? They were following us through the forest."

Wolf gave a low growl, and without thinking about it, Davenport let his hand migrate to the boy's shoulder.

Davenport's fingers fell into Wolf's fur and he gave the boy an affectionate scratch. "I thought of that, too. They were the ones who were watching us when we first landed, weren't they?"

"How could they be?" Alla asked. "The Mad Men were there."

"So the Mad Men and the mud-dwellers were both there at the same time and now the mud-dwellers know about the Ithium? It seems a little too convenient for my taste."

"But the Mad Men didn't know about the Ithium," Breeze pointed out. "They only said they wanted to get you back to the Confederacy. They never mentioned finding the Ithium first. Don't you think they would have gone to more trouble to make sure you had it before they shipped you back to Admiral Joyce?"

Davenport didn't answer. Too many mysteries swirled on this forgotten planet. They couldn't all be just coincidence.

How did the mud-dwellers know to come to the *Artemis Rex*? How did they know to coordinate with the Mad Men—if that's what the mud-dwellers were doing?

Both groups knew each other enough to communicate about the Ithium—if the Mad Men knew about the Ithium at all. The Mad Men must have been on this planet long before those space aliens drove the *Artemis Rex* down to the surface.

Alla's breathing lengthened and Wolf made a low rasping sound under his breath. He was falling asleep and Davenport felt himself starting to drift off. All those questions would have to wait for another time.

Chapter 11

F iddler peeked through the undergrowth. "There's the *Artemis Rex*. It looks deserted."

"Live in hope, darlin'," Dice growled under his breath.

"Who would come after us *here*?" Coon asked. "We've been hiding here for hours and none of those other ships have come back. They must have already searched the area and now they're looking for everyone everywhere else."

"We have NOT been here for hours," Axel countered. "It's only been about fifteen minutes at the most."

"Does it really matter how long we've been here?" Dice got to his feet. "I'm going over there if only to get myself a weapon. This hiding in bushes is bullshit."

He stalked off toward the ship. Axel and Coon glanced at each other. Fiddler waited a second longer and then sprang out to follow Dice. He was so much bigger than the other three. He would be the first target if someone came after them.

Fiddler didn't mind hiding in bushes, but she *did* mind not having a weapon.

She glanced right and left searching everywhere for the Mad Men or whoever it was that kept swooping around searching for the crew. The attackers didn't come back, though.

Dice went inside, and the next minute, furious roars echoed from the cargo hold. "Son of a bitch! The XQs are all gone!"

"There were a bunch of 62s in there when we left," Coon called back. "Did the Mad Men take them all?"

"There are plenty of 62s," Dice bellowed. "I want an 85. I don't want to screw around with some puny, piss-ass 62."

Fiddler chuckled, but she made sure to do it quietly so Dice wouldn't hear. She caught Axel and Coon grinning at each other.

Dice stormed out loading a bunch of pump rifles. He stomped around the *Artemis Rex* and squinted up at the hull sections the boys welded earlier. "How soon can you get this tin can off the ground?"

"It shouldn't take long. We just have to fix the ion reverter...."

"Don't give me a stinkin' scientific analysis! Just fix the damn thing!"

Fiddler went inside to the weapons locker. Coon was right. There were ten XQ 65s in there. She took out two, loaded them, and carried them outside.

She grinned at Dice when he scowled at her. "Mine are bigger than yours."

He bared his teeth and snarled at her, but she only laughed. Axel and Coon started working on the ship. Axel climbed on top of the hull to the spot the boys were working on before. Coon handed things up to him.

Axel rummaged inside the fuselage. Dice and Fiddler circled the ship and searched the surrounding forest for any threat. The more Fiddler didn't see anything, the more the silence got on her nerves.

Wolf was right. Something was out there. Hidden eyes followed her every move. Why didn't they show themselves?

This menacing silence ended last time with the Mad Men attacking the crew. Now, only four of the crew were here to defend the ship. She and Dice wouldn't be able to hold the *Artemis Rex* on their own.

Axel finished doing something and both boys went inside to the cockpit. The forest got even quieter and the darkness made it impossible to see anything.

She instinctively inched closer to Dice. She knew she shouldn't. She should put more space between them to cover more of the terrain, but his bulk and ferocity made her feel safer somehow.

He startled her by growling low under his breath. "I don't like this. This is not good."

"Do you hear or see anything?"

"Naw. It's more just a feeling."

"Wolf smelled something earlier.... right before the Mad Men attacked. Did you notice anything then?"

He snorted. "I wasn't exactly at my peak if you know what I mean."

She tried to smile, but she didn't really feel like it. She swiveled outward and passed her XQ back and forth, but at that moment, a piercing shriek set her hair on end.

She and Dice whipped around fast. They both trained their weapons toward the sound. "Did you hear that?" she whispered and then realized how stupid that question was. Of course Dice heard it.

Another high-pitched yowl followed a second later. "Something's over there." Dice started forward. "I'm going to see what it is. If it's anything dangerous, I want to know about it now before they get the jump on us."

He set off through the forest. Fiddler glanced behind her toward the cargo hold, but the boys were nowhere in sight.

She crept after Dice and found him crouching in the bushes. He aimed his rifles through the foliage at what looked like a village of huts constructed of branches and thatched with leaves.

"Damn mud-dwellers!" Dice snarled. "Pathetic!"

Several fires blazed around an open space in the middle. Fiddler caught her breath when she saw Davenport, Wolf, Alla, and Breeze surrounded by some kind of aliens.

The aliens attacked Breeze, who sprawled on the ground trying to fight them off. He hit and kicked them in a frenzy while Davenport and Alla tried in vain to help him.

Fiddler raised her weapon, but Dice knocked it down. "We need more weapons than this. Come on! We have to rescue them."

He vaulted to his feet and charged back to the ship. "Where are you going?" she demanded when she finally caught up with him. "We have to stop them. We can't let them harm Davenport and the boys."

"I AM helping them!" Dice blasted into the cargo hold and went straight to the weapons locker. He shoved his rifles back in place and started pulling out every XQ he could lay his hands on. He didn't waste time checking what size they were.

He loaded at least six of them. Fiddler glanced behind her toward the cockpit while she waited....and she stiffened when she noticed something. "Dice."

He didn't stop loading his weapons and stuffing his pockets with choke shells. "Huh?"

"Lyons......she's gone."

Dice whipped around fast and narrowed his eyes at the crew quarters farther up the *Artemis Rex's* single deck. All the cabin doors were closed except for one.

"What do you think they did with her?"

Dice snarled something else and snapped one last ammo cylinder into his weapon. He spun the other way and barged outside.

He strode so fast toward the village that Fiddler had to run to keep up with him. The second their feet touched solid the ground, a massive howl erupted from the ship's engines.

The engines fired up to full power. A blast of wind and burning exhaust hit the ground on either side of Dice and Fiddler.

The impact plowed two massive furrows in the soft soil. Two identical sprays of water shot skyward. They created two matched walls of water on either side of the one solid spot of ground where Dice and Fiddler stood.

They both stood rooted to the spot until Fiddler recovered. She raced back inside. "Kill the engines! Kill the engines!"

Axel looked up at her from the tactical cradle where Rodeo usually sat. "You said you wanted to get the ship running."

"You'll attract everyone for miles around! Are you trying to get us killed? Keep it powered down until we're ready to leave."

"Oh." Axel frowned at the controls in front of him. "Sorry."

She peeked out through the cockpit window. "I sure hope you didn't alert everyone within a hundred miles of where we are."

"Me, too," Coon replied.

No one moved or breathed for a second. Fiddler strained every nerve to hear if someone was coming after them, but nothing happened.

"I guess it's all right. Dice and I are going to get Davenport. Stay here."

Axel's head shot up. "You know where he is?"

"Yeah. He's......what the hell is *that*?"

Numerous small bodies moved around outside and Fiddler had to suppress laughter when she recognized them.

She went back outside and really did laugh when she found Dice surrounded by the aliens from the village. They weren't attacking, but Dice sure acted like they were.

They raised their hands to touch, stroke, and admire him. They swayed in ecstasy and murmured in adoring voices that got more excited by the minute.

"What did you do to them, Dice?" Fiddler teased. "Did you snow them with your charm and good looks?"

He bellowed in rage, but they were already streaming past him to surround the ship.

They started caressing the hull in the same attitude of worship and awe. "Alive! It's alive! It carried the Bringer to us and now the prophecy is fulfilled! It's alive!"

"Get the hell off me, you cocksuckers!" Dice roared. "Get your hands off me! Don't touch me!"

He leveled his XQ at them, but they didn't even notice. They paused just long enough to pay him homage and then turned their rapt attention on the *Artemis Rex*.

"What are they doing?" Fiddler called over the tide of voices. "What do they want?"

"How the hell should I know?" he roared. "Get away from me!"

They already were. They left him alone except for more mud-dwellers arriving from the village. Fiddler squinted into the shadows trying to see Davenport and the boys.

"Where did you take Davenport?" she called to the aliens. "What did you do with him?"

She kicked herself for letting them get so near the ship. These creatures might have killed Davenport and the boys.

The mud-dwellers might be about to do the same thing to Fiddler and the others, but she doubted it somehow. These people didn't seem dangerous at all.

That still didn't explain why they attacked Breeze earlier, but before she could ask again, another whine of engine noise interrupted the scene.

She jerked around fast expecting to see the *Artemis Rex* firing up again, but it wasn't. One of the search ships wheeled overhead and swung its searchlight toward the *Artemis Rex*.

The mud-dwellers shrieked and surged away, but it was too late. The search ship unleashed a devastating attack on the *Artemis Rex*.... except that the bombardment didn't hit the Drifter.

A wicked jet of plasma smashed into the mud-dwellers and bodies twirled into the air. Gunfire chewed up the soil leveling the mud-dwellers by the score.

Fiddler lunged for Dice and yanked him out of the crowd. "Get inside the ship!" She whirled for the hatch. "Fire it up, boys! Return fire!"

Dice stumbled and finally charged into the hold behind her just as the boys punched the throttle. The *Artemis Rex* vaulted off the ground with both engines shrieking to full power.

The mud-dwellers ran screaming for their village. The search ship rocketed straight past the *Artemis Rex* raining countless shots on the defenseless villagers.

Fiddler bolted for the cockpit. Coon had moved up to the command cradle where Davenport usually sat while Axel piloted the ship in Bandit's old place.

Axel ripped back the helm to launch into the air. Coon rotated his cradle upward to fire on the search ship.

Fiddler pounced on him and grabbed Coon's arm. "Don't! Don't shoot!"

"What the hell are you talking about? You told us to shoot. They're trying to kill us!"

"They're going for the mud-dwellers! Get down on the ground, Axel! Hurry! If you go up there, they really will kill us."

"You're out of your mind!" Axel countered. "We can't just sit here."

She pointed to the search ship on his controls. "Do you see that? These aren't the Mad Men."

Axel came to his senses and frowned at the identity profile. "What is that? I don't recognize it."

"That ship belongs to Mexia."

Both boys gasped out loud and Coon gaped at Fiddler with his mouth open. "That's impossible."

"Someone must have sent her people out here. Set down on the ground, Axel. Do it before they start thinking we're threatening them."

"What are *they* doing out here?" Coon squeaked. "They're.... they're...."

Fiddler nodded. "Power the ship back down and don't reignite until we're ready to leave the planet."

Axel started to lower the ship to the ground. The mud-dwellers had all retreated into the forest, but Mexia's ship kept hammering them all the way back to their village. What the hell were Mexia's people doing so far out of Confederate space? It made no sense.

Axel set down and started to power down the engines. Coon let go of his controls and started to stand up with another crushing smash vibrated the hull.

Another ship whizzed overhead and unloaded on Mexia's ship. The newcomer plastered the ground outside, the *Artemis Rex*, and Mexia's ship with blistering concussions, but these weren't plasma shots.

"Okay, *that's* the Mad Men!" Fiddler bellowed. "Get us up there and return fire!"

"Make up your mind!" Axel shrieked.

Fiddler pounced into the tactical cradle behind Coon. They both swung their Howitzers upward as Axel erupted out of the trees.

He whipped backward and both Fiddler and Coon unloaded on the Mad Men. "Just don't hit Mexia's people!" Fiddler yelled.

"I got that!" Coon roared. "What the hell are they doing fighting each other?"

"Maybe they're both here for the same thing."

"That isn't the same ship that captured us," Axel called over his shoulder. "It's someone else."

"The Mad Men who captured us were working with more of their own. Where do you think the last stragglers went after Dice chased them out of the ship?"

No one answered her. Coon and Fiddler had their work cut out for them returning the Mad Men's fire. Mexia's people swung around to defend themselves and they didn't take so much trouble not to hit the *Artemis Rex*. In fact, they didn't make any effort at all not to hit it.

Both vessels struck the *Artemis Rex*, either accidentally or deliberately—Fiddler couldn't tell which and it made little difference in the end.

Both ships landed shots that sent the *Artemis Rex* reeling. Axel had to work his hardest to hold the ship stable. Even then, the assault from both enemies stopped Coon and Fiddler from aiming very well.

Dice staggered up to the cockpit, stumbled, and slammed his shoulders against the bulkhead when another belt from the Mad Men jostled the *Artemis Rex* hard to port. "What the hell are you kids doing? We have a rescue operation to...."

An even more vicious barrage smashed into the ship's nose from Mexia's ship. Dice almost fell over and then his fierce eyes locked on Fiddler's controls. "Is that what I think it is?"

"Get us out of here, Axel!" Fiddler ordered. "Bury us in the swamp while they're occupied with each other."

"You don't have to tell me twice!" Axel peeled the *Artemis Rex* sideways. The Mad Men and Mexia's people were too busy bombarding each other to notice the *Artemis Rex* sprint away into the dark.

Chapter 12

Laub and Bandit launched out of their hiding place. "They're attacking the *Artemis Rex!* We have to stop them!"

Emmett jumped from behind the bushes, grabbed both boys, and yanked them down. "Do you want to get your heads shot off? What do you think you're going to do against a ship in flight? You can't get back on board while the ship is in the air!"

The two boys struggled to break out of his grasp. "Let me go!" Bandit growled. "That's my ship!"

Rodeo shot out his arm and jerked Bandit down. "Get down and keep quiet, boy! Don't you recognize that ship?"

"Of course I do, asshole! It's the *Artemis Rex* and it's under fire!"

"Not that! The attacker...." Rodeo rotated his head from one side to the other. He cocked his ear upward toward the battle. "That's one of Mexia's ships."

Emmett, Laub, and Bandit all froze staring at Rodeo. "You're lying!"

Emmett glanced up at the ship swirling overhead. "What are *they* doing here?"

"I don't know, but you can see they aren't shooting at the *Artemis Rex*. They're shooting at the mud-dwellers."

Emmett hunkered lower. He didn't want anyone connected to Mexia knowing he was on this planet. He didn't want them even knowing he existed.

"How do we get back to the ship with them in the way?" Laub asked.

"Just sit tight," Rodeo replied. "If Mexia's people are targeting the mud-dwellers, they might leave the...."

Another shrieking howl of engine noise cut him off as another ship zoomed out of the stars. It rained dozens of shots on the *Artemis Rex* and then laid into Mexia's ship.

"Come on!" Rodeo sprang to his feet.

"Hey, you said....!" Laub cried, but Rodeo was already sprinting into the shadows.

Emmett sighed and charged after him. So much for sitting tight.

Emmett and the three boys hurdled fallen trees and splashed through puddles on a dead race for the *Artemis Rex*.

The bombardment from overhead escalated to a raging din. Plasma licked the ground and the Mad Men's missed shots smashed on all sides. They splintered the soft soil and water geysered from the craters.

Emmett lost sight of exactly who was shooting whom. He only kept his eyes on Laub running right in front of him.

Laub and Bandit both followed Rodeo and that boy could find a shadow in a pitch-black cellar. Emmett didn't have to know where Rodeo was going. Emmett didn't care as long as Rodeo knew where he was going.

Emmett crashed into Laub who crashed into Bandit and all three of them crashed into Rodeo. He halted without warning. "Shit!"

Emmett and the other two boys stared down into a massive crater. A quick glance around revealed that this was the spot where the crew left the *Artemis Rex*.

Emmett almost asked Rodeo what they should do now when both Mexia's ship and the Mad Men came wheeling back. Both ships traded deafening shots and more projectiles pelted into the forest nearby.

Rodeo spun around fast. "Quick—into the woods!"

He herded the others under the trees and all four collapsed behind a different cluster of bushes. "Damn it!"

"Where's the *Artemis Rex*?" Laub husked. "They left without us!"

"They didn't leave!" Bandit moaned. "The ship has been destroyed. We all saw that."

"They didn't. They couldn't." Emmett glanced over at Rodeo. "Could they?"

Rodeo kept turning his head trying to listen.

"What do we do now, Rodeo?" Laub's voice trembled. "I mean.... what do we do?"

"Shhh!" Rodeo hissed. "Let me think."

"What is there to think about?" Emmett demanded. "We're stranded on an uninhabited planet inside Sacron Enigma. We're finished."

"This planet isn't uninhabited. The mud-dwellers are here."

"Like I said, it's uninhabited. We can't be trapped here. We have to find a way off. The question is how."

"Getting off the planet is easy," Rodeo countered. "All we have to do is steal one of the Mad Men's ships, but we have a much bigger problem right now."

"What problem is that?" Laub asked.

Rodeo pursed his lips and listened again. The battle overhead was getting farther away so it wasn't as loud.

"If they really did destroy the *Artemis Rex*," he murmured in a much lower voice, "then we could be sitting at the epicenter of an Ithium release."

A dangerous silence fell over the other three. Emmett glanced at Bandit and Laub and then out at the surrounding forest. Ithium was one of the most toxic radioactive substances known to man. How long did the four of them have left to live if the Ithium had been released?

Rodeo started to stand up. "We aren't alone on this planet. Let's go find the mud-dwellers. They're the only people around here who can help us."

Emmett didn't want to go, but Rodeo's resolve gave him one microscopic scrap of hope. Rodeo sounded awfully confident about stealing a ship from the Mad Men.

Why shouldn't he be? The Chorion Team was Ekol Thaine's most trusted hit team. They might just be kids, but Rodeo knew what he was doing if anyone did. Everything Emmett saw from these boys recently convinced him that.

Emmett got to his feet. Rodeo's resolve had a similar effect on Laub and Bandit. They followed Emmett, who followed Rodeo deeper into the dark woods. Emmett struggled to see every obstacle in their path, but Rodeo didn't have the same problem.

He dodged sections of swamp and stepped over fallen timbers as though he was seeing them in broad daylight.

He headed off to the right. Emmett cast a heartfelt glance toward the crater where the *Artemis Rex* used to be. He was really starting to like that ship.

Emmett and Rodeo froze at the same instant. Emmett gaped at the sight of a bunch of burly human men coming through the trees. They wore ragged clothes, disheveled beards, and they were all armed.

Emmett and Rodeo both ducked at the same time. Rodeo pulled the other two down. "Get down...and keep quiet!"

"Are those....?" Laub asked.

"Mad Men," Emmett replied. "They're either coming to find their friends or...."

The Mad Men paused at the crater. They passed searchlights and their weapons across the massive hole and out into the woods.

Emmett almost asked Rodeo what the Mad Men wanted from the crater, but a few of the Mad Men stopped him when they started talking.

Emmett didn't recognize any of their voices, which confirmed his suspicions. These men must belong to a different group of Mad Men than the ones who captured the *Artemis Rex* crew.

"Spread out, boys," a big, muscular character ordered. "If it isn't here, they might have hidden it somewhere nearby."

"They're after the Ithium," Rodeo whispered.

"The first bunch didn't know about it," Emmett replied. "They only wanted Davenport."

"We don't know that. They didn't mention the Ithium, but they might have been under different orders. They might have been working under a commander who kept certain information to himself and only gave out information to his underlings on a need-to-know basis."

"These idiots sure know about it." Bandit pointed toward the crater. "Look."

"It won't be hidden if Mexia's people blew up the ship," another Mad Man countered.

"They didn't blow up the ship," the first one told him. "We saw them flying away, but that could have been a diversion. They might have wanted us to follow them so we wouldn't find it down here."

"What if they released it here?" someone else asked.

The first Mad Man raised a radioactive counter device and swept it back and forth. "They didn't release it. There's nothing here, which means it's either hidden or back on the ship. As soon as we search here, we'll go after their ship."

"Bastards!" Bandit hissed. "The ship got away!"

"Which means the Ithium is still on board," Rodeo replied.

"Thank Heaven for that," Emmett breathed. "It hasn't been released or they wouldn't be looking for it."

"How do we find the ship?" Emmett asked. "We have no way to locate it or for whoever took it to find us."

Rodeo turned his head the other way. "There's something over there. I hear voices."

He set off in that direction. He moved in a crouch to stop the Mad Men from seeing him.

Emmett kept checking to make sure the Mad Men didn't follow, but the third time Emmett looked, their leader pointed straight at the group of fugitives. "Let's check the mud-dwellers. Davenport might have given it to them."

"Damn!" Rodeo snarled. "Get out of the way!"

He wheeled sideways and shoved Emmett back the way they came, but they couldn't get out of the Mad Men's path fast enough.

The Mad Men started through the forest and spread out in a wide line. They headed in the direction Rodeo had been going. In half a second, one of the searchlights wheeled across Laub and Bandit.

"Shit!" Bandit squeaked and the boys broke into a run.

Rodeo and Emmett stumbled over each other trying to keep up, but it was too late. A shout went up from the Mad Men and they charged forward.

Emmett ran as fast as the others, but he could already see that he and the boys wouldn't get away in time. One of the Mad Men raised an XQ to his shoulder. "Stop where you are or we'll shoot!"

Emmett raised his arms above his head for whatever flimsy protection he could get. Bandit screamed as gunfire erupted in the darkness, but none of the shots hit the fleeing crew.

Emmett dared to look up and saw four Mad Men bite the dust. They pitched onto their faces and the rest whipped backward as plasma erupted from the shadows.

Emmett couldn't believe what he was seeing. His legs kept running without any help from his brain and he tripped over something on the forest floor.

He toppled over Laub, and when they both scrambled to unwind themselves, Emmett got a good look at what was going on.

The Mad Men had their backs to him and they faced off against......

Rodeo caught up with them and hauled Emmett to his feet. "Come on!" he bellowed over the din. "We have to get out of here now!"

Emmett barely heard him. He gaped in shock at the aliens shooting at the Mad Men. It couldn't be, but his senses didn't lie.

"Mexia!" Laub whimpered. "Mexia's people are here!"

"Come on!" Rodeo roared. "Get moving now before they catch up with us!"

He propelled everyone away. They broke into an even more desperate run, this time directly away from the gun battle. Emmett didn't dare to look back. Mexia's people couldn't be here. This made the crew's situation a thousand times worse.

They barely made it fifty feet when the whole catastrophic battle surged deeper into the woods. The Mad Men retreated from Mexia's onslaught and overran the fleeing boys.

Emmett and Rodeo veered left, but there was no way out. Plasma smashed into trees over Emmett's head. Branches crashed on top of him, but he had no choice but to keep running.

Laub fell again. Emmett stalled to try to help him and then Bandit went down with a shriek. Emmett didn't see him get hit, but that one split-second's pause slowed them enough for the Mad Men to overtake them.

The Mad Men stumbled practically on top of where Emmett bent over Laub. Bandit crawled toward them trying to rejoin them and get out of danger himself. Three Mad Men blocked Emmett and Laub from the aliens advancing through the trees.

Three ships hovered over the scene. They shone searchlights at the Mad Men so Mexia's people could see what they were shooting at. The eerie light gave Emmett more than enough clarity on who was shooting at him, the boys, and the Mad Men.

The aliens in the line belonged to countless different species. In fact, Emmett didn't see any two of the same species. None of their weapons matched, either.

Hideous creatures out of his worst nightmares, small lithe warriors almost human in appearance, beautiful sirens with flowing hair and chiseled features—they all advanced on the Mad Men and fired with deadly accuracy.

Emmett shivered and scrambled to pick up Laub. Rodeo caught up with them, strapped Bandit's arm over his shoulder, and hauled Bandit to his feet, but there was only one way to go—away from Mexia's people.

Chapter 13

Davenport's eyes snapped open at the first sound of gunfire. Wolf's head shot up and he growled again. "What was that?" Alla whispered from his own bed.

Davenport crawled to the hut entrance. Wolf tried to pull him back, but Davenport didn't stop. He flattened himself to the ground and slithered closer to the door.

He didn't stick his head out, though. He peeked under the lowest branches that made up the slanted wall. Wolf jammed in next to him and Breeze stretched out on Davenport's other side.

A ship whirled overhead firing plasma bursts down into the mud-dwellers. The mud-dwellers scattered shrieking through the woods. From where Davenport lay, it looked like they had been out in the trees for some reason.

Now the attacking ship drove them back to the village. Some mud-dwellers tried to hide in their houses only to get cut down by wicked blasts from the strange ship.

"That's...." Breeze began.

"Mexia," Davenport whispered back. "What is she doing here?"

"Who cares? Let's get out of here."

"Hold on." Davenport grasped Breeze's arm to stop him from inching away. "Holy shit—look!"

Davenport sprang to his feet so fast the other two didn't have time to react right away. He stormed to the hut entrance and straight out into the battle.

The ship's searchlight swiveled in all directions. That and the sizzle of igniting plasma gave him all the light he needed to see Rodeo, Emmett, Bandit, and Laub clawing their way out of the underbrush.

Davenport headed straight for them. Bandit's eyes popped when he spotted Davenport. A second later, a blast from the ship splintered into the ground right next to Davenport.

He dove aside to avoid getting hit, but the ship kept hammering the village on all sides with no pattern.

Davenport charged Rodeo and grabbed him. "What the hell are you......?"

Another devastating boom echoed over their heads. Everyone ducked as another cluster of ships shrieked into view. They got into an unholy air battle against Mexia's people, but Davenport didn't have time to worry about that.

"Mexia...." Bandit panted. "Mexia......"

"I know!" Davenport roared. "We have to get back to the *Artemis Rex*!"

Laub shook his head, but before anyone could say another word, ten human men charged into the village. They fired behind them and raced past Davenport fleeing an advancing line of aliens coming through the forest.

Davenport took one look at the aliens and bolted. He waited only long enough to grab Rodeo and Bandit and to make sure Emmett and Laub stayed with him.

He spun around to run for his life and changed his mind when he spotted Mad Men lying sprawled and bleeding all over the village.

Davenport raced to one of the dismembered bodies and hefted a giant XQ from the man's severed arms. The boys copied him and they whirled the other way to face Mexia's people.

Davenport's heart sank when he saw how many of them there were. The line of attackers stretched into the woods on both sides.

The battle lit up the village. Mexia's people flooded the woods in such numbers that Davenport couldn't see the end of them. Where did they all come from and why were they here of all places?

He turned his XQ on them. Rodeo, Laub, Bandit, and Emmett appeared at his side all armed with weapons from fallen Mad Men. Breeze and Wolf showed up a second later, but all of them working together couldn't take on so many aliens.

Ships bombarded each other overhead. Rockets and burning plasma pounded the village all around them and still Mexia's people kept coming. Nothing stopped their inevitable advance.

The crew opened fire, but they had to retreat just to keep a safe distance between themselves and Mexia's alien horde. Davenport backed up to the hut the mud-dwellers gave him and the boys to sleep in that night.

He took advantage of his friends' fire to glance behind him. The mud-dwellers had all abandoned their village. Davenport didn't see anything back there but more and more endless woods.

He and the others would have to flee there to get away from Mexia's people. Even then, he and his crew probably wouldn't be safe. Mexia's people would only come after them.

Mexia's search ships charged their enemies and drove everything before them in a hellish barrage of plasma and explosions. Mexia's people cleared the skies so only they remained. Then they wheeled and aimed their guns straight at the *Artemis Rex* crew.

A plasma jet struck a nearby hut and the whole structure exploded in flame. Rodeo, Laub, and Wolf crowded into Davenport on that side and he sidestepped around his former mansion toward the woods.

At that moment, a greprexsite charge blasted out of the deep forest behind Mexia's people. The charge vaulted high into the night sky and smashed one of Mexia's ships to pieces.

The hull detonated in a massive fireball. The rest of Mexia's ships staggered to get away in time and all the aliens on the ground looked up.

Four more charges whistled out of nowhere and bombarded the last three ships to smithereens. The aliens spun backward and unloaded into the darkness, but there was nothing to shoot at.

Davenport's heart leapt and he opened up with his XQ. The rest of the crew joined in, but before they could hit anything, Howitzer fire erupted from the shadows and mowed down half of Mexia's people on the spot.

The surviving aliens roared in fury. They abandoned the *Artemis Rex* crew where they were. Mexia's people barged off into the woods gunning for their mystery attacker.

Davenport took courage and hustled after them. A second later, more charges streaked through the trees from somewhere out of sight.

The missiles smashed into the advancing aliens and cut their numbers down even further. Howitzer fire belched from all directions—or it seemed like it did. Davenport couldn't really tell where it was coming from.

Rodeo grabbed Davenport's elbow. "We should go now!"

Davenport nodded. "Let's get back to the ship."

"We can't!" Rodeo yelled over the noise. "It's gone."

Davenport spun around to stare at him. "What do you mean?"

"Gone! It isn't there anymore. Someone flew it away. I don't know who and I don't know where."

All the lightness evaporated from Davenport's heart and his stomach crashed into his boots. The ship—gone! Now what was he supposed to do?

An even more crushing assault of Howitzer fire ripped the forest to shreds and the rest of Mexia's people hit the dirt. A few tried to crawl away. Some even held onto their weapons.

Davenport let Rodeo pull him backward toward the trees. He didn't want to stick around and find out who had the balls to earn themselves a death sentence by shooting down Mexia's people.

They made it as far as their original hut when a lone attacker staggered out of the woods. Lanky black hair draped half the pale face. The tall, thin figure stalked from the shadows to stand over Mexia's fallen wounded.

Davenport could hardly believe his eyes when Lyons trained her Howitzer down at the last surviving aliens, opened fire, and finished them off.

She lugged a greprexsite launcher in her other hand. When she finally looked up and met Davenport's eye, she almost fell over when she tried to get to the village.

He dropped his XQ and ran over to grab her. She could barely stand on her own and here she was shooting at Mexia's people. "What the hell are you doing out of bed, you crazy witch?"

"Saving your ass," she rasped.

Her hair plastered her sweaty face and she looked like death warmed up, but she didn't let go of her weapons. She kept glancing into the woods to make sure none of Mexia's people got up again.

He lowered her onto a stump by one of the firepits and the others surrounded her all talking fast.

"Have you seen Fiddler?" Emmett asked.

"Did you see where they took the *Artemis Rex*?" Rodeo asked.

"How did you get away from the Mad Men?" Davenport asked.

"I didn't see the ship," Lyons replied. "It was still there when I left it."

"When was that?" Davenport asked.

Lyons shrugged. "I'm not really sure. I woke up and you guys were all gone. I was alone so I armed myself and went outside....and then I'm not really sure what happened. I might have passed out for a while...."

"I'm not surprised," Davenport replied. "You're barely alive."

"I'm alive enough. Anyway, I realized Mexia's people were after you so I.... well, I stopped them, didn't I?"

"Yeah. You did." Davenport had to grin at her. Good old Lyons. "Thanks."

"That doesn't help us find the ship," Rodeo pointed out.

"Which means we're stuck here," Emmett added.

Lyons frowned at the surrounding trees. "Where's Beauty?"

"We haven't seen him for a while," Breeze replied. "He kind of vanished into the swamp."

"Should we be worried?" Laub asked. "How would we ever find him out there?"

"He'll be fine," Lyons replied. "Beauty takes care of himself."

"He was acting awful squirrely on the ship," Emmett pointed out.

Davenport glanced around at nothing. "We're all here except Fiddler, Dice, Coon, and Axel."

"They must be on the ship," Bandit suggested. "They must be the ones who took it somewhere else."

"We hope they did," Rodeo countered. "The Mad Men might have taken it."

"Don't say that!" Bandit gasped.

"It's true. Even if the Mad Men aren't the ones who moved it, they were looking for it. Who's to say they haven't already found it?"

"What makes you say that?" Davenport asked. "How do you know they were looking for it?"

"We saw them." Rodeo pointed into the woods. "They were searching for the Ithium. They thought you might have given the Ithium to the mud-dwellers. The Mad Men were on their way here to check when Mexia's people attacked."

"And after they checked with the mud-dwellers, they were going to search for the ship," Laub added. "They would probably find it, too, since they have ships themselves. They could just scan the surface and locate it with no trouble."

"Let's not let our imaginations run away with us," Davenport told them. "We should...."

He surveyed the village and fell silent when a bunch of mud-dwellers snuck out of the trees. The little aliens stole sidelong peeks in all directions and then advanced in greater and greater numbers.

They surrounded the crew much more quickly this time. They didn't hesitate to paw and stroke and touch everyone, including Lyons.

The mud-dwellers started murmuring. Their voices built to a steady hum of worshipful sighing and crying, but at least they didn't exclaim and declare Davenport the Bringer of the Ithium anymore.

Emmett, Rodeo, and the others tried to shrink away from the mud-dwellers' attention. "What the hell are they doing?" Bandit called.

"Just try to put up with it," Davenport told them. "They think I'm some kind of......"

"The prophecy!" the mud-dwellers cried. "The prophecy is fulfilled!"

"You see what I mean?" Davenport said. "They think I'm some kind of messiah figure because...."

"Salvation!" the mud-dwellers chorused. "Salvation from the Bringer of the Ithium!"

Lyons gasped. "The Bringer of the what?"

"I didn't make this shit up!" Davenport countered.

"No one could make this shit up," Rodeo muttered.

Chapter 14

A deafening clang startled Fiddler for the tenth time. "They must be dismantling the ship," Dice growled from the other side of the *Artemis Rex's* galley. "Bandit will be distraught."

Fiddler finished adjusting the XQ in front of her, but a second later, another crash made her jump. "Hey!" Dice bellowed through the door. "Keep it down in there! We're trying to work."

Fiddler stood up. "Let's get out there. I want to be ready if anyone finds us."

"*When* they find us, you mean." Dice heaved his own weapon off the table. He didn't complain again about the 62 being too small.

The two friends went outside. Axel had parked the *Artemis Rex* in a much denser part of the forest. Faint winks of daylight through the canopy gave the only evidence that morning was coming fast. None of that light made it down to the ground.

The *Artemis Rex's* hull kept knocking and banging behind Fiddler's back as she circled the ship, but no one came to find them here.

Dice went the other way and the pair met back up near the open hatch. "How long is this gonna take?" Dice muttered. "We need to get out of here."

"I've been thinking," Fiddler began.

"Stop right there. Nothing good ever started with the words, 'I've been thinking'."

Fiddler chuckled, but she didn't stop scanning the area for threats she already knew were lurking out there.

"I've been thinking we should hide the Ithium. Davenport mentioned it. So many people are hanging around trying to get it. We should put it somewhere no one knows about but us."

"You mean like....no one not even Davenport?"

"You heard what the Mad Men said. They planned to send him back to Admiral Joyce. It's only a matter of time before they get their hands on him. They could do any number of things to get him to tell them where it is."

Dice winced and looked away. "Let's not talk about that."

"We have to. The Mad Men and now Mexia's people are all trying to get the Ithium. Even if they weren't, there would still be a chance someone would find Davenport and twist his arm to make him tell where it is."

"So what are you saying? The Mad Men were going to kill us all. Then the Ithium would be somewhere on this planet and no one would ever find it."

"Isn't that what we want? We would be dead and not even Davenport would know where the Ithium was. Admiral Joyce would never find it, not even if he put together that it was on this planet. He wouldn't be able to find it even if Mexia or the Mad Men told them where the *Artemis Rex* landed."

"Fine." Dice jerked his horns toward the ship. "Go get it."

She darted inside and went to the crew quarters. She pulled back the mattress in the cabin next to the one where Lyons had been recovering.

Fiddler took out a small, sealed box wrapped in a soft fabric bag. She ripped open the strings and checked to make sure the Ithium cartridge and the chip were still inside the box.

She found Dice still standing guard by the hatch. "I got it."

"Well? Where are you going to put it?" He waved toward the woods. "You have thousands of trees to choose from."

She set off through the dim forest and now she faced a completely different problem. Every tree looked like every other tree.

Dice trailed her at a distance. That left the whole responsibility on her shoulders. She continued for what seemed like a long way. She could still see the *Artemis Rex* gleaming in the shadows when she looked behind her. Bangs and thumps echoed in the stillness.

She stopped at a broad swamp while she searched for the perfect spot. The water surrounded the *Artemis Rex* in a wide, flat mirror. Nothing moved out there. The whole area breathed in a vast silence that swallowed every other sound, even the sounds of the boys repairing the ship.

Then she realized. This was it. This was the hiding place she'd been looking for.

She found a rock wedged among tangled tree roots nearby. She put the rock inside the bag and tightened the strings as tight as she could make them.

A huge dead tree had fallen into the swamp. The top of its trunk stuck out of the water with the rest submerged. The flat disk of its upended roots stood out of the muck even taller than Dice's head.

She circled the swamp, set her XQ aside, and waded out to the roots. She clambered onto the trunk, squatted down, and thrust the bag deep into the water. She wedged it between the roots and the trunk making sure to shove it as far into the mud as she could.

The rock held it there and the box didn't float when she pulled her dripping arm out of the ooze.

"That should do it," Dice growled from the shore. "Good thinking."

She rejoined him, dried her shirt as much as she could, and picked up her weapon. "Now only you and I know where it is. If anything happens to us, the Ithium will be safe."

They started back toward the ship, but Dice kept furrowing his brow and frowning at everything. "What's wrong?" she asked. "Do you have a better idea?"

"It's.... Davenport," Dice muttered. "He's been through the damn ringer for that Ithium. He should know what happened to it. I don't like leaving him in the dark."

"We don't even know where he is. We couldn't find him without flying straight into Mexia's hands."

"I know."

"Besides, he's the one Joyce is targeting. He's the one Joyce hired the Mad Men to find. Davenport knowing where the Ithium is would only make it more likely that the bad guys will find out from him."

"I know."

Fiddler studied Dice on the side. For someone who started out wanting to tear Davenport's head off, Dice sure came around about him.

Davenport was too decent for anyone to stay mad at him for long. The *Echo Omicron* crew might have started out on the wrong side of the law, but Davenport won them over.

Fiddler understood how that felt. She went through the same thing with Davenport. She suffered a stab of guilt when she thought about where he might be on this planet.

The whole criminal underworld was after him. Now Dice and Fiddler put him in a position where he might get tortured or killed for something he didn't even have anymore.

She and Dice returned to their positions outside the hatch. The banging noises had stopped. Axel's and Coon's voices drifted from inside mingled with snatches of laughter.

Fiddler didn't like keeping the truth from them, either. She didn't like keeping the truth from Emmett or the Chorion Team or Lyons or Beauty. They all deserved to know what they were fighting for, but that would defeat the purpose of hiding the Ithium, wouldn't it?

Dice startled her back to the present by hissing between gritted teeth. "Something's out there."

She whipped up her XQ and aimed outward at the dark trees. "Where?"

"Everywhere!"

He swiveled his weapon this way and that covering every angle, but nothing moved out there. The whole forest lay silent as the grave, but as soon as he said it, she sensed it, too.

Some hidden menace lurked in the shadows, but she couldn't tell where it was coming from. It surrounded the ship on all sides.

Axel and Coon came out of the cargo hold still laughing and talking. Coon took one look at Dice and Fiddler and froze. "What's going on?"

"We aren't sure," Fiddler replied over her shoulder. "Arm up—now!"

The boys scooted back inside and reappeared carrying XQs, rifles, and wearing sidearms. They slotted into position with Axel next to Dice and Coon next to Fiddler.

"Are you sure there's anything out there?" Axel asked.

"We're sure," Dice growled.

"Where?" Coon asked. "I don't see anything."

A soft ripple of water answered him. It disturbed the silence for a second and then vanished into nothing.

The friends jolted in that direction until another soft splash blipped from the *Artemis Rex's* other side. The group spun that way, but there was nothing to see.

Another splash made Fiddler jerk back to her right and her blood ran cold when she spotted ten huge aliens striding toward the ship.

More aliens appeared as if out of nowhere. Mexia's people ringed the ship moving fast and sure toward the four friends.

Dice roared and leveled his XQ from one side to the other, but he couldn't decide who to shoot first. Every alien in the circle looked as menacing and determined as the rest.

Fiddler tightened her grip on her weapon and braced herself to go down shooting when another ship howled over the trees. The vessel twirled above the canopy and then drifted to the ground right in front of Dice and Fiddler.

The ship parked between Mexia's people and the crew. The ship's arrival seemed to send a signal to Mexia's people. They all stopped advancing, but they didn't leave or soften their stance. They still aimed their weapons at the four friends guarding the *Artemis Rex*.

"Well, I'll be damned!" Dice snarled. "Look who it is."

The ship's rear hatch popped and Marshall Healey strode out toward the friends.

"What the holy hell is this dipshit doing here?" Dice hissed.

Healey halted in front of Dice and Fiddler. "Thank goodness I found you! I've been looking everywhere for you."

"We *weren't* looking for you," Dice shot back. "What do you want....and thanks a whole hell of a lot for bringing *them* around. You almost killed us all...or was that why you came around looking for us? Are you working for Joyce now?"

"Joyce! Of course not! Do you honestly think I'd be down here talking to you if I was?"

"You can't blame us for being suspicious, Marshall," Fiddler added. "Are you with Mexia's people now? They've came close to killing us."

"I didn't bring them out to kill you. I brought them to stop the Cannibals."

Fiddler's jaw dropped and both boys gasped. "The what?" Dice spat.

"The Cannibals. They're...."

"I know who the hell the Cannibals are, porkchop," Dice snapped. "What the hell are *they* doing hanging around here?"

"If you stop insulting me, I might have a chance to tell you. Joyce called in the Cannibals to go after you. He sent the Mad Men first to capture Davenport."

"We already know that," Fiddler countered. "We already dealt with them."

"Well, after you dealt with them and they didn't turn over Davenport the way he said, he sent out the Cannibals, I brought Mexia's people to stop them."

"They've done a hell of a lot more than stop the Cannibals," Dice countered, "especially as the Cannibals aren't here as you can see for yourself."

Healey scowled at Dice and then at Fiddler. "What's wrong with you people? I helped you get away from Ultra Meridian. What happened? I was trying to help you."

"Well, you didn't," Dice clipped. "You made it a thousand times worse."

Healey flared his nostrils and drew in a long breath. "Look. Just tell me where Davenport is. We need to secure the Ithium before the Mad Men take it back to Admiral Joyce."

Fiddler glanced over at Dice at the same time Dice glanced at her. They exchanged a silent moment of understanding. Neither of them was about to tell Marshall Healey anything. He might have helped them at Ultra Meridian, but that was all ancient history now.

"Davenport is a prisoner in the mud-dwellers' village," Dice finally replied. "We were on our way over there to get him out when Mexia's people showed up. We would have had him a long time ago if they didn't keep interfering and shooting everything that moves. Hell, they might even have shot him themselves for all we know."

Healey stiffened. He didn't look behind him toward Mexia's people standing around. He couldn't exactly call them off now that he brought them in.

"Fine," he told them. "We'll go get Davenport ourselves. Where's the village?"

"Over there." Fiddler pointed toward where she thought the village was, but she couldn't be certain. "You should be able to see it on your scanners."

"All right," Healey replied. "Let's go. Load up in your ship and I'll take the *Prometheus Vox*."

He walked past his own ship to speak to Mexia's people. "Do you believe him?" Fiddler asked. "He *did* help us on Ultra Meridian."

"He helped us on the Needle, too," Axel replied. "He helped us escape from the jail and he helped us get the Ithium from Joyce's office on Atlas Arcane. We wouldn't have the Ithium now if not for him."

"I'm prepared to trust *him*, but not Mexia's people," Dice growled. "They attacked us and I wouldn't put it past them to do it again the instant it serves them. Either they're playing both sides or they're playing for the admiral and shining Healey's ass because he asked them to help us."

"I'm going with the second option," Fiddler replied.

"Either way, what difference does it make if they help us get Davenport back?" Coon shot a significant look past Fiddler's shoulder toward the *Prometheus Vox*. "They're leaving. Healey is loading up."

"Let's go," Fiddler decided. "All of us working together will stand a better chance if anyone attacks us—anyone at all."

"Fine by me," Dice rumbled. "I guess we'll find out who's on whose side once the shooting starts."

The four friends headed inside the *Artemis Rex*, but not without plenty of backward glances toward Healey and Mexia's people.

Healey nodded to the friends from his cockpit, but Mexia's people didn't bother. They faded into the woods where they came from.

Fiddler didn't like taking her eyes off them, but she had to shut the hatch to get to the cockpit. She used the Drifter's scanners to track Mexia's people back to their search ships.... or whatever kind of ships they were.

Sheriff Healey got the *Prometheus Vox* airborne and waited for the *Artemis Rex* to join him before he veered toward the village.

Chapter 15

"Did I miss something in the briefing?" Lyons called over her shoulder.

"They've been like this since the beginning," Davenport replied.

Dozens of mud-dwellers packed around the *Artemis Rex* crew. Their adoration mounted by the second. None of the friends could move with so many mud-dwellers jostling and shoving to get near them.

"I should have stayed unconscious," Lyons yelled.

"I wish I was," Davenport replied.

Hands covered his chest and stomach. The mud-dwellers had given up saying any words. Their humming and murmuring noises blurred into a steady purr that passed from one to the next in an unbroken wave of noise.

"Just don't ask them for anything to eat," Alla reminded everyone. "You'll be sorry if you do."

Davenport almost answered and froze when he spotted another human man standing head and shoulders above the mud-dwellers. Davenport recognized the guy instantly. It was one of the Mad Men that Dice chased away from the first ship that captured the *Artemis Rex* crew.

The guy glared at Davenport, but neither of them could get near or away from each other with so many mud-dwellers crowding around.

"What the shit?" Rodeo snarled.

Davenport's hand flew to his sidearm, but it still wasn't there. He cast around for one of the XQs he stole from the dead bodies earlier, but he didn't see them, either.

The whole crew searched, but not a single weapon remained. The mud-dwellers pushed more Mad Men into the village and Davenport realized with a jolt that the Mad Men were all unarmed, too. What the hell were the mud-dwellers doing?

The mud-dwellers brought more and more Mad Men out of the forest. Davenport counted seven of them with more showing up all the time. The mud-dwellers' movements created a conveyor belt of so many bodies. No one could resist their momentum.

The first guy got within ten feet of Davenport. "We have to get out of here!" Davenport called the boys.

"No shit," the guy snapped.

The mud-dwellers gestured to the Mad Men and then to Davenport's crew. The mud-dwellers waved the two groups together.

"Oh, hell no!" Bandit cried out. "We are NOT making up with THEM."

The Mad Men shot murderous glances at the *Artemis Rex* crew, but no one could move or attack or escape. The mud-dwellers got more enthusiastic until they spiraled into a frenzy.

Davenport waved both hands at them. "We have to go!" He pointed to the woods. "We're going! Thank you for everything. We have to go!"

They pretended not to understand. The Mad Men started to get uncomfortably close, but before the situation could erupt in bloodshed, two ships rocketed over the trees from the same direction.

Everyone whirled around ready to duck for cover from more gunfire. Davenport searched for the attacker and his heart leapt when he recognized the *Artemis Rex*. An instant later, the *Prometheus Vox* swiveled into view with Healey in the cockpit.

Both ships vaulted over the trees on matched trajectories, tilted, and plunged for the village. The mud-dwellers bolted and released Davenport and his friends.

Davenport leapt forward and waved both arms at the two ships. "Don't shoot! Don't shoot!"

They must have understood because both ships streaked past his head, but the mud-dwellers didn't get the message that these were Davenport's friends.

The mud-dwellers charged away to take shelter in the forest. They abandoned the *Artemis Rex* crew and left Davenport alone with the Mad Men.

Davenport was still busy flagging his friends when the first Mad Man jumped him from behind. The guy pounced and pinned Davenport's arms to his sides.

Davenport struggled and tried to throw the guy off. A second later, three more Mad Men tackled them and slammed Davenport down hard on the ground. He couldn't break their grip or throw their weight off.

"Davenport!" Rodeo roared, but his voice kept getting farther and farther away.

Davenport tried to twist around to see where the boys were, but at that moment, gunfire ripped out of the forest. It surrounded the village and the mud-dwellers shrieked as the shots tore into their ranks.

Lyons screamed something and then the whole village exploded in pandemonium. Gunshots mingled with the mud-dwellers' shrieks. Yells and bellows from Lyons and the boys drowned in the din.

Davenport gave one more painful jerk and someone slammed him hard in the back of the head. He hit the ground and everything went black.

He came to a second later, except that this time, he was lying on his back. Four Mad Men pinned him down, but when he tried again to struggle, something sharp cut into his wrists and ankles. They had tied him up.

He stared up at the sky. The *Artemis Rex* and the *Prometheus Vox* wheeled and streaking back and forth up there. They crisscrossed each other's path firing in all directions.

More ships plunged out of nowhere trading shots with both the *Artemis Rex* and the *Prometheus Vox*.

Davenport thought for a split second that his friends just might succeed, but the longer he watched, the more he realized that Mexia's people outnumbered them by at least two dozen.

He no longer doubted that Mexia's people were the ones who carried out this attack. The sizzling and crackling coming from the perimeter sounded like plasma. The Mad Men didn't use weapons like that.

The whole horrible truth hit Davenport like a ton of bricks. Mexia's people must have been working with the Mad Men all along, which meant Mexia's people were working for Admiral Joyce. Now the Mad Men had Davenport tied up.

Where were the rest of the *Artemis Rex* crew? Were any of them alive?

He picked up his head to look around and one of the Mad Men punched him in the face. He flopped down and that left him no choice but to look up at the air battle.

The *Artemis Rex* pivoted in front of his eyes and exchanged shots with some of Mexia's ships. The next instant, a devastating spray of plasma sizzled out of nowhere. It surrounded the *Artemis Rex* and an explosion went off somewhere on the ship.

The *Artemis Rex* wheeled out of control, staggered in midair, and tried to limp away. It made it a dozen yards over the canopy before Mexia's people tracked it down. They bombarded the ship with another blistering jet of plasma and the *Artemis Rex* smashed down into the forest.

Davenport clamped his eyes shut and turned away, but that only brought him into sight of the *Prometheus Vox* suffering a similar fate. With the *Artemis Rex* out of action, all of Mexia's people hounded the *Prometheus Vox* over the treetops.

Mexia's people surrounded Healey pounding the *Prometheus Vox*. They bombarded the Nitrol with punishing crackles of plasma when, without warning, another fountain of combusting plasma rocketed out of the forest.

It struck the *Prometheus Vox* in the belly and the ship somersaulted away. It cartwheeled wing over wing and started to fall. It slammed into a tree and vanished.

The Mad Man sitting on Davenport's left shoulder chuckled. "Take a good long look, porkchop. You and your friends ain't never bothering anyone ever again."

Davenport couldn't bring himself to struggle when the Mad Men yanked him to his feet. His first look at the village only made him feel worse.

Nearly every house had been leveled and he didn't see a living soul anywhere—no mud-dwellers, no Chorion Team, no *Echo Omicron* crew—no one. The whole area was deserted.

Mexia's people had vanished, too—no doubt to go find the fugitives in the woods. Davenport tried one more time to turn around, but two Mad Men grabbed his arms.

He held his breath thinking they were going to drop him to the ground again, but they didn't. Two men hooked their arms through his elbows, and when he stumbled, two more caught his legs.

They lifted him off the ground and carried him into the woods, but they didn't go near the *Artemis Rex* or the *Prometheus Vox*. That would be too nice if they showed him whether his friends were dead or alive.

Instead, they carried him deeper into the woods to a different ship hidden in the shadows. It resembled the first ship—the Mad Men's ship where he and his friends had been held prisoner.

This one didn't have any holes in the side, though. It was perfectly intact and sat idling its engines while it waited for the Mad Men to carry Davenport on board.

He kicked up a fight when they lugged him up the ramp and into the hold, but more Mad Men came out of cabins and compartments to help restrain him.

They never gave him a chance to put his feet on the floor before the hatch closed and the ship rocketed into the sky leaving everyone else behind.

Chapter 16

"This is all your fault," Dice snarled in Marshall Healey's ear.

"I know that," Healey fired back. "You don't have to remind me."

"Did you honestly think you could get Mexia's people to help you?" Lyons smacked her lips. "You aren't as smart as you think you are."

"Will you shut the hell up?" Healey snapped. "I think I know a few more things than you do. Mexia works for Calyx Elkanon and Calyx Elkanon owes Davenport his life. Davenport saved Calyx Elkanon's life when they were both...." He trailed off.

"When he was what?" Rodeo demanded. "If you want us to believe you had some good reason for sending Mexia's people after us, you better tell us why."

Healey let out a deep sigh. "Fine. You'll probably find out anyway. Calyx Elkanon is locked up in Terminus Anathema."

"Of course he is," Alla replied. "He's been there for decades."

"He'll be there for life," Bandit replied. "He doesn't want to leave. He's got too much influence there. He runs his whole empire from inside. Why would he leave?"

"What you don't know is that Davenport spent time in Terminus Anathema," Healey told them. "He got arrested while he was working for Ekol Thaine. That's why Ekol thinks so highly of him—because he got arrested in Ekol's service and Davenport kept all Ekol's secrets. He never spilled one word of what Ekol was up to."

"I thought Ekol thought so highly of Davenport because Davenport was his chief enforcer for so long," Rodeo countered.

"That, too. Anyway, Davenport saved Calyx Elkanon's life inside Terminus Anathema. Calyx has owed Davenport ever since."

"Davenport said something about this when we first went to the Needle," Bandit remarked. "He sent a clearance code from Calyx to get us down on the Needle. He said Calyx still owed him a few favors."

"Calyx owes Davenport a lot more than favors," Healey replied. "That's why I called on Mexia—because Joyce said he was sending the Cannibals out here to clean up the mess the Mad Men couldn't."

The friends scanned what was left of the mud-dwellers and immediately went back to looking at each other instead.

The sight of Mexia's people interrogating the mud-dwellers didn't make for very appetizing viewing. Blood-curdling shrieks came from the unfortunate victims.

Mexia's people surrounded the mud-dwellers while the aliens tormented the little creatures, presumably for information about the Ithium. A mounting pile of mud-dweller bodies grew taller every time Mexia's people tossed one of their victims on top of it.

More aliens stood guard over Healey and the *Artemis Rex* crew. It was only a matter of time before Mexia's people came for the crew next. One look at the crew's downcast expressions told Healey they were all thinking the same thing.

"We have to get out of here," Rodeo murmured.

"How do we do that when both our ships are damaged?" Fiddler asked. "You didn't see the *Artemis Rex*. It's gonna take time to repair all that."

"The *Prometheus Vox* isn't looking so hot, either," Healey added. "We won't be launching in anything like a hurry."

He glanced at the aliens holding the party at gunpoint. The only way he was going to get the time to repair the *Prometheus Vox* was if Mexia's people suddenly evaporated or got transported to another dimension or something equally impossible.

"If you're right about Calyx owing Davenport......" Lyons began.

"I am right about it. I wouldn't have gone near Mexia otherwise."

"If that's true, then Mexia and her people can expect an ugly reception when they get back to Confederate space."

Healey glanced up at the aliens surrounding him. They belonged to Mexia, too, but they didn't react to Lyons's remark. They acted like they didn't understand her even though Healey knew they did.

No one answered for a minute. Whatever reception Mexia's people could expect back in Confederate space didn't help the crew out of this mess now.

"If you're right and the Cannibals are coming," Rodeo went on, "we need to get off this planet pronto."

"How do you say we do that?" Coon asked. "If the Cannibals roll in while we're down here, we won't have time to repair the ship. We'll be Cannibal food just like these idiots."

He jutted his chin at the aliens guarding them, but Mexia's people still didn't respond. They didn't register that they even knew what the Cannibals were.

"We need to come up with a plan," Rodeo announced.

"I'm all ears," Healey replied. "What's the plan?"

Rodeo started to answer when a bunch of Mexia's people strode toward the crew from the pile of dead mud-dwellers.

Healey got to his feet and several of the boys stood up, too. Dice pivoted in front of Healey and blocked the whole party from the approaching aliens.

Dice puffed out his chest to make himself even bigger. He bared his teeth and snarled at Mexia's people. "You got some balls holding us here when you know the Cannibals are coming in."

"Tell us where the Ithium is and we'll let you all go," a giant Storrik replied. "All we want is the Ithium."

"You know where the Ithium is," Axel countered. "You searched the *Artemis Rex* when you captured us. You should already have it."

"The Ithium is not on board the *Artemis Rex*. If you don't tell us where it is, you will meet the same fate as the mud-dwellers." The Storrik shot a deadly look at Fiddler. "We'll start with this one. She's the smallest."

Dice sidestepped in front of Fiddler to protect her from the aliens. "You'll start with me if you think you're tough enough, asshole. We'll see how many limbs you still have left when you finish."

"We already told you. We left the Ithium on the *Artemis Rex*." Laub elbowed Coon. "Tell him. You left it on the *Artemis Rex*, didn't you?"

"One of you must have stolen it," the Storrik boomed. "One of you is a thief."

"Admiral Joyce is the thief and you're working for him," Lyons snapped. "Now you're trying to steal the Ithium from an officer of the law when he's executing his duties. That makes *you* the thief."

"Maybe Beauty took it," Alla suggested. "No one knows where he is or what he's been doing all this time. We were away from the *Artemis Rex* long enough. He could have snuck back to the ship and taken the Ithium when none of us was looking."

The Storrik rounded on him, and this time, Wolf dove between them. He snarled up at the Storrik with as much venom as Dice. Wolf might not be as big, but he posed just as intimidating a figure. Healey would have to seriously think about which of them he'd least like to tangle with when they got mad.

"Beauty wouldn't do that," Lyons countered. "He wouldn't."

"What makes you so sure?" Fiddler asked. "Maybe he thought the Ithium was in danger and decided to hide it—and it *was* in danger."

"What is Beauty?" the Storrik asked.

"He's one of our crew," Lyons replied.

"He vanished into the swamp last night," Breeze added. "He just slipped away when we weren't looking."

"Where's Davenport?" Emmett demanded. "What did you do with him?"

"We did nothing with him," the Storrik replied. "The Mad Men have him."

"Where do *they* have him?" Bandit asked.

"They took him off the planet. They are taking him back to the Confederacy to face justice with the Reserve Wing."

A chill went through the crew and everyone exchanged glances. "Damn it!" Breeze whispered.

"We'll get him back," Rodeo told him.

"Give us the Ithium," the Storrik repeated, "or face the consequences."

"None of us has it," Lyons replied. "You heard what the boys said. We left it on the *Artemis Rex*. If it isn't there, we don't know where it is."

"We will find this Beauty." The Storrik waved to his people. They headed off into the swamp, but not before the big guy made sure his guards stayed where they were. These people took no chances.

"You see?" Rodeo murmured as soon as Mexia's people walked away. "They're working for Joyce to get the Ithium back."

"Not necessarily," Healey replied. "They might be after the Ithium for themselves."

"Does it matter why they want the Ithium?" Lyons asked. "They took Davenport. Now we're sitting in the Cannibals' path without a working ship and no way to repair the ones we have."

"Rodeo is going to come up with a plan." Healey turned to the blind boy. "Aren't you, Rodeo?"

Rodeo turned his ear the other way. "Be quiet! Something's happening."

"What is it?" Fiddler looked around. "Nothing's...."

"Quiet!" Rodeo hissed. "Don't make a sound."

The others scanned the village. Healey still didn't see anything.

Then he heard it. It started as a splash or more of a bloop out in the swamp. It came from beyond the fringe of trees where Healey couldn't see.

Then it got louder.... more splashes followed by shouts... coming nearer.

Mexia's aliens yelled back and forth to each other. Rapid splashing footsteps crossed Healey's line of hearing. More and more splashes continued into a waterfall of sound.

Then he saw them. Mexia's people charged back into the village firing their weapons behind them. Healey didn't see anything they might be shooting at, but the aliens' expressions of abject terror said it all.

The aliens streamed back to the village.... until a mob of creatures caught up with them from behind. They rose out of the forest, out of the ground itself. Swamp water dripped from their gangly limbs and their large, floppy ears.

Healey saw the first one and thought, *Oh, good, Beauty's back*. Then he saw the rest of them. They resembled Beauty in every detail except that there must be thousands of them all pouring into the village en masse.

They bounded on all fours moving fast and sure. They overtook Mexia's people and dragged them down. So many of Beauty's kind swarmed the area that Healey couldn't keep track of them all.

He didn't see what they did, but they left Mexia's people dead on the ground and dragged them down into the muck. Then these swamp creatures flooded forward to pounce on all the others.

Gunshots cracked left and right. Healey instinctively jumped between the *Artemis Rex* crew and the oncoming horde as the swamp creatures overran the village. They streamed around the prisoners without taking the slightest notice of them.

The aliens guarding the party spun backward to confront the horde. They fired into the throng, but the swamp creatures barely noticed. They surrounded the guards and started climbing up their bodies by the dozen.

Razor teeth flashed in their mouths and Mexia's aliens went down screaming in the torrents of bodies. Shrieks and blood-curdling screams cut off suddenly in the silent orgy of blood and death.

Lyons grabbed Fiddler and Emmett. "Let's get the hell out of here!"

"What are they doing?" Fiddler called back.

"Don't ask!" Rodeo yelled and everyone headed for the trees.

Healey pushed the others away. "Get to the *Artemis Rex*! I'll get the *Prometheus Vox* going."

"How will we….?" Fiddler began.

"Go!" Healey ordered. "Get the Ithium to a safe place even if it means you have to disappear. I'll cover you and make sure no one comes after you."

Chapter 17

The *Artemis Rex* crew raced through the trees back to the ship. "Get this bucket of bolts off the ground on the double!" Dice roared.

Bandit and Rodeo bolted for the cockpit. Fiddler went with the other boys to check the hull. "It isn't that bad," Coon decided.

"Not that bad!" Fiddler countered. "Half the starboard wing is hanging by a thread and the engine is completely destroyed. We're sitting ducks."

"We can fix it."

Axel, Laub, and Alla went inside. Fiddler squinted at the damage. It looked a lot worse than Coon made out. "Do you want me to help you?" she asked.

"You want to help us?" Coon pushed Breeze toward Fiddler. "Take him inside and give him something to do so he doesn't get in our way."

Fiddler laughed. Breeze looked offended, but in such a comic way that she knew the boys' teasing didn't bother him.

She took him inside and set him to work cleaning up the supplies that spilled from the storage cabinets when the ship crashed.

Fiddler left him to it and went to the cockpit to talk to Rodeo and Bandit about retrieving the Ithium. They still didn't know where it was, but when she passed the galley, she changed her mind when she spotted Dice.

He had somehow located a whole crate of Barbequed Alligator Tarts. Fortunately for the safety of the whole galaxy, he was still just studying the labels and hadn't started eating them yet.

She walked in and approached him. "Hey."

"Did you know these things have more than the legal limit of Bliostine? They shouldn't technically be legal for human consumption."

"I'm not surprised. Have you ever actually eaten one of those?"

"Have I?" He snorted. "There probably isn't a man on this side of the Omega star cluster that has eaten more of them."

"Then you already know. Anyway, you aren't human so you don't have to worry about it."

"Hmm. You might be right." He tore open the package and dumped the tart into his giant mouth.

"I want to talk to you."

"Here I am," he returned.

Fiddler checked in the corridor to make sure no one else was around to hear her. "It's about the......" She broke off as the engines started cycling up. She cocked her ear to listen. Both engines were firing, including the starboard one. "Wow. That was fast."

"So what do you want to talk to me about?" he asked.

Before she could say a word, the ship boomed and started lifting off the ground. "Shit!" she hissed. "They're launching."

"Hey!" he called after her. "Isn't that what they're supposed to be doing?"

She raced to the cockpit to find Rodeo in the command cradle. Bandit steered the ship out of the trees and into the sky. "Hold it!" she yelled over the engine noise. "We have to go back for the Ithium!"

Rodeo tilted his head in her direction without actually looking at her. "Isn't it on board?"

"No! Dice and I hid it."

Bandit started to turn around, too. "Where?"

"Fly the ship, boy!" Rodeo bellowed. "You're about to crash!"

Bandit tore the ship away from some trees he'd been drifting toward.

"Where's the Ithium?" Rodeo asked.

Fiddler opened her mouth to reply when one of Mexia's ships careened into the *Artemis Rex's* path. Gunfire blasted in the darkness, but it didn't hit the *Artemis Rex*. It came from behind Mexia's ship and smashed it to smithereens right in front of Bandit.

"Holy shit! The Cannibals are coming in! Arm tactical, Fiddler." Rodeo switched to the intercom. "Arm all accessory cradles and fire at will! Cannibals incoming!"

Fiddler sprang into the tactical cradle with her heart in her mouth. This was so much worse than dealing with the Mad Men, Mexia's people, or even the Reserve Wing.

Her controls switched on and her stomach clenched. Thousands of ships blanketed the sky as far as she could see. The forwardmost point of the Cannibals swarm enveloped Mexia's people and bombarded them in a rapid series of flaring explosions.

"Beat it, son!" Rodeo called to Bandit. "Make tracks for Confederate space and step on it!"

"Marshall Healey is launching from the planet!" Fiddler reported. "He's converging."

Healey came over the communications link. "*Artemis Rex*, do you read? Head for Confederate space. I'll cover you."

"Negative, *Prometheus Vox*," Rodeo replied. "We'll go together. No one gets left behind."

Healey smiled at him through the link. "You're a good kid. Just get out of here. We can't let the Ithium fall into the Cannibals' hands."

"We'll work together. Let's go!"

Bandit gunned the engines and sprinted away. Mexia's ships gave the *Artemis Rex* a moment's head start before the Cannibals descended on the planet in a black mass.

The *Artemis Rex* picked up speed as Bandit put more and more space between the ship and the Cannibals, but the *Prometheus Vox* wasn't so lucky.

The Cannibals mowed down the last of Mexia's ships and surrounded the *Prometheus Vox*. "Marshall Healey is taking a pounding!" Fiddler reported. "He's engaging the Cannibals. They're breaking off their pursuit to attack him."

"Pull it around," Rodeo ordered. "We're going back for him."

Bandit didn't question and Fiddler tightened her grip on her weapon. This was it. They were going into battle against the Cannibals, but she didn't hesitate a second. She wouldn't let Healey go down so the *Artemis Rex* could escape.

Bandit slammed the throttle down as far as it would go. The *Artemis Rex* screamed into the battle and all the accessory cradles opened up. Gunfire erupted from the Howitzers as the boys started cutting the Cannibals to shreds.

Fiddler swung her cradle hard to port and unloaded on ten ships whizzing past the cockpit. Rodeo concentrated his firepower to the front to carve a path through the Cannibal horde.

Bandit zoomed in and out of Cannibal ships giving Fiddler and the boys all the targets they could ask for. Fiddler finished wiping out the Cannibals on her side, but the *Artemis Rex* was already diving into a different part of the battle with plenty more enemies to shoot at.

"Get to the *Prometheus Vox*!" Rodeo ordered.

"Where is he?" Bandit looked everywhere. "There he is!"

Bandit slammed the ship hard to port and Fiddler yanked hard against her harness. Her cradle whipped to starboard and she opened up without thinking. She blasted ships to pieces all around her. Fire enveloped the *Artemis Rex* before the ship plunged off in a different direction.

The *Prometheus Vox* sat in one place raining hellfire on every Cannibal ship that came near. Healey whirled the *Prometheus Vox* right and left spraying continuous Howitzer fire from the ship's guns.

The *Artemis Rex* whistled within range and cut the Cannibals away from the *Prometheus Vox*. "Get out, Marshall!" Rodeo barked. "Get on the way to Confederate space! You can break through if we work together."

"I'm trying, son! These bastards are thick as fleas."

"Another wave coming in!" Bandit called. "You might want to bring it around to the rear."

He circled the *Prometheus Vox* so both ships faced the same direction. The *Artemis Rex* cleared enough Cannibals from around Healey's ship that they could all now clearly see the mammoth task before them.

The Cannibal fleet covered the planet in a dense cloud. Hundreds more ships converged from deeper inside Sacron Enigma.

A few of the accessory cradles fired into the cloud, but Rodeo and Fiddler just stared at it. Healey didn't shoot anymore, either.

"Get out of here, son," Healey told Rodeo. "You can't beat this."

"You're coming with us," Bandit told him. "Come on. We can make it together."

"You heard me," Healey replied. "You boys are carrying something much more important. I can slow them down, but I can't stop them. Go on. Go find Davenport and make sure he finishes his mission. You're the only ones who can help him now."

Rodeo gritted his teeth. "Let's go, Bandit! Lay in a course for Confederate space."

"See you around, Marshall," Bandit called.

"See you around, son. Maybe when this is all over, we can share a drink sometime."

Fiddler's throat tightened when Bandit turned the *Artemis Rex* away. Healey remained where he was in the firing line of all those incoming ships.

Bandit nailed the throttle to the wall, but in a second, Fiddler realized not even the *Artemis Rex's* incredible speed would be enough.

The Cannibal force enveloped Healey and the *Prometheus Vox* vanished from sight. The horde kept coming....and coming.

Plasma bursts smashed the *Artemis Rex* in the rear. "Hold your fire!" Rodeo bellowed. "Don't shoot until they come within range. Save your firepower until you know you can hit them."

Fiddler trembled in her seat. Bandit drove the engines to the breaking point. He beat a retreat back along the route the *Artemis Rex* took to escape from Confederate Space. The crew was going back into the hornet's nest of enemies and danger. Would they make it in time?

Another plasma burst rocked the ship and someone yelled from the accessory cradles. "Alla's cradle is hit!" Bandit yelled.

"Steady...." Rodeo countered. "Hold your fire! Not yet!"

Fiddler crushed her firing mechanism in a death grip. She held her breath counting down the seconds until Rodeo gave the word.

The Cannibals crawled up on the *Artemis Rex's* tail. They fired across the ship's bow and again into the rear.

The Cannibals inched up alongside. They matched the *Artemis Rex's* speed, but still Rodeo didn't give the word.

He waited until the Cannibals surrounded the *Artemis Rex*. The enemy peppered the hull with shots, but the Cannibals didn't make any killing strikes on the engines or the outer skin. They were just playing around.

"NOW!" Rodeo roared. He activated the shields at the same time and all the accessory cradles opened up.

Fiddler jerked her weapon around and bombarded the Cannibals on her side. She destroyed seven and left that side of the ship clear while the boys finished off the others.

The pursuing Cannibals buried the ship in gunfire, but the shields protected the *Artemis Rex* from the worst. More Cannibals hurtled out of position around the planet to hunt the *Artemis Rex* down, but the ship was too far ahead by now.

"Coming up on Confederate space!" Bandit replied. "And we got company!"

"Who is it this time?" Rodeo asked, but everyone could already see a giant Reserve Wing force waiting right inside the boundary.

"Are we really flying back to *them*?" Fiddler asked.

"What was that you were saying about the Ithium being back on the planet?"

Fiddler started to answer, but at that moment, the Reserve Wing launched across the boundary in a full-scale assault on the *Artemis Rex*.

Dozens of Stalwarts and even more Daggers surrounded the ship and unloaded with every Howitzer blazing.

"What was that *you* were saying about getting back to Confederate space?" Fiddler hollered.

"Forget the Confederacy!" Bandit screeched. "The Cannibals are on top of us!"

He was right. The moment the Reserve Wing attacked, the pursuing Cannibals caught up with the *Artemis Rex*. The ship jerked backward and an unstoppable force hurled the *Artemis Rex* back into the thickest part of the Cannibals swarm.

Hundreds of ships closed the *Artemis Rex* in a fog of gunfire and flickering shapes. Bandit tried to pull the same maneuver by picking up speed, but none of the gunners could see a thing in the mayhem.

Fiddler couldn't acquire a target. The Cannibals hovered too close and too thickly. Blasts ricocheted off the shields and batted the ship in all directions.

"Get us out of here, Bandit!" Rodeo roared.

"I can't!" Bandit shrieked back. "They're blocking all navigation. I can't even see which way I should be going...."

He didn't finish. Even if he found a way out of this mess and made it to Confederate space, the Reserve Wing would be waiting there to finish them off.

Bandit screamed again and an almighty crash knocked the *Artemis Rex* sideways. The Cannibal throng cleared for a split second—just long enough for Fiddler to see the planet wheeling toward the cockpit.

"Brace for impact!" Rodeo bellowed, but before the ship could crash back into the forest, another devastating smash plastered the ship from starboard. One of the Cannibals wheeled off into space and left the *Artemis Rex* twirling out of control through the atmosphere.

Chapter 18

Davenport eased himself down on the floor and stretched out his cramped legs. He'd been crouching in the lower hold for hours ever since the Mad Men threw him in here. At least they had the decency to untie him, now that they knew he couldn't get away.

The ship launched from the planet, but Davenport didn't see which direction it went. He didn't need to see. It could only be going one way and that was straight back to Admiral Joyce.

He kept thinking over all the details on the journey. He didn't have the Ithium, but the Mad Men didn't know that. Admiral Joyce wouldn't be happy when they got Davenport back to the Confederacy and discovered that he didn't have it.

The Mad Men would be equally unhappy with Davenport, which wouldn't end in any very nice results for him.

He studied the hold around him. It wasn't really a hold. It was more of a subfloor beneath the cargo hold. It wasn't tall enough for him to stand up in.

He'd long since discarded the idea of escape. Escape meant getting out into open space without a paddle, so he better stay put.

The ship's engine noise hummed all around him. Footsteps kept crossing the ceiling above his head. How long would it take before those footsteps stopped directly above his head?

He didn't have long to wait. He thought it would take longer.

The footsteps halted over him and gruff, male voices muttered to each other. At least none of these men was Boss Creed. None of them belonged to the original crew who captured the *Artemis Rex* crew.

The only Mad Men who survived that encounter went down in the mud-dwellers' village—not that being among strangers gave Davenport much hope. These were Mad Men and dealing with the Mad Men never went well.

A shaft of light blasted into the hold when they ripped up a floor section. A beefy guy with tattooed arms stretched down into the darkness and grabbed Davenport by the collar. "Get up here, shithead!"

"Get your hands off me!" he roared. "I can get out by myself."

The Mad Men didn't give him a chance to. Three of them seized him and dragged him onto the floor. They threw him down a lot harder than they needed to and then one of them kicked him.

"Start talking, porkchop!" the first one snapped. "Where's the Ithium?"

"I don't have it, okay? It's back on the planet."

"You're lying. You have it on you. Now hand it over."

"If I had it, don't you think your first crew would have taken it? It was on the *Artemis Rex*. That's where I left it."

"Don't screw with us!" The big guy squatted down and put his face right up next to Davenport's. "You better tell us the truth. If you're hiding it internally, we'll cut you open to get it out of you."

"Internally! What are you......?" Davenport broke off when he realized what the guy meant. "I'm telling you the truth. I left it on the *Artemis Rex*."

The biggest guy clamped his meaty hand on the back of Davenport's neck and hauled him to his feet. The rest of the Mad Men surrounded Davenport in guns while their leader marched Davenport across the cargo hold.

Davenport jerked out of the guy's grasp and knocked that hand away when the guy tried to collar him again. "Quit shoving! I can walk by myself. It isn't like I have anywhere to go or any weapon to get there with."

The big guy glared at him, but he didn't try to molest Davenport again—not yet. This was just the interlude between acts.

They steered him into a crew cabin on the second deck. A single chair sat in the middle of the floor. "Take a seat," the big guy ordered.

Davenport turned around to confront his captors. He didn't sit down. No way. "I already told you I don't have the Ithium. Do you seriously think I would be carrying a hazardous substance around in my pocket?"

"You wouldn't leave it lying around on the *Artemis Rex*, either."

Davenport shrugged and looked away. "I had nowhere else to put it."

The guy pulled his sidearm and aimed it in Davenport's face. "Raise your arms while we search you."

Davenport sighed and laced his fingers behind his head—not that he held out much hope that they would believe him even if they did search him.

Two more Mad Men came forward to pat Davenport down. They got a lot more familiar than he would have liked, but of course they didn't find anything.

"Drop your pants, turn around, and bend over," the first guy snapped.

"You can go straight to hell with that shit! Do you honestly think I would do *that* with an Ithium cartridge? I don't have a death wish."

"You could have fooled me. Stealing an Ithium cartridge from the Reserve Wing sounds pretty suicidal to me."

"I didn't steal it. I confiscated it from smugglers in the line of duty." He picked up his star from the front of his jacket and held it out for the Mad Men to see. "See this? Don't you get it now?"

The big guy scowled and the other Mad Men looked away. That star meant a lot more to them than they wanted to admit.

The big dude lowered his sidearm and dipped his eyes back to the chair. "Sit down, Sheriff."

Davenport didn't move and the Mad Men didn't insist. The big guy backed away and the rest of the Mad Men inched out into the corridor. They left the door open so they could see Davenport across the threshold.

"We have to find it!" one of them hissed. "We can't show up in front of the admiral without it."

"Will you shut your trap about the damn admiral, Red?" the big guy countered. "We wouldn't take the Ithium back to the admiral even if we could find it."

"You're crazy, Robberburn," his companion murmured. "The whole Reserve Wing would be after us if we turned against him."

Robberburn slapped his friend across the side of the head and Red yelped. "Use your brain, dope! Admiral Joyce isn't part of the Reserve Wing. He commands a rogue squadron that isn't under the rest of the Confederate Corps. Do you really think he'd be after the Ithium if he was legit?"

"We can't even get back inside Confederate space without the Ithium," someone else pointed out.

"We're already inside Confederate space, you morons!" Robberburn blurted out and then corrected himself by lowering his voice. He didn't seem to notice that Davenport could hear every word even when they whispered.

"This is nuts, Robberburn," Red murmured. "You can't turn against the Reserve Wing."

"We're already outlaws! How much more outlawed do you think we can get by betraying another outlaw?"

No one answered him. His men refused to meet his eye.

"We aren't turning the Ithium over to the admiral, okay?" Robberburn went on. "We can sell it to Ekol Thaine and make a mint. He's been putting it out on the wires that anyone who brings it to him can name their price."

Davenport had heard enough. He sat down on the chair and lounged back at his ease. These idiots didn't plan to take him to the Admiral at all. They couldn't show their faces in the Confederacy without the Ithium.

So Ekol Thaine was still alive. Davenport's insides flipped. Ekol didn't die on Argus Borealis after all, so that was something to be happy about.

Davenport knew Ekol well enough by now. The crime lord wouldn't put that word out on the wires to screw over Davenport and the Chorion Team.

Ekol was trying to find Davenport. Ekol wanted information that would help him track down where Davenport and the Chorion Team went. That was Ekol down to the ground. He took care of his own.

Robberburn and his men eased back into the cabin. Robberburn scowled at Davenport slouching in front of him. Davenport stretched his legs out even farther. He hooked his thumbs in his pants pockets and relaxed. This one was all his.

"Well?" Robberburn demanded. "You better give us something we can use before we meet up with the Reserve Wing."

"I already told you everything I know." Davenport spread both arms. "You can cut me open. You can beat the shit out of me. You can kill me and dump me in space. You won't find out anything I haven't already told you. I don't have the Ithium. I wasn't carrying it around on the planet and I didn't have it with me when you captured me. I left it on the *Artemis Rex*. As far as I know, it's still there. I can't tell you anything else."

Robberburn glared at him. Some of his men shuffled their feet. Davenport waited and then said, "If you leave me free and don't lock me up again, I might be able to help you. The boys on the *Artemis Rex* are a lot more likely to hand over the Ithium to me than they are to you. They might not look like much, but they can give you a run for your money when it comes to shooting."

Robberburn reacted instantly. Davenport kept a close watch on all the Mad Men for a maneuver just like this one, but they still got the jump on him.

Robberburn shot out one beefy arm and grabbed Davenport by the back of the neck. He tried to hurl Davenport face down on the floor, but Davenport rocketed to his feet in a second.

He seized Robberburn by the wrist and yanked the man forward. Davenport hooked his elbow around Robberburn's neck and punched him in the face more than once.

Davenport kept Robberburn pinned and spun the big man backward so the first Mad Man who rushed him ran straight into Robberburn's backside.

Davenport snatched Robberburn's sidearm from its holster and turned it on the remaining Mad Men. They charged him and ran straight into his gun range.

He popped off two shots and dropped the Mad Men on his other side before a gunshot went off in his face. Searing pain ripped across the side of Davenport's head and he whipped backward.

A second later, they were on top of him and slammed him against the bunk. They tackled him to the floor and pounding blows rained all over him.

Two brutal punches to the back of his head smashed his face into the floor and he blinked stars out of his eyes.

The next thing he knew, they were hauling him across the hold. They paused just long enough to pull up the floor section and then they stuffed him back down into the dark.

He curled in a ball and pressed his hand to the gash in the side of his head. "Son of a bitch!"

He pulled his hand away covered in blood and cursed again. His head throbbed and kept spinning from the blows. The gash sliced through his hair to the back of his scalp and hot blood gushed down his cheek, ear, and neck. Great. Just flippin' great.

He started pulling off his jacket. His shirt was the only cloth he had to stop the bleeding.

He set his jacket aside and his eye fell on his star shining up at him. Maybe everyone was right and he was crazy to keep wearing it, but he couldn't bring himself to take it off. It was all he had left. It was his last remaining evidence that he was who he thought he was.

He sighed again and started unbuttoning his collar. Once he used the shirt to stop the bleeding, he would have to put the bloody shirt back on. He didn't have any other clothes.

He unfastened one button when a rustling sound made him freeze. The engines still vibrated through the hull, but this sound came from right in front of him.

He stared in amazement as a section of metal plate detached from the bulkhead. It lifted out of place and a wrinkled little face grimaced at him from behind it. It was Beauty.

Chapter 19

"Beauty! What are you doing here?" Davenport started to sit up, but Beauty was already climbing into the cavity where the Mad Men dumped Davenport.

Beauty's long, gangly legs folded nearly up to his ears when he crouched down in front of Davenport. Beauty pulled a sooty rag from the space behind him, laid it on the floor, and unfolded it.

He revealed four perfect JimJams tucked inside, lifted one out, put it in his mouth, and gazed up at Davenport in rapt bliss while he chewed.

Davenport cracked a huge grin. "Are those the blueberry-flavored ones, Beauty?"

Beauty nodded and ate another JimJam. He chewed it in silence. Davenport couldn't even resent this creature for enjoying them in front of him without sharing them. Davenport was too glad to see a friendly face.

Davenport leaned back against the wall. His head was really starting to pound now. "You should stay out of sight, Beauty. The Mad Men won't be happy if they find you on their ship."

"They won't find out." Beauty picked up the second-to-last JimJam and stuffed it into his cheek. "They don't know I'm here."

"How did you get here, anyway? We thought we lost you in the swamp."

"You did. I had to talk to a few people."

Davenport frowned. "What do you mean?"

Beauty nodded at a spot behind Davenport's shoulder even though there was nothing there but the wall. "The Mad Men will come back to talk to you again, Davenport."

Davenport snorted. "I'm sure they will. They want the Ithium"

"Robberburn stole me from my home planet. This is the first time I've been back there since then."

Davenport's jaw dropped. "That planet.... HTWV-983.... You came from there?"

"The Mad Men plan to kill you."

"I'm sure they do."

"Don't worry. I'll stop them."

"How will you do that?"

"I'll sabotage the ship. They'll think it's a simple malfunction, but it will be enough to distract them."

"Maybe you shouldn't sabotage the ship while we're flying through space."

Beauty changed his expression and glared at the same spot behind Davenport's head. "I'll get him back. I'll make sure he doesn't get away with this. It might have taken me twenty years, but I'll get him back. You'll see."

Davenport relaxed back against the wall as Beauty picked up the last JimJam. The juice squelched in his mouth when he chewed it up.

He crumpled up the rag and stuffed it into the hole he crawled out of. Davenport suffered a pang. Those JimJams might be the last food Davenport saw for a good, long time, but he still couldn't bring himself to deprive Beauty of the JimJams he loved so much.

So Beauty had been brought to the Confederacy against his will. Robberburn kidnapped him and Beauty hadn't been home in twenty years.

That story stabbed at Davenport's heart. He never knew Beauty's story and now he did. It made this queer alien so much more human somehow.

Davenport wished more than anything that he could go home to Ultra Meridian, but that wasn't likely to happen anytime soon—if ever.

Beauty turned around again and pulled another much cleaner piece of cloth from inside the wall. Davenport didn't pay it much attention until he heard a crinkling noise from inside.

Beauty unwrapped the second package to reveal seven rectangular bars sealed in plastic wrappers. Davenport's chest tightened when he read the labels, *Chunky Tender*.

Beauty picked one up and the wrapper crinkled in his bony fingers. Davenport gulped. He never liked JimJams anyway. He didn't mind watching Beauty eat them all.

ChunkyTenders were another story altogether. He summoned his courage to ask Beauty to give him one, but before he could say anything, Beauty held it out to him. "You like the peach ones, don't you?"

Davenport's throat constricted staring at the bar. Was Beauty really giving him this? Davenport glanced up at Beauty and almost didn't recognize the creature.

Beauty actually smiled at him. Davenport couldn't remember seeing Beauty smile like that except when he was eating.

Beauty pushed the ChunkyTender nearer to Davenport. "Take it."

Davenport took it and studied the packaging. "You shouldn't have done this, Beauty."

"The Mad Men weren't using it. Aren't you going to eat it?"

Davenport ripped the wrapper open and put the bar in his mouth. The peach flavor flooded his tongue. It was the most delicious sensation of his life.

The last time he ate one of these at Ultra Meridian seemed so long ago. It was the taste of a forgotten time, a time before all this Ithium business started, a time when he thought he could live the rest of his life in peace and quiet at Ultra Meridian.

Beauty upended the cloth, tipped the ChunkyTenders onto the floor, scooped them up in both hands, and held them all out to Davenport.

Davenport blinked at them and then at Beauty. He didn't want to believe Beauty really meant what Davenport hoped and prayed he meant.

Beauty shoved them nearer. "Take them. I brought them for you."

Davenport gulped again. "All of them?"

"Of course all of them. I've already eaten enough."

Davenport held the first ChunkyTender in his mouth while he let Beauty dump the rest of the bars into his outstretched hands. Davenport didn't have anywhere else to put them, so he got busy tucking them into his pockets.

That seemed to satisfy Beauty. He smiled again when Davenport took another bite of the ChunkyTender he was eating. Beauty pulled another package out of the hole. He opened it to reveal a large square of gauze, a tube of Skin-Tight, a syringe, and an ampule of painkillers.

Beauty crammed the ampule into the syringe and held it out. "Do you want to do it or should I?"

"Do you know how?"

"Of course I know how. How do you think Dice and Lyons have stayed alive this long?"

Davenport had to laugh. "I should have expected that. Well, if you know how, you can do it."

Beauty straightened up as much as he could, bent over Davenport, and injected the painkillers into Davenport's neck.

Davenport collapsed against the wall with an agonized groan. "Thank you! You don't know how good that feels."

"I know." Beauty unscrewed the tube of Skin-Tight. "Now this."

Davenport kept his eyes closed while Beauty smeared Skin-Tight on the gash in his scalp. Davenport barely felt it and the delicious peach flavor in his mouth erased everything else.

Beauty dabbed the gauze to a few other parts of Davenport's face and put Skin-Tight on them, too.

Beauty finally sat back and took a wrapped JuicyPie from his hole. He opened the package and started eating.

"Where did you get all this stuff?" Davenport asked.

"I stole it from the Mad Men."

"And they didn't see you?"

Beauty shook his head. "They won't see me."

Davenport opened another ChunkyTender and Beauty took the empty wrapper from him. Beauty started stuffing all his goods back into the hole.

"You have to stay here, Davenport. I can't free you or the Mad Men will know you're gone."

"How will you......?"

Beauty started climbing back into the hole. "Stay here, Davenport."

"I don't really have a choice, do I?"

"Don't tell the Mad Men I'm here."

"I won't. Don't worry."

Beauty backed into the hole and pulled the metal plate in place in front of him. Davenport lost sight of him, and a second later, Beauty returned the plate back to its original position. No one would ever know it had been removed.

Davenport put his jacket back on and wilted against the wall. He wished Beauty would have stuck around a little longer. Now Davenport was alone again.

Just knowing Beauty was on the ship lifted his spirits, though. Someone was working to free him and the ChunkyTenders sure tasted good.

A flood of emotion seized him when he opened his third ChunkyTender and started eating it. Beauty must have been paying a lot more attention than Davenport gave him credit for.

Beauty remembered that Davenport didn't like JimJams so Beauty didn't offer him any. Beauty also remembered that peach ChunkyTenders were Davenport's favorite.

Beauty brought those instead and gave them all to Davenport. Beauty didn't take any for himself even though Beauty loved them just as much.

He also brought the Skin-Tight and the painkillers. Davenport couldn't remember any gift that meant as much as this. Not even Ekol Thaine giving him the Chorion Team and the *Artemis Rex* meant as much

Davenport should come up with a way to repay Beauty for this. Even now, Beauty was working to free Davenport from the Mad Men.

Then Davenport remembered. Robberburn destroyed Beauty's life. Beauty was here for revenge.

Davenport made a decision then and there. He would make sure Beauty got payback against these assholes. That was the best way Davenport could help Beauty and show his appreciation for this visit.

Those thoughts barely crossed his mind when he heard footsteps coming back over his head. He tensed and quickly hid the ChunkyTender wrapper in his pocket so the Mad Men wouldn't see it.

He swallowed the rest of the bar and braced himself for another confrontation. The floor panel above his head ripped back and light streamed into the hole.

Red and Robberburn yanked Davenport out, but they didn't bother to take him back to the cabin. They threw him on the floor and Red pulled his sidearm.

He pointed it in Davenport's face. "This is your last chance. Tell us where the Ithium is or it's your ass."

Davenport held up both hands. "Okay! I'll tell you! I hid it at Ultra Meridian."

The Mad Men stood over Davenport. Red still aimed his sidearm in Davenport's face, but Davenport saw his words sink home. None of the Mad Men moved. They stared at him in stunned shock.

Davenport dared to scramble out of Red's range and got painfully to his feet. He straightened up and faced them all.

"Ultra Meridian!" Robberburn exclaimed. "You're lying!"

"My crew and I had it when we landed there a few days ago. We made the admiral think we took the Ithium to Sacron Enigma, but we really hid it on the planet."

The Mad Men exchanged glances and Red forgot to hold Davenport at gunpoint anymore. Red turned around to whisper something to Robberburn, but Robberburn cut him off.

Robberburn shoved past his men and planted himself in front of Davenport. "Where at Ultra Meridian did you hide it?"

Davenport thought fast. "I hid it at the Vultus Wind Mines."

Robberburn staggered a few steps backward and bumped into Red. "That's.... That's Typhon Elexor territory!"

Davenport nodded and pretended not to realize how serious this was. "I've been at Ultra Meridian for a few years now. I got to know everyone down there pretty well."

Robberburn whirled away and lurched across the hold. Red and the others shot Davenport a few backward glances and followed their boss. They put their heads together and held a hasty whispered conference. No one noticed Davenport still standing there as free as a bird.

"What are we going to do?" Red hissed. "We can't go after the Ithium at the Vultus Wind Mines! Typhon Elexor would cut our throats!"

"They'd do a hell of a lot worse than that," another murmured. "We'd have better luck going to the admiral."

"Shut up!" Robberburn snarled. "I need to think."

"What is there to think about?" Red demanded. "We should dump the porkchop and beat it."

"Beat it where?" the other man asked. "There's nowhere left. If we piss off the Reserve Wing *and* Typhon Elexor, we're sunk. That's the plain truth."

"Will you shut up?" Robberburn spat. "This is getting us nowhere."

"Don't even think about going after the Ithium, Robberburn," Red warned. "We won't do it."

Robberburn turned around and fixed his furious glare on Davenport. Was now the time when the Mad Men would kill Davenport the way Beauty said they planned?

Almost in answer to Davenport's thoughts, the steady, familiar hum of the engines died. The hull stopped vibrating and the ship went dead and silent.

A second later, a door opened upstairs and another voice called down. "Hey! We got a problem!"

"Not now!" Robberburn bellowed up to the top deck.

"The engines have completely shut down! We're dead in the water."

Everyone spun around, including Davenport. That was quick.

"What's the problem?" Robberburn roared. "Get them up and running now!"

"I can't! I've tried everything. All our systems are reading normal. If we don't locate the problem soon, we'll have to go through every damn component one at a time."

Another tense silence fell over the Mad Men. Davenport's stomach flipped with excitement. Beauty knew more about mechanics than just about anyone Davenport had ever met.

He really did a number on the Mad Men. They weren't going anywhere—not to the admiral, not to Ultra Meridian, and certainly not to the Vultus Wind Mines.

Robberburn shot Red a look and pointed at Davenport. "Watch him and make sure he doesn't go anywhere." Then he stomped off to the stairs leading to the bridge.

Red had better things to do than keep an eye on Davenport. He barely looked at Davenport. Red went over to his friends and they started whispering to them instead. Davenport could just imagine what they were saying to each other.

Various noises that might have been bellows came from upstairs. They made Red and his buddies even more nervous.

Davenport had to suppress laughter. Where was Beauty? What was he doing on the ship at this very moment?

Davenport only hoped Beauty didn't take the whole sabotage thing too far, but then again, Beauty did know a lot about ship engines.

Everyone spun around when the upstairs bridge door banged opened. Robberburn came out, turned to shut the door behind him, and called down to his men. "Don't worry. We have it all worked out now. It was just the......"

A crushing boom smacked the ship hard from port and every man on the deck went flying off his feet. Davenport, Red, and all the Mad Men slammed against the far wall and then another blow struck from directly above them.

The ship jolted downward and then tumbled ass over tea kettle in all directions. Bodies banged and bumped against Davenport as they all somersaulted across the hold floor and crashed into the stairs.

Davenport barely had time to grab hold of the railing before another brutal strike pitched the whole ship on end and everything went black.

Chapter 20

Gunfire pounded the *Prometheus Vox* and Healey wrestled the controls to stay on course. The constant hammering of weapons on his hull made the earlier damage even worse and the engines coughed.

He fought the helm to stabilize the ship, but he couldn't concentrate with the Cannibals surrounding him on all sides.

More ships came out of nowhere until he couldn't see beyond them all. They whizzed past his cockpit pelting him with shots and then zoomed off into space behind him.

He struggled to see somewhere he could land. He caught a moment's glimpse of HTWV-983 before another flock of Cannibals cut off his view.

They raced across his bow and another barrage nailed his starboard wing. The blow knocked the *Prometheus Vox* on end and another group of Cannibals sprinted past the Nitrol's underside.

Every one of those fast-moving fighter craft bombarded the ship's belly with shots and the impact hurtled Healey backward in his seat. A blaring alarm screeched from the controls as the ship tried to correct.

Healey wrenched the helm hard to port and somersaulted away from the attackers, only to pitch into another crowd of them crowding on his other side.

Hundreds of shots lambasted his cockpit. The alarm screeched louder than ever as the hull started to give way. He had to get out of this before they destroyed him.

He gunned the engines and bolted for the only sanctuary left to him. He plunged for HTWV-983, but thousands of Cannibal ships already revolved around the planet. He could only guess how far he was from the surface.

He didn't care anymore. He had to land, and with a little luck, the planet would hide him until he got airborne again—*if* he got airborne again.

He made one last check of the surrounding space. Thousands of Cannibal identity profiles blocked out the stars. He spotted the *Artemis Rex* in the farthest distance. The Drifter was making one last desperate break for the Confederate line.

He put the *Artemis Rex* and the boys and Davenport and the Ithium out of his mind. He had enough on his plate right now. They would all just have to take care of themselves. He would deal with them later if he ever even made it off this planet alive.

He tilted the *Prometheus Vox* to the surface and nailed the throttle to the wall. The Cannibals in orbit turned to meet him, but he just didn't care anymore.

Gravity took hold and he dive-bombed the Cannibals at terminal velocity. He blasted his Howitzers straight in front of him.

He took dozens of shots all over his hull, but he concentrated all his firepower on breaking through their blockade and getting into the atmosphere.

Five Cannibals fighter craft tried to stand in his way, but as he plummeted straight for them, three darted out of his path. His fire detonated the other two and the *Prometheus Vox* blasted through their burning wreckage to the forests below.

He grasped the helm in both fists. He had to brace his legs against the console to drag the ship level. Even then, he was flying way too fast to slow down.

He zoomed parallel to the canopy, but as soon as he got into that position, rockets and plasma bombarded him from the atmosphere. The Cannibals smashed the *Prometheus Vox* down into the forest.

He braked hard and veered around several enormous trees before he slowed enough to see where he was going. He had to find a place to hide.

His readings showed him dozens of Cannibal ships landing on the planet's upper continents, so Healey flew as far away from them as he could get before he dared to land.

He found himself a nice quiet, out-of-the-way spot on the planet's night side. The Cannibals hadn't made it this far, but it was only a matter of time. They would swarm the whole planet and find him eventually. He had to work fast.

He stole a quick glance at the readouts, didn't see any Cannibals nearby, and sprang out of his seat. He couldn't sit here staring at the readings until the Cannibals came back.

He dove into the back and got out his tools. He scrambled under the Nitrol's belly and groaned when he saw the damage.

He dreaded the moment he had to pull on his welding helmet and fire up the torch. He wouldn't be able to see or hear as long as he had it on, but he had no choice.

He got busy welding as fast as he could. He patched several holes, pulled off the helmet, and strained his ears to listen in the gathering darkness. This planet didn't seem to understand the concept of sunshine.

He fixed all the hull damage without seeing or hearing anything. Then he got to work on the wiring and systems malfunctions. They would take a hell of a lot longer.

He hustled in and out of the ship checking the controls and then going back to different places to reconnect or reinitialize.

He finally returned to the cockpit for the last time, and when he ran full diagnostic software on all the Nitrol's systems, they came up clear.

He hopped into his seat ready to launch out of the forest when an alert came over the controls. *Proximity breach—unidentified aliens approaching.*

He took one look at the readings and gulped. A whole army of Cannibals was coming his way.

He leapt into the back and snatched two Howitzers before he heard gunfire in the distance. His heart sprang into his mouth. This was it. The Cannibals were coming for him.

He charged outside checking his weapons as fast as he could. He got to the hatch and his stomach dropped all over again when he saw them all.

There must have been hundreds all spread out in a line. They advanced firing into the trees, but they weren't alone.

They marched forward one unstoppable step at a time. They drove at least forty of Mexia's people before them and the two sides traded shots back and forth.

Healey stood rooted to the spot taking in the scene as fast as his mind could think. The Cannibals weren't coming for him. They hadn't even seen him yet. They were too occupied with wiping out Mexia's last holdouts.

He made a split-second decision and raced into the trees. He didn't know where he would hide, but if he could conceal himself until the whole battle passed, he just might be able to survive this. He just didn't know how he would get off the planet afterward.

He sprinted between massive trunks putting as much distance as he could between himself and the *Prometheus Vox*. He cast this way and that for any place to hide—any place at all.

Then he saw a hole under the roots of a gigantic tree. The opening disappeared into a dark cavity just big enough for a man to crawl inside.

He jammed himself in, scooted backward, and aimed his biggest Howitzer through the gap to blow away anyone who came near him.

He panted for air while he awaited his fate. The crash and belch of gunfire snuck closer by the second. It was practically on top of him.

From here, he could just see the *Prometheus Vox* gleaming in the distance. Mexia's people backed into the clearing still unloading into the trees. They paid no attention to the ship.

They backed around it and several of the Cannibal shots peppered the ship in spots Healey just repaired, but he didn't care. He would hide here and watch the Cannibals destroy his ship rather than show himself.

They *would* destroy it, too. As soon as they finished off Mexia's people, the Cannibals would come back, strip the *Prometheus Vox* of any useable parts, kill and devour anyone they could find, and then move on to their next target. That was the Cannibals' way.

Mexia's people inched toward the ship's nose. They paused there to bombard the Cannibals as the savage aliens pushed into the clearing.

Healey shivered when he saw the Cannibals at close range. Their grim visages would give anyone nightmares. Their blood-streaked fangs extended from wide, grinning mouths. Their dark, expressionless eyes locked on their prey, but at least they were looking at Mexia's people instead of Healey.

The Cannibals entered the clearing on long, angled legs lined with thin, wiry muscle. Their bony bodies and skeletal stature belied their strength, speed, and ferocity.

Their numbers made them even more fearsome. They always attacked in force. Shooting one of them or even several of them only made it more certain that the rest of their horde would come after whoever did it.

More and more Cannibals advanced into the clearing. Their flank swept toward the ship and Mexia's people retreated further toward the trees on the other side. The *Prometheus Vox* sat directly between the two sides.

Gunfire from both sides pinged off the hull. Both sides used a combination of lasers and plasma weapons that carved the Nitrol to pieces. Hull sections banged into the dirt and one of the landing struts gave way.

The Nitrol toppled onto its side and Mexia's people ducked for cover behind the ship.

The Cannibals must have expected this. As soon as Mexia's people got out of range, the Cannibals charged. Their line surged into the clearing and both ends wrapped around the ship to trap Mexia's people there.

At least a hundred Cannibals swooped in, surrounded Mexia's people, and unloaded. The noise echoed through the trees and assaulted Healey's ears. He shrank lower in his hiding place, but he never stopped aiming his Howitzer outward to defend himself.

The Cannibals descended on Mexia's people and cut them to the ground. The Cannibals stood over their fallen victims firing downward to finish off the last survivors.

The clearing fell silent except for the Cannibals talking to each other in their guttural, grunting language. They searched the surrounding area and Healey retreated to conceal himself.

The Cannibals returned to the ship's hatch and went inside to search it. They came out a second later and scanned the woods.

Healey held his breath. His heart wouldn't stop pounding and he tightened his grip on his weapon. If they came after him, they would cut this tree down to get him out of it. The Cannibals didn't leave survivors.

A few Cannibals ventured into the trees. Some went in different directions from the way Healey ran to get here. They returned without finding anything and they discussed the situation some more.

Then they loped off the way they came. Healey collapsed in his hiding place, too overwrought and breathless to move. He had to get out of here. He had to get back to the ship, repair it all over again, and launch before the Cannibals came back, but he didn't leave his hiding place.

He waited for what seemed like an eternity. He had to make absolutely certain the Cannibals didn't come back while he was repairing the ship.

The hull would need even more welding this time, which would leave him blind and deaf to any danger. He would also have to search the atmosphere and the area of space around HTWV-983 before he launched. He couldn't fly into another vast flock of the Cannibals or he'd be dead for certain.

He finally summoned the will to climb out. He swept his weapon back and forth in all directions, but the whole forest had gone quiet again.

He strode back to the ship making sure to cover every possible angle. He kept his Howitzer by his side while he got out his tools, but he didn't dare to put his helmet back on.

He used the visor as a shield in front of his eyes so he could weld while keeping his eyes and ears free. The whole job took ten times as long because he kept looking around and startling at the slightest sound.

He finally went into the cockpit and sat down. The first thing he did was to scan the forest for the Cannibals. His chest tightened when he saw them coming straight for him.

He scrambled through his readings. The Cannibals were still at least a quarter of a mile away, but they were coming back for the *Prometheus Vox*.

More Cannibal ships patrolled the planet, but they mostly concentrated on the light side. They weren't paying much attention to the night side.... not yet.

That would change as soon as he launched. He had to work fast.

He ran through his diagnostics again. They were normal. He fired the engines and adrenaline seared his insides when the Cannibals on the ground burst into a run to catch up with him. They closed the gap.

He gunned the engines and launched as they sprinted out of the trees. They leveled their weapons at the ship rising through the canopy.

He unloaded with his Howitzers and cut them down as the ship broke the topmost branches. He punched the throttle and vaulted into the atmosphere. More Cannibal ships rocketed toward him from the planet's other side. They raced to intercept him. He didn't have a moment to lose.

He veered into orbit as more Cannibal ships converged from farther out in space. Their shots zinged past the hull, but they were still too far away to hit him.

He ripped away from the planet and plunged the ship to full speed on a dead sprint for Confederate space. The Cannibals gained on him and he spotted the Reserve Wing standing guard across the line.

Healey opened a channel to the biggest Stalwart on the block. "Confederate Marshall Lawrence Healey to Reserve Wing Stalwart. I'm on a law enforcement mission for the Confederate Sheriff's Service. You are ordered to stand down and let me pass by the authority of Admiral Killian Joyce. I repeat. This is Confederate Marshall Lawrence Healey on law enforcement business for the Confederate Sheriff's Service. You are ordered to stand aside and block the Cannibals from following me into Confederate space. Do you read?"

No one answered. The Stalwarts and Daggers stood in formation across the boundary, but he didn't slow. The Cannibals crawled up on his ass and unloaded at the *Prometheus Vox*. Some of their shots missed him and hit the Reserve Wing instead.

He got within range of the boundary before the Reserve Wing reacted. As soon as the Cannibals came within shooting distance, the Confederate forces erupted out of position, flooded the boundary, and streaked into Sacron Enigma.

They plunged for the *Prometheus Vox*, surrounded the Nitrol, and then dove past to engage the Cannibals.

Healey exploded in relieved laughter. He was free. The Cannibals stayed inside Sacron Enigma fully occupied with the Reserve Wing.

He rocketed across the boundary and kept on going. He didn't slow down at all. The Reserve Wing obviously came out here on Joyce's orders. Healey didn't want to deal with them.

Now he had to find the *Artemis Rex* and hopefully locate where the Mad Men took Davenport. The entirety of space left a pretty big territory to cover.

He had to narrow it down some. Admiral Joyce would still be holding court at Ultra Meridian. None of Davenport's crew would go there.

Healey put on as much speed as he could while he thought fast. He also had to get word back to Calyx Elkanon that Mexia had betrayed Davenport. Healey didn't want to stick around to see the consequences of that, either—assuming any of Mexia's people survived to get off of HTWV-983.

Healey veered back toward Pandora's Needle while he thought the matter over. The Reserve Wing database might be able to tell him where the Mad Men took Davenport. It also might be able to turn up some location data on the *Artemis Rex*.

He was just passing through the Luurlats system when a message came through his controls.

"Nitrol *Prometheus Vox*, you are under arrest by the Confederate Sheriff's Service. Cut your engines and prepare to be taken into custody."

"I'm a Confederate Marshall, buddy," Healey replied. "I'm on duty for the...."

"Negative, Nitrol *Prometheus Vox*. You are under arrest by the Confederate Sheriff's Service. Cut your engines and prepare to be taken into custody. We will fire at the first sign of resistance."

Healey smacked his lips in annoyance. He reverse-throttled to slow down and prepared himself to flex his new Marshall's authority on whatever pissant sheriff dared to mess with him.

Then he spotted the identity profile of the ship moving to apprehend him. Healey collapsed back in his seat with a shaky sigh of relief. The profile on his instruments read, *Vindicator*. Healey was safe.

Chapter 21

The *Vindicator* swiveled in front of the *Prometheus Vox*. Seven more attack Drifters surrounded the Nitrol as the *Prometheus Vox* eased inside.

The *Vindicator's* rear hatch cracked open to reveal eight powerful characters standing guard inside the flight deck. They all wore body armor and they were all armed with giant XQs.... all except the square-shouldered man at the center.

Salt-and-pepper grey flecked his black hair. He hadn't shaved in a few days, but he stood over all the others in such an obvious attitude of authority that Healey's heart skipped a beat.

Healey didn't have to steer. A tractor beam pulled the *Prometheus Vox* into the *Vindicator's* hold and the hatch clanged to lock the Nitrol inside.

Healey walked out to face the people who apprehended him. They all wore Sheriff's stars and two of them were women.

The eight deputies leveled their weapons at Healey, but he didn't react except to raise his hands.

The big guy at the center strode forward under his deputies' cover, halted right in front of Healey, and leveled Healey with a hard stare. "I know you. You're Lawrence Healey.... from Pandora's Needle."

"That's right. I tried to explain to your deputy that I'm in the line of duty here, but he wouldn't listen."

"That doesn't matter." The big sheriff glanced down at Healey's star. "So they promoted you, huh? We hadn't received word that you were made a Marshall."

"That's because it just happened. I don't know that my brain has quite caught up with the truth yet."

The guy snorted, but he stopped short of actually smiling. He stuck out his hand. "I'm Deacon Pritchard."

"I know who you are. Everyone knows who you are." Healey glanced around at the deputies who still held him at gunpoint even as he shook their boss's hand. "The Wide Patrol is legend in the service."

Pritchard completely ignored the compliment. "Well? What's the story? What are you doing out here? Nitrol *Prometheus Vox* is flagged as wanted by the Sheriff's Service."

Healey's head whipped around so fast he made himself dizzy. "What? That's impossible!"

"I can show you the entry in the database. Why do you think we apprehended you?"

Healey's hand flew to his head. "That son of a bitch! He screwed me over!"

"What son of a bitch?" Pritchard asked.

Healey hesitated. He wasn't exaggerating about the Wide Patrol. Sheriff Deacon Pritchard and his posse of deputies were notorious throughout the Confederacy for getting the job done when no one else could.

They earned the name the Wide Patrol because they had a habit of working outside their original jurisdiction. They still called the Osaids sector their home territory, but they'd been known to pop up just about anywhere.

People traveled from all over the galaxy to beg for the Wide Patrol's help solving problems no one else could solve. The Wide Patrol had even been known to take on the Reserve Wing itself when the situation called for it. They never turned down a job when someone really needed their help.

The Wide Patrol didn't back down from putting a toe over the line into doing something illegal, either. No one really knew just how far they would go, but no one in the whole Confederate chain of command dared to question their commitment to law and order.

That was the one iron rule the Wide Patrol always kept. If they broke the law, they did it to stop someone from doing something a whole lot worse.

The Wide Patrol never went after non-combatants, civilians, or the defenseless—ever. They were the knights in shining armor that everyone in the galaxy knew they could count on.

Even knowing all that, Healey stopped himself from spilling his guts to Pritchard—not that Healey doubted Pritchard's integrity. No one would do that. If Healey was going to trust someone, it would be Pritchard.

Pritchard cocked his head and his sharp eyes pierced Healey to the core. "You better talk to me if you ever want to get off this ship. The entry in the database includes orders to send you up to Terminus Anathema for crimes against humanity."

Healey threw caution to the wind, took a deep breath, and launched into the story. "Do you know Mace Davenport? He's the Sheriff of Ultra Meridian."

Pritchard nodded. "I've heard of him, but I don't know him personally. What about him?"

"He confiscated a stolen Ithium cartridge. He took it off a smuggler's vessel, and a few minutes later, the Reserve Wing attacked from orbit. They destroyed his jail and stole his safe containing the Ithium and a computer chip designed to trigger it......and then Admiral Killian Joyce tried to kill him."

Pritchard stiffened. His eyes flashed even more dangerously. "That is a very serious accusation."

"I didn't want to believe it, either. Davenport showed up at the Needle with a bunch of assassins on Ekol Thaine's payroll."

"So what did you do?" Pritchard asked.

"I threw him and his whole crew in jail—that's what. I didn't believe a word he said....and then I started looking into it. I still probably wouldn't have done anything about it, but while I still had him in custody, Admiral Joyce contacted me from Atlas Arcane. He ordered me to transport Davenport down to the planet on the double."

Pritchard pursed his lips and waved to his deputies. They all lowered their weapons, but they didn't slacken their posture. They surrounded Healey squaring their shoulders and watching his every move. He wasn't free by a long mile.

"Stay here, Marshall," Pritchard told him. "I'll be right back."

Pritchard turned away, shot a fierce glare at one of his men, and walked off. He climbed the stairs to the *Vindicator's* top deck and left Healey standing there surrounded by some of the most notorious deputies in the whole damn service.

Healey tried not to look around at them, but a second later, a man to his right spoke up. "You got Cannibal damage to your hull there, Marshall."

Healey spun around and faced the man who spoke to him. The guy must have been at least six-foot-three with a cap of dirty-blonde curls on top of his head, sparkling blue eyes, and a sandy mustache on his upper lip.

He blew a bubble of chewing gum, let it pop, and went back to chewing it while he leveled Healey with a challenging grin. The name on the guy's star read, *Bolander*.

"Shut your trap, Ace," another man barked from across the circle. "Mind your own business and do your job."

Healey whirled the other way to face the second man who spoke. This one was much shorter. He must have been at least four inches shorter than Healey.

Healey barely had time to read, *Treese*, on the guy's star when one of the women spoke up.

Her soft undertone didn't fit her position on this patrol, but that gentle tone rang through the hold with a force of authority Healey had rarely heard anywhere else in the whole Sheriff's Service.

"If the Cannibals are moving in, we better know about it," she murmured. "If they're here, we have to drop everything and starting arming for doomsday."

"The Cannibals aren't here," the other woman cut in. Her badge read, *Swygert*. "Open your eyes, Wommack. Do you see any Cannibals *here*?"

"They aren't here," Healey explained. "They're in Sacron Enigma going after Davenport. Admiral Joyce called them in when the Mad Men couldn't capture Davenport on their own."

"So the Mad Men are going after Davenport, too?" Bolander chuckled. "This job just gets better and better."

"All of you shut your mouths!" Treese barked. "The next one of you says a word before the boss comes back will be on latrine duty for a week."

That shut them up and Healey took advantage of the lull to examine them more closely.

They looked like the most unlikely bunch imaginable. Healey wouldn't have pegged such a diverse group as sheriff's deputies, but their reputation throughout the Confederacy didn't lie.

Bolander kept grinning at Healey and popping chewing gum bubbles. Wommack actually smiled at Healey, but Swygert turned her head away and refused even to look at him.

Treese studied Healey back with as much penetrating interest as Pritchard did. John Treese had a reputation almost as big as Pritchard's. Treese was Pritchard's chief deputy and he was as tough and determined as his boss.

Healey thought fast. If Bolander noticed Cannibal damage to Healey's hull, Pritchard must have seen the same thing. He wouldn't miss a detail like that.

A door slammed and Pritchard came back. He started talking as soon as he got on the stairs. "You people can stand down. Get up to the bridge, Ace, and keep your eyes peeled for Cannibals, Reserve Wing—anybody."

Bolander laughed and lowered his Howitzer out of position. He shot Healey a huge, cheeky grin and headed over to the stairs. As soon as Pritchard got to the floor, Bolander sprang up the stairs three at a time and vanished onto the bridge.

Pritchard pulled up in front of Healey and sliced his forefinger at the rest of his deputies. "Wommack, you and De Rosa go over to the *Anarchy* and start arming our patrol for battle. Yarborough, take Grant and Swygert back to their ships and stand ready to defend the *Vindicator* in case someone gets the jump on us."

"Are you going somewhere, Boss?" a massive guy named De Rosa asked.

"I've got something I need to take care of first and then the *Vindicator* will be ready to rock, too. Go on, Bill. If anyone comes near us, start shooting and ask questions later. That includes the Reserve Wing. John, you're with me."

The rest of the Wide Patrol walked away in different directions. Pritchard kept an eye on his people until they all got well out of earshot. Only Treese remained.

Pritchard finally faced Healey and he didn't look happy—not at all. "Follow me, Marshall."

Pritchard crossed the deck going in a different direction. He opened the door to a crew cabin adjacent to the hold. Pritchard motioned Healey inside and Healey saw at one glance that the cabin had never been used.

Treese followed Healey inside and the Pritchard shut the door behind all three of them. Pritchard straightened up and locked eyes on Healey.

"Well, Marshall, I've just traced some of the movements you mentioned and I've confirmed enough of your story that I'm willing to listen to the rest. Let's hear it. Tell me everything."

Healey skimmed over the parts he'd already mentioned. He fast-forwarded to his most recent encounter with the admiral at Ultra Meridian and everything that happened after that.

"So the Mad Men have Davenport now," he finished. "They'll be taking him back to Ultra Meridian to hand him and the Ithium over to the admiral. I just wish I could figure out why Joyce flagged me for arrest. He's the one who tasked me with finding Davenport in the first place."

"He didn't flag you for arrest," Pritchard replied. "The Reserve Wing just flagged you when you crossed back over from Sacron Enigma. They couldn't stop you with the Cannibals around. They must have wanted someone else to pick you up for them."

"Swell," Healey growled. "Just flippin' fantastic."

Pritchard gave him an ironic grimace. That was as close as he ever came to actually smiling. "That means Admiral Joyce still thinks you're on his side. There's another transmission going out on the wires that he's on his way to rendezvous with the Reserve Wing and another unidentified vessel. He must be on his way to meet up with the Mad Men and take custody of Davenport, which means we have to get there first."

Pritchard opened the cabin door, stepped through it, and started barking orders over his shoulder.

"He wants you to find Davenport, so that's what you're going to do. John, you get over to the *Fortitude* and deploy the rest of the Patrol. You deploy, too, Marshall, and I'll need you to transmit the identity profile of the Mad Men's vessel to the rest of us."

"That's going to make it a little tough since I don't have it," Healey replied.

"Don't worry about it. We can trace it from HTWV-983. Go!"

Pritchard veered onto the stairs and Healey lost sight of him. Treese and the rest of Pritchard's deputies raced away while Healey returned to the *Prometheus Vox*.

The minute he sat down in the seat, voices assaulted his ears from the other attack Drifters. "*Fortitude—Anarchy—Stormspike—Celestis—*hold position while the *Prometheus Vox* deploys," Pritchard ordered.

"There goes our only chance at stardom, boys," Bolander drawled. "Our moment of fame in the presence of a real, live Confederate Marshall."

"Take a good, long look, Ace," De Rosa boomed over the intercom, "'cuz you ain't never gonna be no Confederate Marshall."

"Do I look like I want to be a Marshall? Hell, I can't even tie my bootlaces without the Boss slapping me upside the head."

"*Prometheus Vox*, you are clear to deploy," Pritchard interrupted.

An alarm went off on Healey's controls as the Drifters powered up and locked and loaded their weapons. The *Vindicator's* engines kickstarted and the hatch boomed open to let the *Prometheus Vox* out.

"*Prometheus Vox* is clear," Treese interjected. "*Fortitude, Anarchy, and Celestis* moving in."

Three Drifters advanced into the *Vindicator's* hold and Healey caught a glimpse of the deputies rushing to their cockpits. A second later, the three ships re-launched with their deputies at the helm.

"Transmitting identity profile and location of the Mad Men vessel," Pritchard announced. "Wide Patrol—hit it."

Chapter 22

The Wide Patrol rocketed away in unison, but the Drifters couldn't match the *Vindicator's* speed. The larger ship outstripped them all and Healey had to fly at his top speed just to keep up.

They closed on the coordinates in no time, but Healey didn't have to follow the location Pritchard mentioned.

A massive swarm of alien attack vessels revolved in a blur with at least seventeen ships belonging to the Mad Men. They traded shots and several of the Mad Men's ships stood still and nonoperational at the center of the battle.

"Holy living shit!" Swygert muttered. "Look at 'em all!"

"Those ships belong to Mexia," Pritchard remarked. "What the hell are they doing out here?"

"Which ship is Davenport on?" De Rosa called. "That identity profile isn't coming from any of these."

"It doesn't matter," Pritchard ordered. "Neutralize the attackers and apprehend the Mad Men. We'll figure it out later."

"Neutralize and apprehend," Bolander replied. "I live to obey."

"Now I've heard everything." Pritchard rocketed into the swarm and opened fire. The rest of the Wide Patrol gunned their engines. They surrounded the aliens firing inward toward the center, but it was hard to acquire a target without hitting the Mad Men, too.

The Mad Men only made the situation worse by shooting at the Wide Patrol at least as often as they hit the aliens. The Mad Men must have identified the Wide Patrol and panicked. Any sane person would rather fight Mexia's gang than get arrested by the Wide Patrol.

Healey took a turn around the perimeter searching everywhere for some sign of which ship might be carrying Davenport. He had barely started when a laser blast pelted across his bow.

He whipped around to see a giant alien battle craft charging him from inside the swarm. Healey yanked his Howitzers into position and unloaded on the beast, but it was too big.

He skidded out of the way and plastered shots down its starboard flank as the thing thundered past him, but it could move a lot faster than he realized.

It barely cleared his wing when it wheeled and came hurtling back for another charge. Healey punched the throttle and vaulted over the thing's roof spraying fire across the hull.

He ducked behind its guns where it couldn't hit him, but as soon as he got there, more of Mexia's ships plummeted out of the swarm to attack him.

The battle swallowed him and he fired at everyone and everything just trying to keep them from blowing his ship apart. He spotted the battle craft that first attacked him plunging back into the cloud.

This one ship dwarfed every other vessel on the field, including the *Vindicator*. It seemed to be coordinating all the others. The smaller, speedier ships revolved around it in wider and narrower orbits depending on what was going on.

Healey gritted his teeth and blocked out every other ship on the field. He rushed the thing and concentrated his fire on its laser ports.

It recognized him instantly and trained all its weaponry on the *Prometheus Vox*. Healey skimmed underneath the enemy ship and pounded the underside with Howitzer fire, but nothing scratched its iron surface.

That left only one option. He pulled into a tight skid under the thing's tail and sprang over the top of it. He zoomed back toward the nose and laid into the laser ports with a vengeance.

He hit two of them and the thing attacked in fury. It nailed him hard across the port side and the *Prometheus Vox* lurched to starboard.

Healey dropped the throttle to the wall and rushed the thing at top speed. Lasers glanced off his cockpit, but that only gave him the perfect target. He bombarded another port and it exploded in his face.

He sprinted back the other way, but when he turned around, he had to check himself before he recognized which ship he was fighting.

Three Drifters surrounded the thing and Healey read their profiles in a heartbeat. The *Stormspike* hurdled the alien vessel and blasted into the port wing. Part of it snapped off before the *Stormspike* raced across the fuselage and laid into the starboard wing on the way past.

The *Fortitude* made another turn around the enemy's tail, veered into a dangerous reverse slide, and fired straight up the thing's tailpipe. The *Anarchy* rocketed out of nowhere and fired a well-placed charge directly into the enemy's bridge.

"We got your back, Marshall!" Treese called. "One more pass and that'll be all she wrote."

"The main propulsion system is overloading!" Wommack replied. "Clear out, Ace! She's gonna blow!"

"Here comes another one!" Bolander replied. "Right behind you, Wommack!"

Bolander corkscrewed around the stricken vessel and plastered three smaller vessels creeping up on Wommack from behind, but she wasn't there anymore.

She throttled past the imploding enemy and went to town on another dozen trying to surround the *Celestis* and the *Fortitude*.

The *Celestis* fired a few times and veered out of the cloud to rush another group of attackers trying to ambush Treese. "Get back, you bastards! Are you hit, John?"

"I'm okay, Bill," Treese replied. "Watch out! Here they come again."

De Rosa pulled the *Celestis* out of a dive and bombarded four more attackers materializing from inside the swarm. He hit two of them before the other two pinned him down.

"Don't hit the Mad Men, De Rosa!" Pritchard ordered. "We still don't know which one of them is carrying Davenport."

"I can't hardly tell one from the other," De Rosa muttered.

"We need to identify which ship he's on."

The words barely got out of Pritchard's mouth when more of Mexia's people swooped in and another Mad Men ship detonated right off De Rosa's bow.

"Shit! Was that the ship Davenport was on?"

"I see him!" Healey called. "His ship is hit! The reactor is melting down! We need to take him on board as soon as possible."

"How can you tell?" Pritchard asked. "They all look the same."

"That one has an alien life form on board. It's native to HTWV-983."

"That's good enough for me." Pritchard turned back to Mexia's attackers. "Clear these assholes off the field, Wide Patrol. We got work to do. Marshall, you come with me."

"Yes, Sir," Healey replied and he steered over to the *Vindicator*.

Most of Mexia's people were starting to withdraw from the foundering vessel Healey identified. The enemy concentrated on other more operational ships, including the Wide Patrol.

"Draw them away, Ace!" Pritchard ordered. "You, too, Yarborough! Clear the area!"

"Come and get it, little chickens!" Bolander pelted in and blasted through the flock. He clipped one of the enemy vessels across the wing and showered the others with Howitzer fire.

He cartwheeled around them and annoyed them until they rounded on him, but he was already rocketing away. "Suckers!" he yelled as they all fell in line to hound him away.

Yarborough pelted back in the *Conquest*. He collided full tilt with one of Mexia's ships that had crawled up Bolander's tailpipe. A second later, Yarborough exploded through the fireball heading in the opposite direction.

"That's my boy!" Bolander cheered. "Give 'em hell, man!"

"Watch your ass, kid," Yarborough boomed. "Here comes another bunch from port."

Healey lost track of everything the Wide Patrol was doing. They flew faster, shot faster, and reacted faster than any Reserve Wing squadron he had ever seen. They attacked with frightening viciousness and left nothing in their wake.

He stood guard while the *Vindicator* backed up to the Mad Men's ship. "Nitrol *Diving Bell*," Pritchard called, "you are under arrest by the Confederate Sheriff's Service. Hold your fire and prepare to be taken into custody."

No one answered. Healey scanned the ship. "It's reading without power so they probably can't hear you. There are plenty of human life signs aboard, though."

"Swing around, Marshall. Stand ready to fire if anything goes haywire. Swygert—quit messing around and come in here to defend us."

"You got it, Boss."

Healey pivoted backward and aimed his Howitzers into the *Vindicator's* open hatch. The ship reversed and swallowed the Mad Men's vessel.

"I got him!" Pritchard announced. "Break off and return to the Luurlats system."

Chapter 23

D ice shoved a Howitzer into Fiddler's hands. "Go! Go! Go!"

Fiddler raced for the hatch. The boys grabbed more weapons from Dice and followed Fiddler outside.

Fiddler's heart pounded scanning the dim trees all around the *Artemis Rex*. Lyons bumped into Fiddler from the other side. "How close are they?"

"The cockpit sensors showed Mexia's people two hundred yards that way." Rodeo nodded past the ship toward the north.

"I don't give a shit about Mexia's people," Emmett snapped. "Where are the Cannibals?"

"A hundred yards that way." Rodeo indicated to the west.

"Shit sandwich!" Dice snarled.

"Coon, take Axel and Laub and get working on the ship."

"But what if the Cannibals come?"

"All the more reason we'll need to fly away before they get here."

The three boys started to retreat. Fiddler didn't turn around. She strained her eyes to see everything that wasn't creeping up on the crew.

"We just HAD to get stranded on a planet with the Cannibals," Lyons muttered.

"We were so close, too," Bandit lamented. "We could have been over the line if they hadn't caught us."

"I hate to tell you this, but we never would have made it over the line with the Reserve Wing there," Rodeo replied. "They were standing guard to stop us from returning to the Confederacy."

"Admiral Joyce has every angle stitched up," Dice growled.

"You can do that when you're an admiral," Lyons replied. "He's got every resource we don't. All he has to do is tell everyone we're criminals. He can bring in every sheriff, bounty hunter, and ship in the galaxy to hunt us down."

"Why are we trying to get back to the Confederacy, anyway?" Bandit asked. "We're safer here."

"Safer with the Cannibals?" Emmett countered. "I don't think so."

"Shhh!" Rodeo hissed. "Here they come!"

"Which ones?" Alla whispered.

"All of them!"

A twig snapped and Fiddler spun around to train her weapon in that direction, but she still didn't see anything. Another sound startled her from her right and she wheeled the other way.

The rest of the group did the same thing. They spread out to ring the ship, but the boys made it even worse when they fired up their welding torches and started sawing into the hull behind Fiddler's back.

The tension racked her nerves to the breaking point. Why didn't the enemy show themselves? She would rather get into a shooting war against the Cannibals than wait any longer.

Another snap made her jump, and this time, she jolted to high alert when the Cannibals emerged from the *Artemis Rex's* other side.

She jerked her Howitzer up and opened fire. Dice, Lyons, and Emmett joined her, but when the boys tried to help out, Mexia's people showed up from the opposite direction. Both armies flanked the *Artemis Rex* all gunning for the crew.

Fiddler concentrated everything on the Cannibals. They were much more dangerous and there were a hell of a lot more of them. They advanced through the woods in vast numbers. Their gruesome, dripping fangs told Fiddler exactly what they planned to do if they won.

She mowed them down as fast as she could, but still they came. Yells and a few screams punctured the din with the boys trying to drive off Mexia's people.

Almost as soon as the battle started, the Cannibals and Mexia's people both noticed each other with both groups trying to get the quarry the other wanted.

The Cannibals turned their guns on Mexia's people and the two invading armies fired at each other instead. A three-way battle broke out between all three groups.

This didn't make the *Artemis Rex* crew any safer. Plenty of Cannibals and aliens from Mexia's side kept up a continuous bombardment on the crew. The majority turned on each other, but they still threatened to mow the crew down if this kept up.

Fiddler retreated back to the ship. Lasers and plasma ricocheted off the hull and one of the shots hit Wolf. He went down screeched and roaring, but he still kept shooting through it all to drive the enemy off.

Bandit and Rodeo sprang to his side to defend him, but the battle was already swinging away from the *Artemis Rex*. The Cannibals overpowered Mexia's aliens and drove Mexia's people back into the forest. Both parties started inching away into the trees.

More aliens swiveled away from the *Artemis Rex* to protect themselves from the Cannibals. The Cannibals advanced to drive them deeper into the woods and left a carpet of bodies behind them.

Fiddler didn't dare to hope the Cannibals would leave the *Artemis Rex* alone and she was right. As soon as the Cannibals drew level with the crew, they split again. Half their number went after Mexia's people and at least fifty Cannibals advanced toward the ship.

Dice charged forward bellowing and laying down fire with his XQ, but he had to retreat before so many Cannibals. He planted himself in front of the hatch while Fiddler, Lyons, Emmett, and the boys took refuge behind the fuselage.

The Cannibals widened their net to cover every angle. They curved the ends of their line to surround the ship. They would capture and kill the crew any second now.

Fiddler jerked her weapon from one side to the other, but nowhere was safe anymore. The Cannibals bombarded her with such heavy fire that she had to hunker down. If she faced right, they targeted her from the left. If she fired to the left, more Cannibals threatened her from the right. She couldn't hold out much longer.

At that moment, the *Artemis Rex's* engine shrieked to life. Fiddler barely had time to get away from the landing gear in time. The ship sprang off the ground, wheeled, and opened fire on the Cannibals.

The Cannibals turned their guns up toward the cockpit where Alla sat in Bandit's usual cradle, but it was too late. The *Artemis Rex* sliced a deadly arch of Howitzer fire and leveled the Cannibals in a splayed semi-circle of twitching bodies.

The ship sank to the ground and the engines wound down to silence. The crew crouched in place. Fiddler held her breath still watching and waiting for something, but the forest returned to its former stillness—all except for the rattle of gunfire in the distance.

"That was sudden," Laub remarked.

"We have to get off this planet." Rodeo turned to his boys. "Get back to work. We'll protect you as well as we can."

They raced away and went at it with all their energy. Rodeo headed for the hatch to go back inside, but Fiddler stopped him. "I have an idea. I think we should go back for the Ithium."

"What for?" Dice boomed. "Why did we hide it in the first place if we're only going to go back for it?"

"That was before we knew Mexia's people and the Cannibals would be all over this planet. If Mexia's people know about the Ithium, all they have to do is scan for the location we landed when we hid it."

"They still wouldn't find it. It's too well hidden."

"I'd just as soon not take that chance." Fiddler turned back to Rodeo. "I'll go get it while you fix the ship."

"It's too dangerous. If Mexia's people saw you, you could lead them right to it.... or, if they captured you after you retrieved it, they would have both you *and* the Ithium."

"That's why you and the boys should stay here. They'll come after you instead and you can distract them. They might not notice one person running off into the woods."

"You can't go alone," Lyons interjected. "I'll go with you."

"Neither of you is going anywhere with anyone else," Rodeo countered. "I just said it's too dangerous."

"We should leave the Ithium here," Dice added. "That's the whole point of hiding it in the first place. Even Davenport said so."

"So now you're doing what Davenport says?" Fiddler returned. "I wonder what he'd say if he knew you changed your tune so quickly, Dice."

He scowled and looked away. "You and Dice are the only people who know where the Ithium is," Rodeo went on. "Let's keep it that way. You and Lyons going after it would only draw attention to it."

He went back inside, and a second later, Dice and Emmett left to go help with the repairs. Fiddler turned to Lyons. "Well?"

"Well what?"

"Should we go after it?"

"No," Lyons replied. "I agree with him. It's safer where it is."

Fiddler huffed and looked over her shoulder. Should she go after the Ithium on her own?

Why was she even thinking that when she was the one who wanted to hide it in the first place? Wasn't that the whole reason the crew fled to Sacron Enigma?

She sighed and gave it up. They were probably right. The Ithium was safer where it was.

She went back to patrolling around the ship. The boys had finished welding, but they were still working on the wiring both inside the ship and on the outer hull.

Fiddler made a circuit back to the ship's nose. She scanned the surrounding woods, but she still didn't see anything. That didn't mean the Cannibals and Mexia's aliens wouldn't come back any time.

The boys kept shouting at each other behind Fiddler's back. "Try it now!" Laub called.

What sounded like Bandit yelled back at him from the cockpit.

"Not that one!" Coon roared. "Are you trying to kill us?"

More muffled responses came from inside and then a whoop. "Yes! That's it! Cycle it faster."

A deafening crash made Fiddler spin around. She had her weapon to her shoulder before she noticed Breeze tangled up to his neck with Alla at the base of the hatch ramp.

"Get off me, you idiot!" Alla bellowed.

Dice stormed over to them, seized Breeze by the shirt, and yanked him off. Dice ripped him away with such force that Breeze flew out of his grasp and landed on the ramp.

Emmett strolled around the ship to check out the scene and Lyons watched from the other side of the ship's nose. She shot Fiddler a knowing grin and both women went back to checking their surroundings. Breeze might be a walking safety hazard, but he rarely did any serious damage.

Lyons and Fiddler parted to head back the other way when Fiddler heard another sound. It didn't come from the boys.

She leveled her XQ toward the trees. "Did you hear that?"

Lyons jumped and brought up her weapon to aim at the same spot. "What was that?"

"I didn't see anything, but this is the same thing that happened right before the...."

A laser ripped out of the trees, and in a flash, a whole horde of aliens erupted from the forest. The laser zinged past Lyons. Fiddler lunged for her and tackled her to the ground as more lasers and plasma bursts bombarded the *Artemis Rex*.

The two women rolled away and Fiddler swung onto her knees. A clump of bushes gave her some scant cover to shoot at Mexia's aliens advancing on the ship.

Lyons scrambled up next to Fiddler. Dice and Emmett both wheeled to defend the hatch. "Get inside!" Dice bellowed. "Come on, Laub!"

Laub started climbing down from the fuselage when a brutal crack of plasma struck the hull right in front of him. He pitched over backward and screamed when he landed hard on the ground.

Breeze and Alla scrambled to their feet, but they were both unarmed. They charged inside just as Wolf and Rodeo came through the hatch blasting away with their XQs. They joined Dice and Emmett defending Laub and Coon.

Coon rushed Laub and helped him up. Laub limped a few paces and pivoted behind Dice and Emmett to run up the ramp. That left Lyons and Fiddler cut off from the rest.

"Lyons!" Dice bellowed.

Lyons and Fiddler rose a little out of their hiding place, but they ducked again when Mexia's people split into two flanks. The aliens kept inching deeper and deeper into the clearing. Some of them turned backward to assault Lyons's and Fiddler's position.

The two women returned fire, but with Mexia's people coming closer all the time, Fiddler spent more time hunkering down than shooting.

"We have to get out of here!" Lyons yelled over the noise.

"No shit!" Fiddler countered.

"Lyons!" Dice roared again.

Lyons peeked out. Dice and Emmett tried to rotate around the ship, but Mexia's people advanced in such numbers that they ended up driving Dice and Emmett back toward the hatch.

Fiddler didn't see any way she and Lyons could got to the ship with so many enemies in their way.

At that moment, the engines exploded to life and the ship vaulted off the ground again. The *Artemis Rex* spun around and gunfire erupted from the Howitzers, but Mexia's people anticipated this.

Instead of retreating, the aliens sprinted under the ship's belly and fired straight up into its underside. They hit one of the engines the boys had just been working on.

It exploded in a raging fireball that threatened to consume the ship. The *Artemis Rex* slammed down hard on the ground and even crushed a few of the aliens before the rest surrounded the ship.

Fiddler grabbed Lyons's elbow and started to tow her backward away from the fight. Lyons resisted and tried to straighten up.

She tried to catch a glimpse of Dice and Emmett, but she had to dive for cover as Mexia's people overran the clearing. The two women wouldn't be getting back to that ship anytime soon unless they went back there as prisoners.

Mexia's people marched ever closer to Fiddler's hiding place. She gave Lyons one last tug and then Fiddler rocketed to her feet. She unloaded her XQ at the aliens. "Run!" she bellowed. "I'll cover you!"

Lyons fired a few times and then bolted into the trees. Fiddler's sudden move slowed the aliens just enough for her to break away, too.

Fiddler raced between enormous tree trunks with lasers and plasma bursts spitting all around her. They smashed into branches and rained debris on her head.

One vicious plasma jet hit her in the back and sent her sprawling. She landed face down in damp moss with shots ricocheting all around her.

She struggled to pull herself up when Lyons came storming back. Lyons straddled Fiddler and bombarded the oncoming aliens with hellfire. "Get up!" Lyons roared. "Hurry up!"

Fiddler pried herself out of the muck and floundered to get hold of her XQ. Lyons kept up a steady rain of shots and Fiddler staggered away.

Lyons caught up with her a second later. Between the two of them, they carved out just enough of a gap between themselves and Mexia's people. The two women finally broke through the foliage and made a break for freedom.

Chapter 24

"**G**reat!" Bandit muttered. "Just great."

"Keep quiet," Rodeo told him.

"What difference does it make?" Bandit shot a glance at the aliens surrounding the *Artemis Rex* and he grimaced. "We're dead meat. It's only a matter of time before they kill us all."

"Or torture us," Dice added.

"Will you all shut up?" Rodeo hissed. "This is getting us nowhere."

"*We* aren't going anywhere," Bandit pointed out. "We're Mexia's prisoners."

"Look on the bright side," Emmett chimed in. "We didn't get captured by the Cannibals. At least Mexia's people will try to defend us against the Cannibals."

"If they don't kill us first," Dice finished.

"They haven't killed us yet," Rodeo replied, "which means they want something from us."

"They must want the Ithium," Coon suggested. "Don't you remember that Storrik in the village? They know it's here."

"Dice is right. They might be planning to torture us to tell them where it is."

"I can't wait," Dice growled. "I'm the only one here who knows where it is. I would so love to see them try to torture that information out of me."

Just then, a bunch of Mexia's aliens stomped out of the ship's hatch. Banging and thumping noises had been coming from inside the *Artemis Rex* while the aliens searched the ship.

Rodeo turned his ears in that direction. "They better not have done any more damage to my ship."

"What are you going to do if they did?" Bandit moaned. "Every time we repair it, it gets even more damaged. We're never getting off this rock!"

"Will you shut your trap!" Rodeo hissed. "How am I supposed to hear anything with you jabbering nonstop?"

"Do you hear anything, Rodeo?" Emmett asked.

Rodeo fell silent and listened some more. "They've searched the whole ship—again. They're talking about all the places they already looked. Now they're in the cockpit checking the logs."

"Holy shit, this is bad!" Bandit rubbed his arms and rocked on his seat.

Rodeo almost said something else, but he stopped himself when three Ghrukeds marched over. They towered over the prisoners seated on the bare dirt. "Where is the Ithium? Tell us now if you wish to live."

"We don't know where it is," Rodeo replied. "We told your Storrik earlier. We had it on the ship. If it isn't there, we don't know where it is."

"I don't believe you," the first Ghruked boomed. "If it is on your person, we will tear you apart to find it."

Dice raised his great, ugly, horned head and bared his fangs at the creature. "It isn't on the ship because I hid it."

"Where did you hide it?"

"None of your business."

The Ghruked raised his laser pistol and pointed it at Dice's head. "Tell us now or die."

Dice only glared at him. "I'll give you a clue. It's somewhere on this planet."

The creature flicked something on his weapon and it started to hum with a high-pitched whine. The Ghruked tightened his grip on it to fire when one of his pals caught his arm.

They exchanged a subtle glance and the first Ghruked lowered his weapon. The prisoners started to relax when the alien fired straight down into the dirt next to Dice's foot.

The shot exploded dirt and torn moss all over Emmett. He sprang clear with a startled cry and the others caught him.

"Get inside the ship now," the Ghruked ordered. "We will take you with us, and if we don't find the Ithium, we will dispose of you in the swamp where you belong."

More of Mexia's people prodded the crew inside the cargo hold. Aliens surrounded the crew with weapons and shoved everyone down on the floor again.

"This is NOT the way I planned to spend my morning," Coon remarked.

"No, you planned to spend your morning repairing the ship for the twentieth time," Axel replied. "I'm with Bandit on this one. If the *Artemis Rex* takes any more damage, it might get so damaged that we shouldn't screw around repairing it at all."

"What are you complaining about?" Emmett countered. "My daughter is stranded on this planet somewhere. We have to figure out how to get Fiddler and Lyons back."

"Lyons can take care of herself," Dice rumbled.

"Don't you even care about your own crewmates?" Axel asked.

"Of course I care about them. It just looks like we're the ones who need rescuing right now. Fiddler and Lyons are free to move around—unlike us. Beauty isn't here, either, and you don't see me worrying my head over him."

Just then, another deep boom shook the *Artemis Rex*. The aliens all migrated through the hatch and it closed from the outside. They locked the crew inside by themselves.

Rodeo sprang to his feet. "Come on! To the cockpit!"

He, Bandit, Coon, and Emmett dashed to the cockpit and Rodeo sprang into the command cradle. He worked over the controls with expert precision. "They're taking us on board! Look!"

Emmett looked up through the cockpit window to see a giant ship descending on top of the *Artemis Rex*. A massive yawning trapdoor widened in the alien vessel's underside. It descended from the atmosphere and loomed right on top of the *Artemis Rex*.

"Get us out of here!" Emmett yelled. "You can't let them take us inside their ship."

"We can't!" Bandit countered. "We don't have any engines!"

The trapdoor touched the ground and closed with the *Artemis Rex* inside an even bigger hold. The whole thing boomed once and then dead silence fell over the ship.

Bandit and Emmett stared up through the cockpit window, but the hold outside fell into impenetrable darkness. The trapdoor sealed the *Artemis Rex's* fate. No light came through from outside and the cockpit controls glowed red on the boy's faces.

Rodeo took one last look at his controls. "They're launching!"

"This is not good!" Bandit whimpered. "This is not good at all."

"Come on!" Rodeo sprang out of his cradle. "Let's go! We don't have much time."

"Where are you going?" Emmett asked.

"We have to get busy repairing the ship."

"What for?" Bandit yelled. "We can't fly anywhere."

"We can't fly anywhere *now*!" Rodeo called back. "As soon as we figure out how to get out of this hold, the *Artemis Rex* needs to be ready to fly. Come on, Coon. Get your tools out."

Chapter 25

D avenport peeled himself out of a pile of bodies. Someone groaned nearby, but Davenport couldn't see anything in the pitch darkness.

He groped around and finally found a vertical wall. He started to push himself up when someone crashed into his knees and kicked him.

"Knock it off!" Robberburn bellowed.

Hands pawed at Davenport's shins, but he managed to keep himself upright. He tried to work his way down the wall and ended up stepping on someone.

The guy yelped, but Davenport couldn't see enough to figure out where to put his feet. He didn't know where he could go if he did. He should go to the bridge and see what the situation was, but before he could move, the whole ship shuddered, banged, and then fell silent again.

"What was that?" Red asked in the darkness.

"Get up, boys," Robberburn ordered. "We need to...."

A loud clang cut him off and the ship's rear hatch popped. Streaming bright light flooded the Mad Men's vessel and Davenport strained to see beyond it.

A bunch of armed figures strode inside and lined up across the opening. Davenport still couldn't see them clearly.

Robberburn and the rest of the Mad Men started to pry themselves off the floor, but the strangers didn't give them a chance. Davenport's hand flew to his hip, but he still didn't have a sidearm. He had no way to defend himself.

The strangers halted in front of him and Davenport's stomach dropped when he saw who it was. A big, powerfully built guy with greying hair nodded down at Robberburn and the other Mad Men. "You boys are under arrest."

"Who the hell are you?" Robberburn snapped.

The guy raised his eyebrows. "You don't know who I am?"

"Of course not! How the hell should I?"

The guy snapped his sharp eyes to Davenport. "You do, don't you? You know who I am."

Davenport nodded and straightened up to face him. "Yes, Sir. I do."

The guy stuck out his hand. "You don't have to call me that, son. We're both sheriffs."

Davenport shook Pritchard's hand. "You don't know what an honor it is to get arrested by you."

Some of Pritchard's deputies laughed, but Pritchard didn't. His eyes twinkled, but that was all.

"What the hell are you......?" Robberburn started to stand up to confront the Wide Patrol.

Lightning quick, four deputies dropped their weapons down and aimed straight at Robberburn's head. He froze on the floor and his men cowered.

Another man shouldered the deputies aside and hustled up to Davenport's side. "Davenport! You're alive! Thank God."

Davenport blinked down at Lawrence Healey, the Confederate Marshall who saved Davenport's bacon more than once. Did he bring the Wide Patrol here?

"You better come with us, son." Pritchard shot a ferocious glare at the Mad Men. "We need to question you."

"Yes, Sir."

Davenport stepped out of the muddle of Mad Men on the floor. He ended up stepping on Robberburn's hand and made Robberburn bellow. Robberburn tried to get up and retaliate, but Pritchard's deputies stopped him from getting in Davenport's way.

Davenport finally got clear of the mess. Healey pulled him behind the deputies and Pritchard backed away leaving his deputies to guard the prisoners.

Davenport cast a backward glance at the Mad Men, but the Wide Patrol hardly intimidated him less. He never expected to get questioned by Deacon Pritchard. Pritchard left Davenport in no doubt at all that he was under arrest along with the Mad Men.

Pritchard led the way outside the Mad Men's vessel and Davenport discovered that they were in the hold of a much larger ship. More deputies stood guard out there and Pritchard said something to one of them.

The guy fell in with the three sheriffs. Pritchard climbed the stairs. Healey stayed behind Davenport with the deputy in the rear.

Pritchard opened a door and all four men stepped onto the *Vindicator's* bridge. Davenport looked around, but he didn't recognize the class or make of this ship. It wasn't any Reserve Wing class, but every detail of its controls and layout had been meticulously attended to.

"Come over here and take a seat." Pritchard waved to a station at the front of the bridge. It occupied a position directly beneath and forward of the large command chair in the center.

Davenport lowered himself into the seat and looked down at the navigation controls. He swiveled the other way to face Pritchard, but Pritchard wasn't looking at him.

The deputy went to a tactical station against the back wall and started working the controls with fast, sure movements. Pritchard crossed to his chair, but he didn't sit down. He tapped away at his own instruments and barely looked sideways at Davenport.

"Marshall Healey has been telling me all about your run-in with Admiral Joyce," Pritchard said over his shoulder. "The wires are all buzzing with the news that Mexia's people rallied from the Needle to go out to Sacron Enigma to get you. I'm guessing Calyx Elkanon sent them for some reason—maybe to steal you from Ekol Thaine."

"I called Mexia's people," Healey interrupted.

Pritchard and his deputy reacted instantly. They both spun around to stare at Healey and Davenport did the same thing. "You.... did.... what?"

"Admiral Joyce told me he sent the Cannibals to find you. I had to do something."

"What did you do?" Davenport croaked. "How did you....?"

Healey shrugged. He wouldn't look at anyone. "I went downstairs and told Mexia that you were in danger.... but it didn't do any good. As soon as Mexia's people showed up on HTWV-983, they betrayed us and went after the Ithium themselves. They were questioning and killing the mud-dwellers. They almost started on me and the *Artemis Rex* crew when Beauty's people attacked and got us clear."

Pritchard sighed and went back to what he was doing. "That was a ballsy thing to do, Marshall."

"What was I supposed to do—let the Cannibals raze the planet? They could have released the Ithium without even realizing it."

"They're on the planet now." Pritchard brought up something on the big bridge screen in front of Davenport. "Mexia's people are still down there, too."

Davenport started to stand up. "Can you locate the *Artemis Rex*?"

The deputy spun forward so fast Davenport barely had time to freeze in place before the guy leveled his XQ at Davenport's head. Davenport finally got a decent look at the man's star. The name on it read, *Treese*.

Davenport lowered himself very slowly back into his seat, but Pritchard pretended not to notice anything out of the ordinary. "The *Artemis Rex* isn't on the planet anymore."

"Where is it, then?"

"What about Chorion life signs?" Healey asked.

"They better not be dead," Davenport muttered. "The Cannibals better not have hurt them."

Pritchard frowned at his instruments. "I'm not reading any Chorion life signs anywhere in Sacron Enigma. Are you picking up anything, John?"

Treese went back to his work. "Nothing.... oh, wait. I'm not picking up anything in Sacron Enigma, but I am reading a bunch of Chorion life signs on an alien freighter crossing Confederate space. They have an Adik on board, too."

"Dice!" Davenport shot out of his seat without thinking. He was on his feet before Treese could do anything, and this time, the deputy let it go. "Where are they?"

"They're on a ship flagged as belonging to Mexia....and they're on an intercept course for us."

Pritchard sat down in his chair. The two arms folded toward him so the controls rested right at the level of his hands.

"They've got the *Artemis Rex* on board, too...but it's only the one ship coming over. The rest are still on HTWV-983."

"What are they doing?" Healey asked.

Pritchard's face twisted in a wry grimace. "They're fighting the Cannibals...and it looks like they're going to be at it for a while. Get downstairs and deploy the patrol, John. Get our people out with orders to intercept that ship."

"You got it." Treese set off for the exit, but at that moment, an alarm went off on Pritchard's controls.

He scowled at it. "Belay that order, John."

Treese and Healey went over to Pritchard's seat to look over his shoulder. "What's up?" Healey asked.

Davenport started to do the same thing, but Pritchard shot out one hand. "Not you! Stay where you are."

Davenport froze fearing the worst until Healey gasped. "Holy crap! It's a transmission from Admiral Joyce."

Pritchard waved Davenport to one side. "Go over there, Sheriff. Stand next to the screen."

Davenport backed away and flattened himself to the wall hardly daring to breathe. Did Admiral Joyce know Davenport was on this ship? Did Joyce suspect that the Wide Patrol had Davenport in custody?

Pritchard got to his feet and squared his shoulders at the screen. His chiseled countenance became even more stern than usual as he faced front.

Treese took his place at Pritchard's elbow and kept his weapon in full view. Healey did the same on the other side before Pritchard opened the link.

Pritchard stiffened to his full height when the link established. "Admiral! What an unexpected surprise."

"I didn't expect to see you and your deputies out here, Sheriff," Admiral Joyce began.

"Well, you know...." Pritchard drawled. "We do have a tendency to get around."

"I realize that." Admiral Joyce's voice betrayed the slightest hint of irony and Davenport's heart soared. He would give anything to see the admiral's face right now, but Davenport couldn't show himself.

"What can I do for you, Sir?" Pritchard asked.

"You apprehended a ship belonging to the Mad Men."

"That is my job, Sir. The Mad Men are notorious, lawless criminals. They're blacklisted throughout the Confederacy. You of all people should know that."

"Of course I know that. I'm not interested in the Mad Men. They had a prisoner on board—a prisoner they were transporting to me. If you took their ship in custody, you should have found him on board, too."

Pritchard's eyes widened with exaggerated surprise. "Oh, you mean Sheriff Davenport.... from Ultra Meridian?"

"Of course I mean Davenport! The Mad Men were bringing him to me on my orders. They apprehended him for me. If you have him, I'd appreciate it if you could hand him over."

Pritchard scowled and rubbed his rough chin like he really had to think about it. Davenport could have laughed out loud. He was starting to really like this guy.

The Wide Patrol was Pritchard's command and everyone in the whole Sheriff's Service idolized Pritchard, but this performance was making Davenport respect him even more.

"I don't know about that, Admiral. I have to question Davenport and then...."

"Nonsense!" Admiral Joyce barked. "I'm on my way to rendezvous with you now. I'll board your ship and...."

"I think not," Pritchard cut in. "If you rendezvous with us, we'll discuss that when you get here. Davenport is in Sheriff's Service custody. If you want to transfer him to Reserve Wing custody, you'll have to go through the proper channels and complete the proper requests. Even then, we would still have to question him along with all the other prisoners."

"Since when did you become such a stickler for the rules, Sheriff?" Admiral Joyce snarled.

"I've always been a stickler for the rules, Admiral. You won't find a bigger stickler than me." Pritchard turned to his controls and tapped something into them. "I'm sending you the official log of our attack on the Mad Men. Davenport was captured on board an illegal transport in the company of known fugitives. That means he's subject to automatic arrest. You can register a request for transfer, but you'll need to show cause either by displaying evidence of his innocence or his guilt of crimes under Confederate law."

He turned his shoulder to the admiral and went to work on the controls. Admiral Joyce's voice dropped to an even lower menacing growl. "Are you going along with this, Marshall Healey? I thought we had an understanding."

"We do," Healey replied. "You ordered me to apprehend Davenport and bring him into custody. That's what I'm doing. You can see on the logs that I helped the Wide Patrol intercept the Mad Men. Davenport would have been killed if the Wide Patrol didn't intervene and then you wouldn't have been able to question him at all. Isn't that what you wanted?"

Admiral Joyce snorted and Pritchard turned back around to face the screen. "You should have all the relevant information now, Admiral. If there's nothing more, we'll see you when you get here."

"Very well," Admiral Joyce growled and cut the link.

Pritchard strode straight over to Davenport. "We don't have a choice about meeting with him. He already knows you're on this ship and we can't fight the Reserve Wing, so we'll have to do this another way. We can get more incriminating information out of him if we show you to him."

Healey came over to join the other two. "He's been very careful never to mention the Ithium to me. He gave me this job on the understanding that you were deranged and making it all up. If we meet with him, we might be able to get him to spill his guts in front of me and Pritchard here. That will be two more sheriffs who know the truth. We'll be better able to stop him once we do that."

"Treese can come with us," Pritchard added. "That will make four."

"What about my crew?" Davenport asked. "You might be able to exonerate me, but I wouldn't be alive today without them. I won't leave them hanging out to dry."

"The Ithium is on the *Artemis Rex* and the *Artemis Rex* is on board Mexia's ship," Healey pointed out. "They're on their way here, too, probably to sell your crew to Joyce."

"Like I said, it will work out better for all of us once we're all in one place," Pritchard added. "We can use the meeting to get the Ithium away from Joyce, but we have to at least show you to him, even if it's only for a few minutes."

Davenport let out a shaky sigh. "All right. I'll go along with it, but I won't make any promises about what I'll do after that."

"Of course not." Pritchard crushed his shoulder. "None of us will."

Chapter 26

E mmett stuck his head into the *Artemis Rex's* cockpit. "What's taking so long?"

"What's taking so long is that you keep interrupting me," Rodeo snapped over his shoulder and then turned back to the command cradle controls. He switched on a communications link with the back of the ship. "How's it looking, boy?"

Wolf's low growl came through it. Rodeo turned to Bandit. "Try it now."

Bandit tapped his own controls and then gripped his control stick. "The engines are cycling up. The power system is holding. Gyroscopes all online and registering inflight stability at optimum."

"What are you doing?" Emmett asked again. "We aren't in flight and the engines aren't cycling up."

Rodeo turned halfway around, but not so far that he faced Emmett completely. "Would you like to take over here and show us how it's done?"

Emmett pulled his head in. "No."

"Then shut the hell up. We're running a simulation to make sure the ship's systems are all online. We're in the hold of another ship. It isn't like we can fire the engines in here, can we?"

Emmett fell silent again as the boys continued their work. In the middle of the operation, Dice stormed up to the cockpit and almost pulverized Emmett by sticking his huge horned head inside. "What the hell is taking so long?"

Rodeo didn't even bother to turn around this time. "Adjust your attitude five degrees ascendant."

"I asked you a question!" Dice bellowed. "How much longer are we going to be stuck in this crate?"

Rodeo finished what he was doing. "Your starboard thrust is still seventy degrees out of balance. Bring it online and then recalibrate the boost modulators." He finally turned his head with deliberate slowness. "Do yourselves a favor and go back to the hold. Get every weapon you can lay your hands on and make sure they all have ammunition. Don't come up here again until you finish that."

Dice scowled at him and then glanced down at Emmett. Emmett shrugged. He had no idea what these boys were up to and he wasn't sure he wanted to know. They were turning out to be one of the most ruthless and resourceful crews he had ever worked with—if not *the* most ruthless and resourceful.

Dice grunted something and turned away. Emmett followed him back to the cargo hold. "What do you think they're up to?"

"Planning an escape, I hope. Why else would they want every weapon armed?"

Emmett didn't answer. Maybe Rodeo gave Dice that job just to shut him up and keep him out of the boys' hair. Emmett wouldn't put it past Rodeo to pull something like that.

They found Breeze, Axel, Laub, and Coon already tearing into the *Artemis Rex's* impressive stash of weapons. All the battles they'd fought since leaving Nyx Anonyma certainly put a dent in their stores, but there were enough medium XQs to satisfy even Dice.

Wolf and Alla showed up a minute later. They put away their tools and came over to arm up—at least Alla did. Wolf stood back glaring at everyone.

"Rodeo says we aren't on HTWV-983 anymore," Coon began. "We're flying through space."

"I wonder where we're going," Alla replied.

"We're only going one place, fool," Axel countered. "Mexia's people are taking us back to the Reserve Wing."

"How do you figure?" Alla asked. "How can you be sure? Did Rodeo say that?"

"He didn't have to. Use your brain, boy! We told Mexia's people ourselves that the Ithium was on the *Artemis Rex*."

Alla wilted. "Oh."

"Which means we have to break out of this shithole before we get there." Dice locked in his ammunition cartridge and hefted his XQ. "Let's rock and roll."

"How do we do that when we don't have a plan?" Coon asked.

"Are you telling me Rodeo doesn't have a plan?" Laub asked. "I'll never believe that."

Almost as though it was meant to be, Bandit and Rodeo arrived from the cockpit at that moment. Bandit started helping himself to the weapons, but Rodeo had other things in mind.

"Now," he began. "The *Artemis Rex* doesn't have the firepower to blow our way out of this rig so we have to get creative."

"Yay!" Laub squealed. "I love it when we get creative."

"One of us is going to go out into the hold and plant Aswalt mines along the hull. We'll blow our way out and then drop away into space."

"Oooo! Rodeo!" Alla's hand shot up. "Can I go? Can I plant the mines?"

"Hell no!" Coon countered. "You'd fall all over yourself. We might as well send Breeze and let him blow up the whole ship with us on board."

"No one is blowing up anything," Rodeo ordered. "Wolf is going."

"How do you know Mexia's people aren't standing guard outside?" Emmett asked. "They'll shoot him for sure."

"I already know they're standing guard which is why we have to create a diversion."

A chill ran up Emmett's spine. "What did you have in mind?"

"Nothing you need to worry about." Rodeo turned to his boys. "Laub, you and Breeze get over here by the hatch. When I give the word, you start banging on the hull and making a racket. You go, too, Dice."

"No way!" he boomed. "I'm not going anywhere that anyone is calling a diversion."

"Nothing will happen," Breeze told him. "I'll make sure they attack me instead of you."

"Then why am I here?"

"Who's more distracting than you, Dice?" Rodeo steered him over to the hatch, but Dice wouldn't stop scowling. "Put your guns away, boys. Don't give them a reason to blast your heads off."

"This is the stupidest plan ever," Dice grumbled.

Rodeo only laughed, parked Dice, Breeze, and Laub by the hatch, and led Wolf away. Bandit tore into another carton and brought out ten enormous Aswalt mines. He lugged them after Wolf and the three of them vanished into the crew compartment where Lyons had been recovering from her injuries.

"I don't like the sound of this," Emmett murmured.

"What are you complaining about?" Dice snapped. "You aren't the one creating a distraction by throwing yourself in front of Mexia's people."

"Neither are you," Breeze told him. "I am."

Dice glared at the boy, but Breeze only smiled at him. The boy looked about as far from dangerous as anyone possibly could look. He looked like the least intimidating member of the Chorion Team. He even looked less dangerous than Rodeo, but both of them were misleading.

Breeze and Laub brought out two enormous spanners from their tool kits. Both boys started pounding the rear hatch until the din echoed through the ship.

A second later, Rodeo returned along with Bandit, who was now empty-handed. "What are you going to do?" Emmett asked.

"You'll see."

Rodeo went over to the hatch. He signaled the boys to keep hammering. Then he waved the others to stand back out of sight.

Rodeo waited until Emmett and the rest of the Chorion team moved back against the bulkhead. Then Rodeo unsealed the hatch. It purred down and slammed on the hold floor.

A bunch of Mexia's people stood outside aiming their weapons at Dice, Breeze, and Laub.

Breeze smiled his most disarming smile. He and Laub raised their arms in an attitude of surrender as they advanced down the ramp to meet their captors.

The aliens shouldered their weapons and aimed straight at the boys, especially when Rodeo motioned Dice to follow and go outside.

The boys got within ten feet of the aliens. Breeze started talking unbelievably fast, but he didn't speak in any language Emmett could recognize.

Breeze jabbered away making elaborate hand gestures. He spoke earnestly into the alien's faces in a fervent, urgent tone. Even Emmett started to wonder if Breeze might be sincere in trying to tell them something important.

The aliens stiffened and then started to relax. A huge Enzai furrowed his brow and peered down at Breeze's bright little face. The Enzai concentrated hard trying to figure out what Breeze was saying.

Emmett's heart skipped a beat when three more guards stormed over and tried to talk to the Enzai about what was going on. The guy held up his hand for silence and cocked his head to listen more intently to whatever Breeze was saying.

All five guards surrounded Breeze and Laub. Two of the guards spoke to each other and then shook their heads. They had no idea what Breeze was trying to tell them.

At that moment, a black shadow skimmed across Emmett's line of sight. It darted from one side of the hold to the other against the back wall and vanished into darkness again. None of the guards saw it.

Then Breeze pulled his master stroke. He stuck his arm behind him, took hold of Dice's elbow, and started guiding Dice down the ramp. The guards reacted instantly. They all jerked up their guns to protect themselves from Dice, but he didn't do anything. He took a few steps nearer.

Breeze started talking faster—a lot faster. The faster he talked, the more venomous Dice looked. The guards became increasingly agitated. They bellowed at Breeze to stand down, but instead, he kept moving farther down the ramp.

Emmett braced himself for an explosion. Dice and Breeze in the same place.... with a ticket from Rodeo to cause a diversion—what could possibly go wrong?

Nothing happened. The tension spiked off the charts as seconds ticked by, but neither Dice nor Breeze did anything. Breeze jabbered away and gesticulated wildly while he made his non-existent point.

Dice glared at the guards like he might blow at any second, but he didn't. He just scared the living shit out of them by standing there looking murderous.

The guards held him at gunpoint and never took their eyes off him which only made him glare at them more ferociously.

The black shadow rocketed back across the hold and vanished the way it came. Rodeo tiptoed over to the crew quarters and came back with Wolf. Rodeo whispered in Wolf's ear and then whispered something to Bandit.

Bandit disappeared into the cockpit and Rodeo came back to the hatch. Emmett couldn't breathe. The tension out on the hold floor spiked to the breaking point. He didn't see how any of them could get out of this without the guards opening fire.

Rodeo stood perfectly still without moving or saying anything. Breeze waved his arms in the guards' faces and then turned to Dice. Breeze's face lit up like a kid at a carnival. He motioned up and down in front of Dice like Breeze might be displaying the huge alien for sale at a market.

Breeze turned just enough to face Dice. Breeze never took his eyes off Dice's smoldering features, and at that moment, a colossal ka-boom detonated across the hold.

The shockwave flattened the guards before they had a chance to turn around. The impact hurled them all bodily into the *Artemis Rex's* hull where they smacked hard and bounced off.

Breeze, Dice, and Laub ducked and then sprang for the hatch. They sprinted inside and Rodeo slammed the hatch closed behind them just as Bandit fired the engines to full throttle.

The *Artemis Rex* vaulted off the floor and whipped around so fast that everyone in the cargo hold toppled against each other. Emmett scrambled to unwind himself from the boys, but they were already springing away with unbelievable speed.

Rodeo lunged for the cockpit as Howitzer fire exploded outside the hull. Emmett got to his feet and gulped when he saw the scene beyond the cockpit window.

Bandit punched the engines. The *Artemis Rex* streaked through the breach Wolf had blown in the hold. The beautiful stars welcomed the Drifter into clear, open space....and so did Mexia's people.

The ship blasted into a curtain of gunfire from seven other ships surrounding the vessel that held the *Artemis Rex*. Pounding blasts smashed the *Artemis Rex* in the nose and knocked it straight back into the breach the boys just escaped from.

The Drifter missed the opening and crashed into the hull. Bandit gunned the engines one more time before all seven alien attackers slammed it back again.

The *Artemis Rex* floated away from its captor, but Rodeo didn't give Bandit a chance to make another dive for freedom. "Cut it, boy," Rodeo murmured. "It's hopeless."

Chapter 27

Fiddler pulled Lyons down behind a fallen log. "Get down! They'll see you!"

"What are they doing?" Lyons stole a peek through a gap between the trunk and the ground. At least she stayed low enough that the aliens in the distance couldn't see the two women.

"They're searching for the Ithium, of course." Fiddler hunkered lower and moved her head nearer to Lyons. "This is where the *Artemis Rex* landed earlier—where Dice and I hid the goods."

"So where are they? Where are the goods?"

"Over there." Fiddler pointed toward the swamp.

"How did Mexia's people find this place? You didn't tell them, did you?"

"Of course not! They must have tracked the ship's movements since we landed on this planet.... or maybe they checked the ship's logs. How should I know? See? They're using radioactivity scanners."

"They aren't having very good luck. They haven't left the landing site."

"We should steal the Ithium back," Fiddler suggested. "If they're scanning for radioactivity, they might find it even if it takes a while. We can't let that happen."

"Do you think you can get to it without attracting any attention?"

Fiddler almost answered that she didn't when a ship howled down through the canopy. Mexia's aliens didn't have a ship so of course their friends had to come pick them up.

The ship descended and the aliens boarded. They made one last pass with their scanner and turned their backs.

"How convenient," Lyons remarked as the ship soared away. "Real nice of them to clear off so we can get on with moving the stolen goods."

"None of us stole this stuff," Fiddler countered. "Except for you. You stole the Ithium."

"I didn't steal anything. I received the Ithium from a client with a contract to transport it. I didn't do anything.... except maybe try to smuggle it past Ultra Meridian. I really should have known better than to try to pull one over on Davenport. That was the mistake I made."

"Well, I didn't steal the chip, either," Fiddler added. "Emmett accepted it for a legitimate business job.... Well, it might not have been *strictly* legitimate, but we didn't steal it."

"Are we really talking about who stole what?" Lyons fired back. "Are you getting the Ithium or not?"

"Oh. Yeah."

Fiddler climbed out of her hiding place and retrieved the bag from the swamp where she left it.

"Now what do you want to do?" she asked Lyons when the two rejoined.

Lyons wandered across the *Artemis Rex's* landing site. "I guess standing around here waiting for them to come back isn't an option."

"Maybe the mud-dwellers can help us," Fiddler suggested.

"You mean like maybe they have a ship hidden somewhere that will get us off this planet?" Lyons shrugged. "We might as well. We have nothing else to do."

They set off walking. Fiddler wrung out the dripping bag and stashed it in her pocket.

She looked up to find Lyons studying her on the side. "The mud-dwellers want those, you know. It might not be such a great idea to carry the goods right into their village for them."

"The mud-dwellers thought Davenport was the Bringer of the Ithium. They don't even know me."

Lyons snorted. "Keep telling yourself that, honey."

Fiddler took her turn to examine Lyons's profile. "What is it with you, anyway?"

"What do you mean?"

"How did you go so rotten? What made you turn to crime in the first place?"

"You're one to talk. You're no Virgin Mary, sweetheart. Let me count the number of illegal things you've done in your life."

"I'm not a career criminal like you," Fiddler countered. "I have my Core. I do what I have to do for them....and Emmett. I don't go out of my way to do illegal things that might destroy the whole galaxy."

"I don't, either."

"Don't you care about anything or anyone?" Fiddler insisted. "Don't you care at all whether what you do hurts other people?"

Lyons looked away. She surveyed the woods around her for a while before she answered. "I used to think my crew meant that."

"What—you mean Dice and Beauty?"

Lyons shrugged again. "Maybe I thought that because they were all I had. We went through a lot together, but I guess I never really did feel that way about anything.... until now. I really hated Davenport, but now...."

Fiddler didn't answer. She didn't want to think about Davenport.

When this whole adventure started, she linked Davenport with the Ithium. Saving Davenport meant saving the Ithium from the people who wanted to use it.

Now Fiddler had the Ithium and Davenport was.... somewhere else. Knowing him, he would be in some kind of danger. He might be alone or injured or a prisoner.

Lyons's words struck home and chilled Fiddler's heart. Lyons was right. Davenport had become something much, much more than the Bringer of the Ithium or the Carrier of the Ithium or anything Ithium-related.

He had become the sun around which their crew revolved. The Chorion Team, the *Echo Omicron* crew, the Armageddon Core, Ekol Thaine's vast criminal enterprise—hell, even Marshall Healey revolved around Davenport.

Davenport had become a lodestar guiding all of them to some destiny none of them ever expected for themselves. Fiddler never saw herself as responsible for anything more than her friends and Emmett.

Now she was halfway across known space, stranded on a hostile planet, dodging cannibalistic aliens, and risking her neck for something beyond her comprehension.

She had the Ithium in her pocket right now along with the chip to activate it, but now she found out that didn't really mean anything. She was doing this for Davenport. She was doing this because it was what Davenport would have done but couldn't.

No one knew how to risk his neck like Davenport. He barely thought of the risk. He did it because he was a good man. He dedicated himself to the law and he did what he had to do to uphold it.

Fiddler would have scoffed at that not so long ago. Now she could only mimic his principles and hope for the best. She would almost rather abandon the Ithium entirely if it meant saving Davenport's life.

What would the universe be without people like him? He somehow made all this worthwhile. He made the universe something other than a fetid cesspool of criminality and corruption. Only he could do that.

Lyons woke her from her thoughts by touching Fiddler's arm. "There's the village."

The women peered through the trees. The mud-dwellers migrated around their clearing picking up the fallen timbers of destroyed houses. Others carried the bodies of Mexia's many victims into the woods. Soft splashes told Fiddler how they were disposing of their dead.

Lyons sighed. "Here goes nothing."

She started walking toward the village and Fiddler fell in behind her. Fiddler kept casting backward glances into the woods. Maybe this wasn't such a great idea after all, but as Lyons said, she and Lyons couldn't exactly stand around in the forest for the rest of eternity.

Lyons made it to the village first and the reaction came swift and sure. The mud-dwellers dropped what they were doing, waddled over, and started swaying, stroking, and murmuring over her.

They surrounded her in an ever-growing throng of worshipful utterings. They caressed her clothes and hair and exclaimed over every detail of her sudden appearance.

Fiddler hesitated, but it was too late. The mud-dwellers spotted her, surrounded her, and prodded her into their midst. They herded both women into the village where the whole bobbing, swaying, bowing mass could adore the women more easily.

"Go on!" Fiddler called over the mud-dwellers' heads. "Ask them if they have a hidden ship we can use to get off this planet!"

"Whatever you do," Lyons yelled back, "don't say......"

"The Ithium! The Ithium! The Bringer of the Ithium!" the mud-dwellers started chanting.

They came dangerously close to touching the box in Fiddler's pocket, but they showed no sign that they knew the Ithium was right in front of them.

"I told you not to say it!" Lyons bellowed.

"I didn't! I didn't say anything!"

"What are they doing?" Lyons frowned down at the mud-dwellers nearest her. They gazed back up at her in undisguised adoration. They chanted about the Ithium while worshiping her, too.

"I don't think they know," Fiddler replied.

"Why are they talking about it, then?"

"I don't know, but I think we're okay. We just have to……"

The mud-dwellers started steering the two women toward one of their fires. A bunch of clay pots full of dirt dotted the ground around the fire rings.

The mud-dwellers waved at the women and then toward the pots. Fiddler stared down in horror as one of the mud-dwellers thrust his bony fingers into the soil and drew out a long, wriggling nightcrawler.

The little alien held up the squirming creature in front of Lyons. The mud-dweller went into an elaborate pantomime of motioning the thing toward Lyons's mouth.

Lyons blinked at the insect. Then her eyes flicked to the little person holding it up for her in such obvious delight. Neither she nor Fiddler could mistake the alien's meaning.

"Uh….no," Lyons said. "No and no. I don't think so. I'm not hungry. Thank you, but no."

Fiddler had to laugh. "Go on. It might be the greatest delicacy you ever tasted. It might be better than Apricot Mint."

"You better be careful," Lyons fired back. "They'll be trying to feed you next."

Her words produced an electric effect on the mud-dwellers. They all started scurrying around in a dither. They even forgot to worship the two women in their excitement to bring a bunch of new stuff from one of the few huts still standing.

Fiddler watched in rising alarm as the mud-dwellers skewered a large arthropod on a spit, set it up to roast over the flames, and then added what looked like swamp water to a large cauldron. She could even see sticks and bits of grass floating on the surface as it came to a boil.

The mud-dwellers chittered to themselves while they worked. Then they came back to raise their arms in adulation to the two women.

"I have an idea," Fiddler yelled over the aliens' heads. "Let's not stick around for the main course."

"Um…excuse me!" Lyons called to the congregation at large. "We need to meet up with our friends, and for that, we need to fly away from this planet. You know…. fly away?" She flapped her arms toward the sky in a flying motion.

The mud-dwellers bobbed their heads, nodded, beamed at her, and then went back to what they were doing.

"Nice try," Fiddler told her.

"Um…. excuse me!" Lyons yelled louder. "We need to go! Do you have any….?"

"You know they don't," Fiddler cut in. "Why are you even asking?"

The arthropod on the spit erupted a squirt of juice that hissed and popped in the flames. The sound attracted Lyons's attention and she glanced down at it.

She took one look at it and her expression changed. "Okay. New plan."

"You mean first plan."

Lyons glanced over her shoulder again, this time toward the forest. "We need a ship."

"Uh-huh," Fiddler replied. "Where are we going to get one?"

"There are only two options: the Cannibals and Mexia's people."

Fiddler spun around and stared at her. "You're insane."

Lyons shrugged. "We need a ship. They have ships."

"How do you say we get a ship from either the Cannibals or Mexia's people?"

One of the mud-dwellers distracted Lyons by bumping into her legs. The little creature shouldered his way to the fire and started ladling the now steaming swamp water into a wooden bowl.

He held that up to Lyons, too. She gazed back down into his eyes and went very still. More mud-dwellers paused their work to watch her appreciate their hospitality. Fiddler didn't see how Lyons could get out of taking it and drinking it.

Lyons seemed to come to the same conclusion. She sighed, shook back her long, black hair, and started to extend her hand for the bowl when gunfire erupted out of the trees.

Fiddler and Lyons spun around to face the new threat. Fiddler's heart dropped into her stomach as hundreds of Cannibals advanced through the trees making a beeline for the village.

They opened fire on the shrieking mud-dwellers who scattered to the four winds. A bunch of ships descended behind the Cannibals and blasted the village to kingdom come.

Lyons charged Fiddler and seized her by the sleeve. "This way!"

They raced into the woods with dozens of mud-dwellers scurrying around their feet. The fugitives sprinted deeper into the trees as the Cannibals advanced and swarmed the village.

More gunfire blasted into the trees from behind. Fiddler stumbled and Lyons caught her by the shoulder. "This way!"

Lyons swerved to the right and almost ran straight into the Cannibals' fire. "No!" Fiddler tried to correct their course, but before she could run another step, a shot smashed into a tree trunk right next to her head.

Both women went down under a barrage of gunfire. Lyons scrambled over to Fiddler. "You okay?"

Fiddler nodded panting hard. They both crawled behind a tree stump as the Cannibals drew nearer. "What do we do now?" Fiddler whispered. "We can't let them find us."

"The ship!" Lyons hissed. "We have to get to one of their ships."

Fiddler shook her head fast. "You're suicidal. We are NOT stealing a ship from the Cannibals!"

"Yes, we are. Come on."

Chapter 28

Lyons crawled away heading straight into the Cannibals' route. Fiddler followed her if only to stop Lyons from going near them.

Lyons paused and Fiddler grabbed Lyons's ankle. "What are you....?"

"Shhh!"

Fiddler inched up next to Lyons's side and realized that Lyons might not be so suicidal after all.

The Cannibals advanced in their usual line. They swept the forest for any unfortunate mud-dwellers who stumbled or happened across their path. The Cannibals gunned down anyone who came within range.

As soon as Fiddler got to Lyons, she realized that the Cannibals were advancing at an angle to the women's hiding place. The Cannibals at the far end of their line came close to the thick log that concealed the two women from view.

Lyons pointed back toward the village and Fiddler's heart flipped. The Cannibals' ship stood in the center of the mud-dwellers' clearing. The vessel gleamed in the dim sunshine. Its rear hatch stood open.

Five Cannibals guarded it. That was it, but Fiddler still quailed at the thought. Were she and Lyons really about to attack five Cannibals and steal their ship in broad daylight? Both women were unarmed. They would need one hell of a lot of luck to pull this off.

Three Cannibals approached the log. They had to climb over it to keep hunting down the mud-dwellers.

Lyons grabbed a fistful of Fiddler's shirt and tugged her under the log. A tiny gap between the log and the ground gave just enough space for the two women to crawl under it.

The Cannibals stepped onto the log, but they kept searching farther ahead. They didn't look down. Lyons backed farther under the log and emerged on the back side as the Cannibals hopped down to keep going after the mud-dwellers.

Fiddler's heart hammered her ribs. She didn't dare to breathe. She collapsed on the ground and didn't stick her head up to see if the Cannibals were moving farther away. She let Lyons do that.

Lyons ducked down next to her. "They're leaving. Let's go."

Fiddler grabbed her. "Hold it right there. How do you plan to defeat those Cannibals who are guarding the ship?"

Lyons shot her the craziest grin yet. Fiddler was really starting to hate Lyons's grin. "I don't plan to defeat them, genius. I'm going to lure them away."

Fiddler rolled her eyes to Heaven, but Lyons ignored her. She shot one last glance over the log, hunkered down, and started crawling back to the village.

Fiddler would have vastly preferred to stay where she was. Going near the Cannibals was the absolute last thing Fiddler wanted to in life.

Then again, if by some miracle this worked and Lyons stole the ship from the Cannibals, Fiddler wanted to be on hand to fly away. She didn't want anything to delay her getting there to make her escape.

She finally threw caution to the wind and followed Lyons, but not without plenty of backward glances to make sure the Cannibals didn't come near them.

Lyons stopped her about thirty yards from the village. She yanked Fiddler even lower if that was possible. "Listen!"

"Ow!" Fiddler yelped.

"Be quiet and listen!" Lyons hissed. "You skirt around the village to those trees over there. As soon as the Cannibals leave the ship, you get on board and fire that mother up. Understand?"

"What—me? I thought *you* were going to steal the ship."

"I am, but I need you to get on board and get the thing up and running until I get there."

"That's stupid," Fiddler argued. "As soon as I fire the engines, the Cannibals will come running back."

Lyons cracked another lunatic smirk. "That's when you open up with the big guns. Just don't hit me. Understand?"

"How the hell will I know where you are?" Fiddler shut her eyes and held up her hand. "Don't answer that. I already know where you're going to be. You're going to be running for your damn life with a hundred Cannibals on your ass. I won't be able to shoot without hitting you."

"Just do it. I'll take care of myself."

"Sure," Fiddler grumbled.

Lyons shoved Fiddler's shoulder. "Go over there. Be ready to take the ship as soon as it's clear."

Fiddler didn't want to think about what Lyons was going to do. At least Lyons was the one drawing the Cannibals away. This plan would leave Fiddler free to take the ship while the Cannibals' backs were turned.

A fleeting thought passed through Fiddler's head. If everything went wrong on the ground, she would be on board with her finger on both the trigger and the throttle. Lyons was taking all the risk. Fiddler could always fly away without Lyons if she had to.

She pushed that thought out of her mind. She wouldn't leave Lyons to her death. No way.

Fiddler had come a long way since the day she attacked Davenport in his own jail to free Emmett from custody. Fiddler had developed a sense of loyalty for the *Artemis Rex* crew that she'd only ever experienced for her own Armageddon Core.

She snuck through the trees making sure not to snap any twigs, step in any puddles, or make any other noise. She made it as far as the position Lyons instructed her to take. Fiddler checked behind her. Lyons grinned again and gave Fiddler a thumbs up.

Fiddler concealed herself in a thick patch of bushes and held her breath to watch. She expected Lyons to leap out and assault the Cannibals. Why in God's name would Lyons do that? She would have to be deranged even to think of it.

As soon as Fiddler got under cover, an ear-splitting shriek echoed through the woods. It didn't sound human and it set Fiddler's hair on end. She tensed every nerve as that otherworldly screech split the stillness again and again.

The Cannibals stiffened to high alert and aimed their weapons into the undergrowth where the noise came from. Fiddler strained her eyes to see something over there, but she couldn't even see Lyons anymore. Was Lyons there or did something else make that noise?

That spine-chilling scream pealed through the trees. The stillness between cries made it sound even more agonizing. The Cannibals guarding the ship inched nearer to the tree line, but they didn't leave the village. They must be under orders not to leave the ship.

All at once, something flopped in the bushes where Lyons and Fiddler had just been hiding. Fiddler suffered another moment of confusion when whatever it was flopped again. Was it some creature from the swamp? It didn't look human, but Fiddler couldn't really tell from here.

The Cannibals on guard got even more agitated. They trained their guns on whatever it was. Branches swayed and leaves rustled to show where the thing was, but no one could see *what* it was.

Fiddler held her breath and fought down rising anxiety. Her chest ached from her heart about to break through her ribs. Could Lyons really pull this off without getting devoured right here?

Whatever it was thrashed even harder and that horrible scream ripped out of the woods one more time. That did it. The guards entered the trees and left the ship completely unguarded.

Fiddler didn't give herself an instant to doubt. She crept behind more trees into the village. All the Cannibals were facing the other way and moving farther into the trees every second.

Fiddler tucked her head, clamped her parched lips tight together, and sprinted for the ship. She dashed up the ramp and her tension rocketed into the stratosphere. She couldn't see the Cannibals anymore. She didn't know where they were or if they were coming after her right now.

She sprang into the pilot's seat and fumbled for the controls. She didn't take a moment to draw breath. She seized the helm and punched the engines to full throttle.

A deafening howl of engine noise shattered the stillness. Now she KNEW the Cannibals were coming after her.

She yanked back on the throttle, lifted the ship an inch off its landing gear, and slammed the helm hard to port. The vessel whipped around and she opened fire without even looking for a target.

Lasers sliced into the trees, severed huge trunks, and sent curtains of foliage raining to the ground. Cannibals raced back to the village. Fiddler took a split second to make sure they weren't chasing Lyons and then Fiddler opened fire.

She cut down every Cannibal in sight, but she didn't see Lyons anywhere. The Cannibals who attacked the village poured out of the trees returning. They all leveled their guns at the ship.

Fiddler couldn't let them damage this vessel. The ship was Fiddler's only way off this planet and also her only way to save Lyons.

Fiddler opened up with another hellish barrage. She sliced bodies in half and lopped off limbs and heads. She left a carpet of dismembered body parts everywhere, but no matter where she turned, she still didn't see Lyons.

Fiddler checked the ship's instruments to make sure no more Cannibals were coming. She gulped when she spotted a bunch of Cannibal ships coming toward her. Several hundred ground troops closed on her location. She couldn't stay here any longer.

At that moment, an alarm on her console went off. It showed a single human life sight closing fast on the village.

Fiddler looked up to see Lyons charging out of the undergrowth. She waved her arms and her mouth moved in silent shouts to Fiddler.

Fiddler whipped the ship backward and descended just enough for the rear hatch to touch the ground. Lyons sprang aboard and Fiddler punched the throttle with all her might.

Lyons yelled in surprise and almost pitched out the back before she slammed the hatch shut. She staggered to the cockpit and dropped into the seat next to Fiddler as the ship vaulted high into the atmosphere.

"Phew!" Lyons exclaimed. "That was fun!"

Fiddler gritted her teeth and concentrated all her attention on the Cannibal ships closing in. "You might want to man the guns."

Lyons perked up and her cheery expression changed as soon as she saw what Fiddler was looking at. "Woops."

"Hold onto your panties," Fiddler muttered. "We may need to get wild."

Lyons didn't answer. She slipped her arms into a safety harness on the back of her chair. Fiddler had completely forgotten about the harness, but she couldn't take her hands off the helm right now.

She banked to starboard and pushed the throttle to the wall. The Cannibals gained, but they were still too far away. They crawled up on the ship, but at the last second, Fiddler made her move.

She ripped the ship into a slide and dove for the planet's surface. "Stand by!" she hollered to Lyons.

"What are you gonna do? You're flying straight into their range."

"Get ready to fire!"

Lyons hunched over her controls. Fiddler tilted the ship straight down into a vertical dive and aimed for a large lake buried deep in the wilderness.

The Cannibal ships copied her move for move. Fiddler was going to have to pull one out of her ass to get them off her tail.

She leaned all the way over backward hauling the helm up. She strained every muscle to drag the ship level and just in time.

The Cannibals screeched in behind her as she ran level to the lake's glassy surface. Fiddler took her eyes off the controls just long enough to make sure the enemy was running level, too.

"Fire!" she roared. "Double trouble!"

Lyons punched the lasers to the maximum and both beams struck the water. She cut two identical troughs into the lake and two matched fountains of vertical geysers erupted in the ship's wake.

The Cannibals plowed straight into the walls of water while Fiddler rocketed clear on the other side. She ripped the ship back into the atmosphere.

"Whoo!" Lyons whooped. "You've been taking lessons from Bandit, girl!"

Fiddler slumped over her console when she saw the Cannibal ships floating in the drink behind her. They got farther and farther away as she steered back toward Confederate space.

Lyons bumped Fiddler's shoulder still laughing and running her hand across her forehead. She got up and muddled around in the back doing something. Fiddler didn't turn around to see what.

Lyons came back and flopped in her chair. "What do you want to do now? Any idea where the boys are?"

Fiddler frowned at her controls. "We got a problem."

"What—that this ship is too small and belongs to the Cannibals?"

Fiddler pointed to the navigation chart. "That. The Reserve Wing is guarding the line. They tried to block the *Artemis Rex* from crossing. They must be under orders to stop anyone who comes back through."

"What do you want to do about it?"

Fiddler looked up and caught Lyons's eye. "We don't have to go back to Confederate space. We're in Sacron Enigma...."

"And we have the Ithium," Lyons replied. "We could stash it somewhere else where Mexia's people won't get it. We'd be safe over here, and if we choose our spot wisely, the Reserve Wing will never find us OR the Ithium."

"I don't like the idea of running away and hiding."

"We can't rendezvous with the others if we don't know where they are." Lyons pointed to something else on the chart. "Mexia's people are fighting the Mad Men. Let's not go over there."

Fiddler sighed and leaned back in her seat. She gazed through the cockpit window at nothing and her mind flipped back to Davenport. What would Davenport do right now?

"I know! We'll take the goods back to Ultra Meridian."

Lyons's jaw dropped. "You're stupid."

"The third component is at Ultra Meridian."

"All the more reason NOT to take the other two there. If we got caught, someone would have all three."

"Not necessarily. I know a few places at Ultra Meridian where we can hide the first two where no one will ever find them."

Lyons groaned. "Famous last words. Davenport is from Ultra Meridian. He must know all the good hiding spots."

"Not by a long way." Fiddler sat up straighter and took the helm. "We're going. It's the perfect solution."

"About as perfect as stealing a ship from the Cannibals?" Lyons asked and both women laughed.

Chapter 29

Sheriff Deacon Pritchard halted in front of the door, turned to Davenport, and pulled out a pair of steel handcuffs. "I need to cuff you, Sheriff."

"Like hell you will!" Davenport fired back. "You can shove that shit right up your...."

"Keep your voice down!" Healey hissed. "He'll hear you."

Pritchard shut his eyes in saintlike patience. "Please. It's only for appearances. Admiral Joyce needs to see that Healey and I are bringing you to justice."

"Justice!" Davenport spat. "You call that justice?"

"I call it being smart so we can all go on doing our jobs without him any the wiser."

Pritchard didn't wait for Davenport to agree. Pritchard snapped the cuffs open and started moving them into position to clip them on Davenport's wrists.

Davenport didn't move when Pritchard picked up one of Davenport's wrists and started cuffing his hands together. Davenport felt numb.

Getting taken into custody by the Wide Patrol actually made him hope he might be able to get his life back. The Wide Patrol was notorious for solving problems no one could solve. If this Ithium debacle didn't qualify, Davenport didn't know what did.

Davenport went limp while Pritchard moved his limbs around where Pritchard wanted them. If Pritchard couldn't fix this, maybe it couldn't be fixed at all.

Davenport never let himself think that before. What if he never got his life back? What if this whole disaster ended with him being outlawed for life?

He shuddered at the thought. He couldn't go back to the wrong side of the law. Becoming a sheriff was the only thing that gave his life any meaning. If he went back to being a criminal, he wouldn't know who or what he was anymore.

He didn't have time to think about it. Pritchard turned away, opened the door, and led the way into Admiral Joyce's stateroom on Stalwart *Rambler*.

Davenport followed Pritchard with Healey behind him and Treese coming last. The cuffs made Davenport acutely aware that the three sheriffs were escorting him in handcuffs just like a real prisoner. Whatever they said to him in private, he was still their prisoner. He was totally at their mercy.

Pritchard stepped aside and Davenport came face to face with the man who tried to kill him. Admiral Joyce stood up straight behind his desk and eyed Davenport with distaste.

The admiral's expression changed in a flash when he saw Davenport cuffed. Davenport made a mental note never to doubt Deacon Pritchard again. The man was a genius.

A smirk of sadistic triumph peeled across the admiral's lips as Pritchard and Healey positioned Davenport in front of the desk. Both sheriffs flanked Davenport in such an obvious guarding posture that no one could misunderstand their meaning.

"Well, *Sheriff*?" Admiral Joyce sneered the word while he leered in Davenport's face. "Are you ready to hand over the Ithium?"

Davenport stiffened. Bingo. This jackass fell right into Pritchard's trap. Admiral Joyce admitted in front of three impartial witnesses that he was after Davenport for the Ithium. Point #2 for Pritchard.

Davenport locked his teeth to get through this. If he played his cards right, maybe Pritchard and Healey would get enough information to finish this son of a bitch once and for all.

"I already told these two," Davenport growled. "I don't have the Ithium. I had it when we left Ultra Meridian, but I don't have it anymore."

"Ah, yes!" Admiral Joyce consulted something on his desk. "You left Ultra Meridian in a ship belonging to Ekol Thaine—a certain *Artemis Rex*. Isn't that right?"

Davenport froze. What did Joyce know about the *Artemis Rex*?

Davenport didn't have to wait long to find out. "The boys who stole the Ithium from my safe on Atlas Arcane were registered on board the *Artemis Rex*. As it happens, I know where the *Artemis Rex* is."

He tapped something on his console and the door popped behind Healey. The four sheriffs spun around to stare as a bunch of uniformed Reserve Wing officers came in dragging the Chorion Team with them.

All eight boys were bound hand and foot so they couldn't move. The officers dumped the prisoners on the floor at Healey's feet.

"You see?" Admiral Joyce crowed. "I have my own ways of getting information. Of course, we couldn't bring the Adik here. He's in custody in the *Rambler's* hold, but I'm sure you can all tell me what I want to know just as easily."

Rodeo cocked his head listening to every word the admiral said. Then he raised his face and trained his sightless eyes on Davenport. "Sir! Are you okay? We've been trying to find you.... You're injured...."

Healey touched the boy's shoulder. "Settle down, son. We'll talk later."

"None of you will talk to anyone until you tell me where the Ithium is." Admiral Joyce turned back to Davenport. "You claim the Ithium is on the *Artemis Rex*."

"That's where I left it."

"It isn't there now. My men searched it....and Mexia's people searched it more than once. The Ithium isn't on board." Joyce turned to the boys. "Where did you put it?"

"We didn't put it anywhere...." Bandit began.

"Shut up!" Rodeo snapped.

Admiral Joyce grinned even more. "So you *did* put it somewhere. I knew it. We have ways of making you tell us whether you want to or not."

"If the Ithium isn't on the *Artemis Rex*, I don't know where it is," Davenport replied. "You can do what you want to me. You won't find out something I don't know."

"You've been a thorn in my side since we first met, Sheriff. You wouldn't cooperate with me by telling the truth." Joyce pressed another button on his desk and the door opened for the second time. The same bunch of officers entered. "Take these prisoners down to the medical lab."

"Medical lab!" Pritchard repeated. "What are you going to do with them?"

"We'll use truth serum on Davenport to make him tell us where the Ithium is. If by some distant chance that doesn't work, we'll start on these next." He motioned to the boys.

"Truth serum is outlawed in the Confederacy and we're in Confederate space." Healey began. "You're...."

He broke off and his next words hung heavy in the air. Killian Joyce was a Reserve Wing admiral. If he would resort to such illegal activities to get what he wanted, there was no limit to how far he would go.

"You can go back to Pandora's Needle, Marshall. Your job here is done." Admiral Joyce barked over Healey's shoulder. "Take them away."

The officers fell on the boys again and started dragging them out of the room. Rodeo twisted out of their grip trying to get to Davenport. "Don't worry, Sir. We'll think of something."

Admiral Joyce laughed at him. The officers shoved Laub toward the threshold, but before they could push him over it, he flung his legs out in front of him. Two officers held onto both of his arms and that left his lower body free.

He hurled his legs forward and jammed his feet on either side of the doorjamb. He wedged himself there so tightly that they couldn't move him.

They yanked and tore trying to dislodge him, but they didn't count on his great strength. He barricaded the door with his crewmates and all the officers inside.

Wolf exploded at the same instant. He lunged for the nearest officer and slashed his teeth down the man's neck. The officer staggered away screaming and pressing his hand to the wound.

Blood spilled from the cut, but Wolf had stopped short of actually severing any major blood vessel. He just made it look that way.

Wolf rounded on the men nearest him. He spat and yowled in a frenzy swiping his teeth in all directions. Having his hands tied behind his back made little difference.

The first officer's pained shrieks set off all the others. They bolted from Wolf to get away from his ferocious attack, but they had nowhere to run and nowhere to hide.

He charged across the room and bowled them into Pritchard and Davenport. Wolf made the officers scurry for cover, but they couldn't get past Laub.

Wolf caught four of them and inflicted bites and gashes to anyone who came within reach. Others hurt themselves by crashing into the walls and the desk.

Admiral Joyce bellowed orders at everyone, but no one could hear him over the noise. The officers yelled to each other trying to warn each other of impending attack. They tried to coordinate some response, but Wolf's attack took them completely by surprise.

Wolf made it to the room's back corner and turned around to hound the enemy the other way. Three officers collided with the boys trying to find some shelter. One of them bumped into Breeze and he toppled in an insoluble knot of arms and legs.

He hit the floor completely ensnared with the officer who tripped over him. The officer screamed and two others got caught in the chaos.

Healey backed away from them and pushed Davenport out of danger. Both men ended up moving against Pritchard as Wolf burst past them chasing the other officers into Breeze's trap.

"I said take them away!" Admiral Joyce roared. "Get them out of here!"

None of his officers even heard him. Davenport inched another step away and suppressed the urge to laugh at the scene. Good old Breeze. That boy really knew how to cause a diversion.

Wolf charged past Healey with a hair-raising screech. He pounced on the officers trying to avoid Breeze's kicking, thrashing limbs.

Wolf landed on one man's back, rode him to the ground, and dove for the man's neck from behind. Wolf sank his teeth into the guy and the guy screamed in blood terror.

At the moment when the whole office threatened to explode in pandemonium, Deputy Jeremy Yarborough stormed in from outside followed closely by Ace Bolander and big Bill De Rosa.

Yarborough knocked Laub's legs to the floor and the deputies forced their way into the office. They all carried their Howitzers pointed at the ceiling, but their presence cooled the atmosphere instantly.

The deputies glanced around at Breeze tied up in knots with three officers, Wolf still straddling his victim's back mauling his neck, and the four sheriffs wedged in a corner trying to stay out of the line of fire.

"Anything wrong in here, Boss?" De Rosa boomed.

"No, we're all good, Bill," Pritchard replied. "Take these boys and Davenport downstairs to the medical lab and guard them until I come. Don't let them out of your sight. Understand?"

"You got it." The deputies turned to the boys.

Laub stood where Yarborough put him. Laub didn't try to resist again. Wolf stopped his savage assault at one look from Yarborough. Wolf climbed off his hapless victim and got to his feet. He didn't attack again and returned instantly to his usual subdued posture.

The officers mixed up with Breeze unwound themselves from him. Davenport could never figure out how they did it now when they couldn't do it a second before. Breeze must have released them somehow.

They picked themselves up and limped out of the room. They had to dodge the deputies blocking their path. The deputies didn't make it any easier for them by moving out of the way.

Pritchard turned to Davenport, pulled out the key to the cuffs, and started unlocking them. "What are you doing?" Admiral Joyce demanded. "This man is a prisoner."

"He's still a prisoner, but he won't bother you. He's going down to the lab under guard from my men. I'm sure he'll be perfectly safe." Pritchard shot Davenport a piercing glance. "Won't you?"

Davenport read the man's eyes in a split second and nodded. He didn't know yet what Pritchard planned to do, but at least Davenport would be with the Wide Patrol instead of the Reserve Wing.

As soon as the officers left, the three deputies moved aside to clear a path for the boys to leave the office. Most of the Chorion Team checked Davenport for approval first and he nodded to them, too.

Laub went first and then the rest of them filed out. Rodeo waited until last. He frowned while he cocked his head from side to side listening. He even flared his nostrils at the deputies. Then he stalked out of the office to join the rest of his crew.

Pritchard released the cuffs and Davenport rubbed his wrists. Admiral Joyce fumed behind his desk, but he didn't argue as the four deputies escorted Davenport outside, too.

Chapter 30

T he door closed to Admiral Joyce's office, but Healey couldn't stop staring at it. Joyce's medical people were going to use truth serum on Davenport. He would tell them for certain where the Ithium was and Healey couldn't stop it.

He scrambled for some way to intercept Davenport on his way downstairs, but Healey couldn't leave the admiral's presence until the admiral gave him permission.

Pritchard faced Joyce and snapped Healey out of his thoughts. "Well, there you go. You got what you wanted. Me and the Patrol will just shimmy on out of here and head back to Osaids where we belong."

"You have my gratitude, Sheriff. I'm sure the Wide Patrol will earn another commendation for bringing this dangerous criminal to justice."

Pritchard shrugged that away. "We don't need any more of those. We'll just get back to work if it's all right with you."

He started for the door without waiting for permission. Healey really needed to take some lessons from that guy.

Admiral Joyce waved at Healey. "You're dismissed, too, Marshall. You can go back to Pandora's Needle and relax. You've done an excellent job."

Healey could only mutter, "Yes, Sir."

He headed for the door, and when he got outside, he accosted Pritchard. "What the hell are you doing?" Healey whispered in Pritchard's face. "You can NOT be serious about just packing up and shipping out! Davenport is downstairs undergoing truth serum right now. If he tells Joyce's people where the Ithium is, we might as well all hang up our stars."

Pritchard didn't budge. He blinked a few times when Healey's breath hit his face. Other than that, Pritchard didn't act like Healey's behavior came as any surprise. "When did I say I was packing it up?"

"You just told Joyce you were skedaddling back to Osaids. What the hell is wrong with you? Don't you give a shit that some maniac is trying to use the Reserve Wing to release Ithium inside the Confederacy?"

"Will you pull your head in?" Pritchard murmured back. "Davenport and his boys are in custody with my deputies right now. Do you think that just happened by accident?"

Healey clamped his lips shut. He should have known Deacon Pritchard wouldn't let this Ithium bullshit slide.

"I'm going downstairs right now to find out what's going on," Pritchard went on. "If I was you, I would...."

At that moment, the office door yanked open from the inside. Admiral Joyce stuck his head out and glared at the two sheriffs. "What are you still doing here, Marshall? I thought I told you to go back to the Needle."

Healey hunched his shoulders again. "Yes, Sir. I was just going."

Admiral Joyce stepped out of his office and shut the door behind him. "You can come downstairs with me, Sheriff."

Pritchard and Healey exchanged a glance. Now Healey had no choice but to leave. He broke away and Pritchard and Joyce walked off in the other direction.

Healey took off toward the hangar where he left the *Prometheus Vox*. He entered the stairwell and started down it, but when he got to the hangar level, he just kept on going.

It didn't take long for him to find what he was looking for. Four floors above the *Rambler's* bottommost hold, deep, thunderous vibrations resounded through the walls and floor coming from below.

Healey picked up the pace. Whatever was down there was kicking up one hell of a ruckus.

He paused at the very last landing. He couldn't go any lower than this, but he already knew he'd come to the right place. That reverberating boom rocked the ship and blood-curdling screams came through the door.

Healey eased the door open just a crack and pressed his eye to the opening. Barred cells flanked the corridor beyond with a wide aisle down the center—not wide enough, though.

Dice stood in the center of the aisle. He had swollen to at least four times his normal size and his enraged bellows resounded through the *Rambler's* hold. This was the sound Healey had heard from four floors up.

Dice expanded before Healey's eyes and his countenance transformed into a monstrous mask of pure alien rage. He thrashed so ferociously that his horns nearly touched the arched ceiling.

Ten people tried in hopeless desperation to hold onto thick chains. The chains attached to sturdy metal bands around Dice's bulging arms, legs, and neck. These dopes tugged the chains trying to restrain him.

He roared out of control, thrashed his arms, and tossed the puny wretches off their feet. One of them stumbled a step too close to him. He wheeled and backhanded the sucker straight into the bars where the would-be handler flopped motionless to the floor.

Healey held his breath as one man darted between his comrades. He dodged the chains, lunged in, and jabbed Dice with an electric prod that cracked and sizzled against Dice's body.

He exploded in rage, threw back his horns, and thundered to the skies. He slashed one massive arm, caught four chains, and sent the handlers flying.

The poor fool with the prod got trapped nearer to Dice and Dice's swipe didn't touch this guy. That left him alone with only his prod to defend himself against Dice's vengeance.

More handlers charged out of nowhere. Fifteen of them surrounded Dice trying to catch hold of the whipping chains, but Dice didn't notice them. He glared down at the guy who shocked him and Dice's eyes narrowed to venomous slits. Healey didn't envy the guy one bit.

The guy froze brandishing his prod in front of him. Dice looked right down on top of him. No way could the guy get away in time and he didn't look like he was going to try it.

He thrust the prod at Dice and it sputtered again, but it didn't touch him. It didn't have to. That crackling sound triggered Dice's rage and he raised one giant fist on high. He brought it down in a crushing blow on the guy's head and dropped him to the ground.

The prod fell away and none of the new people dared to get close enough to grab it. Dice wheeled to confront them and Healey saw his chance. He didn't much care to go near Dice right now, but Healey thought he knew another way he could help the *Artemis Rex* crew.

Healey stepped out of the stairwell, but he didn't advance. He glued his spine against the wall, drew his sidearm, and took careful aim.

He didn't shoot right away because Dice was moving around too much. He spun backward, flexed his massive shoulders, and roared at the handlers trying to creep up on him from behind.

They backed off and he pivoted a different way to drive off another bunch moving in from the side. As soon as he turned his back, someone ducked in and grabbed the fallen prod. They didn't learn from their friend's mistake.

Some brave soul rushed Dice and stabbed the prod into his back. It sizzled against his lower ribs and he went ballistic. He roared even louder and wheeled in a full circle. He swiped his arm in a ring flattening everyone before him.

They toppled and started to scatter, but he was already too far gone even to see them anymore. He seized the chains in both fists and stormed down the corridor slashing and whipping them against the bars, the floor, the ceiling—everything.

He roared continuously and barely stopped to draw breath. He turned at the end of the corridor to make his way back, and when he got there, he noticed his fallen adversaries trying to crawl away to safety.

He stopped over the man who shocked him in the back. Dice glared down at the man's unconscious form, snarled through bared fangs, and tightened his grip on his chains.

Healey couldn't wait any longer. He leveled his sidearm at Dice and fired. The shot pinged on the iron lock of his neck collar and the collar unclipped.

Dice whipped around fast and his ferocious eyes fixed on Healey, but Healey didn't lower his gun. He fired a second time and the band on Dice's bicep snapped off. The chain and manacle hit the floor with a clang.

Dice turned all the way around and took a menacing step toward Healey. Healey fired a third time and the manacle on Dice's other arm dropped away.

Dice looked down at it and blinked. Healey fired twice more into the bands around Dice's legs, but Dice didn't react.

Healey holstered his weapon. He did what he came here to do. He opened the stairwell door behind his back. He slipped into the stairwell without turning his back on Dice and then Healey took off running for the hangar.

Chapter 31

Rodeo leaned close to Davenport's ear. "We gotta get out of here."

"Any ideas?" Davenport glanced over his shoulder. Deputy Yarborough walked right behind him, close enough to hear every word.

Yarborough looked like a younger version of Pritchard—beefy, mustached, and flinty, but maybe not quite so impenetrable. He looked like the kind of guy that actually might be able to laugh and smile under the right circumstances, but this was definitely not that time.

Davenport was starting to have serious misgivings about these men. If they really planned to take him and the boys to the medical lab for treatment with truth serum, he would have to start treating the Wide Patrol as his enemies, too.

"The *Artemis Rex* is ready to fly," Rodeo murmured. "We just have to get back to it and fly away."

Davenport snorted. "Great. Let's go."

Rodeo swiveled his head to one side. "Which members of the Wide Patrol are here?"

"You know about the Wide Patrol?"

"I know a few things. Which ones?"

"Yarborough, Bolander, Treese, and De Rosa."

Rodeo nodded. "Good."

"Keep moving, boy," Treese called from the back of the group.

Bolander led the way through several corridors and into the stairwell. They exited in another corridor. Bolander stopped to open a door at the end and let everyone through into a blinding white hall.

He turned off into what looked like a closet. The deputies herded the whole party inside and De Rosa locked the door behind them. Only then did Davenport realize that it was actually something like a medical clinic.

Treese hustled over to Rodeo, pulled out a pair of pliers, and snipped the cable binding Rodeo's wrists together. "Keep your voices down so no one hears you. Do you have any weapons?"

"Weapons!" Bandit countered. "You're joking, right?"

Treese went over to him and then went through the whole group freeing all the boys. "Damn it. We should have armed up on the top deck."

"We couldn't do that with the admiral's men around," Yarborough pointed out.

"We still have Wolf and Breeze," Axel pointed out. "They're weapons."

Some of the others giggled and then stopped when the deputies scowled at them. The instant Treese freed Wolf, the boy shoved between Bolander and De Rosa to plant himself at Davenport's side.

Davenport squeezed the boy's neck and gave him a shake. "You did great up there. You were magnificent."

Wolf growled back. "So what are you gonna do?" Rodeo asked. "You aren't really going to take us to the medical lab, are you?"

"We have to," Treese replied. "The admiral will check that we followed his orders."

"We won't go," Davenport insisted. "We'll resist."

"Cool your jets, son," De Rosa boomed. "The Boss has a plan."

"Are you sure about that? He didn't act like he has a plan."

"He never acts like he has a plan," Bolander replied. "That's his genius."

"His genius is that he never has a plan," Yarborough countered. "He just does it."

"Does what?" Bandit asked.

Yarborough started to say something until Rodeo cocked his head and held up his hand to stop him. Footsteps passed in the hall outside and faded.

"How far away are they?" Bolander whispered.

"They're going into the lab." Rodeo turned his ear to the side wall. "It's clear now."

Bolander eased the door open, peeked out, slipped into the corridor, and shut the door behind him.

"Do you know these guys?" Davenport asked Rodeo.

"They get around," Rodeo whispered back.

"I'm getting that."

Bolander came back. "It's clear. Let's go."

Yarborough and De Rosa headed for the door. Treese leaned in close to Davenport. "Try to stay calm. We'll get you out."

"How?" Davenport asked.

Treese silenced him with a shake of the head as the deputies herded the boys back into the corridor. They filed farther down the corridor and into a different room.

Davenport balked as soon as he crossed the threshold. A sick feeling crept into his stomach when the door clicked shut behind him.

He and the boys stood in a bare, tiled room. Prison bars separated the prisoners from a lab on the other side. An examination chair complete with restraint straps and a restraining headrest sat in the center beyond the bars.

Davenport whipped around, but De Rosa's vast bulk blocked him from getting back to the door. De Rosa rooted himself there and hefted his weapon across his chest. Davenport wasn't getting out that way.... or any other way for that matter.

"You sons of bitches!" Davenport roared. "You sold us out!"

"Keep quiet!" Treese snapped. "Sit down over there and don't make me shut you up."

Davenport didn't move. He narrowed his eyes at the deputy, but Rodeo pulled Davenport away.

Davenport didn't sit down. Wolf, Bandit, Laub, and Coon did, but the others remained standing. Davenport didn't stop glaring at Treese. These assholes tricked him. They never planned to help him at all.

Bolander crossed to the opposite wall, propped his shoulder against it, pulled out a piece of chewing gum, and put it in his mouth. "You might as well relax. No one is going anywhere 'til the Boss comes down."

"I'll tell you what you can do with your Boss," Davenport hissed.

Bolander laughed in his face. Davenport started thinking about how he and the boys could take these four deputies when another door opened behind him.

Five nurses and three doctors enter the lab beyond the bars. They started checking the examination chair, setting up a few rolling tables, and laying out all kinds of medieval medical equipment on it. They also laid out several ampules of clear fluid.

Davenport shuddered. He didn't want to think about what these people were going to do to him to find out where the Ithium was, especially since he had no idea where it was.

Rodeo startled Davenport again. "We need to free Dice from the hold."

"Can you tell where he is?" Treese asked.

"I think I heard bellowing about five decks down....and maybe some screaming."

Davenport turned around to find Treese and Yarborough both flanking Rodeo. They listened to him like they knew all about him. Now Davenport knew for certain Rodeo knew these men from before.

Rodeo cocked his head the other way. "Beauty is on this ship, too."

"He is?" Bandit asked. "Are you sure?"

"Don't you damn well ask me that, fool!" Rodeo spat. "Am I sure!" He snorted and shook his head.

"He was on the Mad Men's ship with me," Davenport replied. "He must have stowed away on HTWV-983. He crippled the Mad Men so the Wide Patrol could overtake us."

"Good for him." Treese turned back to Rodeo. "Where is he?"

"I can't tell. He's in the pipes. I can't locate him."

"He can take care of himself," Bolander added. "We got enough to worry about just dealing with you nine without breaking our necks over him."

Davenport glanced back and forth between Rodeo and the four deputies. "Hold it. Are you telling me you know about Beauty, too?"

"We know more than any living person would ever want to know about the *Echo Omicron* crew," De Rosa rumbled. "Trust me on that."

"And the Chorion Team," Yarborough added.

"None of this gets us anywhere," Treese cut in.

"Does your boss really have a plan?" Davenport asked.

Another bang interrupted them, and this time, Davenport's hopes drained away as a dozen armed Reserve Wing soldiers entered the lab beyond the bars.

They lined up across the back wall behind the examination chair. They presented their guns and stood at attention in a way that told Davenport loud and clear why they were here.

Their arrival solidified the medical people. They came to some understanding and turned to stare at the prisoners. Davenport's blood ran cold when one of the doctors advanced toward the bars. "Are you ready?"

Davenport gulped and stepped forward. "I'm ready."

"Not you." A different doctor consulted some device against the wall. "We're taking the regressive."

"What?" Davenport asked. "What does that mean?"

The doctor nodded toward Wolf. "Him—the regressive. Our orders are to test him first."

"No way!" Davenport stepped between Wolf and the medical team. "You are NOT taking him!"

"Those are our orders. If you resist, we'll have no choice but to restrain you all." The doctor turned to the soldiers and sliced his finger through the air. "Bring him in."

He pushed a button on the wall and the bars started to slide out of the way. The soldiers stepped forward, shouldered their guns, and aimed at the prisoners.

Davenport reacted without thinking and sidestepped the rest of the way in front of Wolf. Laub, Bandit, Rodeo, and Coon all did the same thing. They surrounded Wolf to block him from the guards.

"You are not taking him!" Davenport bellowed. "You'll have to kill us all first. What do your orders say about that?"

None of the medical people answered. They moved well back out of the way as the soldiers advanced.

Davenport braced himself for a fight. None of the boys were armed. Wolf, Breeze, and all the others fighting together couldn't overcome more than a dozen Reserve Wing rifles.

Davenport screwed up his courage to charge. If he acted fast enough, he might be able to get one of their guns away from them and turn it on the others.

The four deputies reacted before Davenport could move. He didn't even see Bolander push himself off the wall before all four men surrounded the *Artemis Rex* crew. They aimed their XQs back at the soldiers in a tense standoff.

"Put your guns down on the ground and back out of the room!" one of the soldiers yelled. "Put your guns down before we open fire!"

"Back off!" De Rosa bellowed. "You're about to carry out an illegal medical procedure on a Confederate citizen. You are ordered by the authority of the Confederate Sheriff's Service to stand down and lower your weapons!"

Another soldier yelled out followed by another ultimatum from Treese. The room erupted with both sides yelling at each other and ordering each other to stand down.

Davenport dared to glance behind him. Maybe he could make a break for the door before both sides started blowing each other to pulp.

He was just about to say something to Rodeo when the door swung open. Davenport's heart soared when Deacon Pritchard strode in. Then Davenport's heart took a steep dive all over again when Admiral Joyce followed Pritchard inside.

"What the hell is going on here?" Pritchard demanded.

Both sides started talking fast. No one could hear anything until Pritchard raised both hands. "Quiet!"

Everyone shut their mouths, but they didn't slacken their posture or lower their guns. The four deputies glared across at the soldiers. The soldiers fidgeted and kept shifting their weapons from one side to the other trying to cover both the deputies and the *Artemis Rex* crew.

"You men have no right to raise your weapons against Reserve Wing staff on board this ship," Admiral Joyce began. "You were under orders to bring these prisoners to the medical lab, not to threaten my people."

"You ordered your medical people to use truth serum on Davenport, not on Wolf," Yarborough fired back. "Truth serum is banned and Wolf isn't a suspect in any crime. None of these people are."

"That will be for me to decide," Joyce returned. "These people are my prisoners and I'll say whether any of them is a suspect in any crime."

"That isn't good enough," Treese countered. "We're sworn to uphold Confederate law, even when the perpetrator is Reserve Wing brass."

Joyce narrowed his eyes at the man. "You could wind up in custody yourself talking that way, Deputy. These people are my prisoners. You brought them into custody on my orders. You've done your job. You can clear your patrol off the *Rambler* now, Sheriff. I'm sure you have better things to do with your time."

No one moved for a minute and then Pritchard bumped his knuckles into Treese's shoulder. "Put your guns down."

"Hell no!" De Rosa boomed. "We are NOT standing around watching them use truth serum on these kids!"

"We aren't standing around. We're clearing off."

Davenport spun around and gasped. "You're just going to leave us here? You're just gonna let him get away with this?" Rodeo started to pull Davenport away, but Davenport only surged forward trying to fight his way to Pritchard. "I trusted you! I believed in you!"

"Them's the breaks, kid. See you around, Sheriff." Pritchard bumped Treese again. "Let's go."

The four deputies hesitated and then Bolander raised his XQ to aim it at the ceiling. De Rosa and Yarborough stayed in position and then they turned away, too.

Pritchard opened the door and let his men out of the room. A heavy weight plummeted into Davenport's stomach when the door shut. Now he faced the soldiers with no one to protect him and the boys.

Chapter 32

Admiral Joyce smirked in smug triumph and pointed at the medical people who cowered in the corner. "Carry on. I'm looking forward to this."

The soldiers charged the crew in a flash. Davenport and the boys started to fight back, but the soldiers quickly overpowered them. Breeze thrashed and struck out with all four limbs, but it wasn't enough.

Five soldiers caught Davenport and wrestled him across the room. They pinned him against the wall and held him there. Now he had no choice but to see exactly what was about to happen. He yanked and kicked, but he couldn't break their grip.

Wolf went nuts the instant the soldiers touched him. He screeched and slashed his teeth everywhere. More soldiers poured into the room and packed the cell so tightly that no one could move.

It took a while, but they eventually tackled Wolf to the floor. So many soldiers piled on top of him that they finally got hold of his limbs.

They carried him to the examination chair, crushed him into it, and strapped him down.

They fixed the metal restraining straps across his chest, stomach, and all his limbs. His hair-raising screeches echoed through the *Rambler*, but the chaos only seemed to delight Admiral Joyce all the more.

Soldiers piled on top of the other boys, too. None of them could get near Wolf and he couldn't get away. His wild black eyes raced around the room and he slashed his fangs at any of the medical team who came near him. They finally strapped his head in place, too, and that drove him even more frantic.

The first doctor who addressed Davenport came forward under heavy guard from the soldiers. He loaded a syringe with a vial from the table at his side.

Wolf yowled louder than ever. His countenance contorted in fury and terror. His eyes skipped across Davenport and made Davenport feel even sicker. What could Admiral Joyce possibly hope to gain by using truth serum on Wolf? The kid couldn't even talk.

Davenport didn't have to think too hard to come up with the answer. Admiral Joyce didn't care about getting Wolf to talk. The admiral wasn't doing this to get information out of Wolf because that wasn't possible.

He was doing this to torment Wolf in front of his friends. Admiral Joyce wanted to soften up the others. He wanted them to cooperate when it came time to ply Davenport and the Chorion Team for information.

The doctor lowered the syringe to Wolf's arm. Wolf let out a scream that tore Davenport's brain in half. Davenport cringed and had to look away. Alla gave a low, dry sob on the other side of the room.

The syringe thunked back down on the tray. The sound made Davenport look up.

Wolf collapsed in the chair. His head would have lolled to one side if the metal strap didn't hold it in place. His eyelids drooped and his vision bleared out of focus. All his limbs went slack and he stopped fighting.

Admiral Joyce filed between the soldiers to Wolf's side. "Hook him up to the stimulation electrodes."

"That isn't what we agreed," the doctor argued. "You said you were going to use truth serum. You didn't say anything about electrodes."

"Do as you're told or I'll get someone who will. You're only here because General Cornelius recommended you. You can go back to the clinic at Chiton's Hold if you don't like it."

The doctor compressed his lips and threw something else down on the table. "I'd rather be there than here. I never should have agreed to this."

He stormed out of the room and slammed the door. Minutes of breathless silence dragged by. Only Wolf's tortured breath disturbed the stillness.

Admiral Joyce heaved a sigh and turned to the next doctor in line. "Hook him up. Now."

The second doctor got to work with fumbling hands. He wouldn't look at Wolf or the admiral while he unwound the electrodes and tried more than once to disentangle the muddled wires.

Admiral Joyce fumed in anticipation and started pacing the room, but he didn't tell the poor guy to hurry up.

Davenport gulped at the sight of Wolf. The boy was always on alert, always tense and watchful, always quick to react to anything. Now he sagged in the chair, a lifeless blob. He didn't even blink anymore.

The doctor finally hooked up the electrodes to Wolf's body, but it took way too long. "What's the hold-up?" Joyce barked. "What's wrong with it?"

"It's his hair, Sir. The electrodes don't stick properly. I'm not sure we can get good contact. It might not work."

"I don't care! Do it anyway. Hook him up and give him the first dose setting."

The doctor tucked his chin and went at it. Davenport jerked against the soldiers holding him just to satisfy himself that he wouldn't be able to get to Wolf.

The soldiers still aimed their guns at Davenport and the boys. Even if Davenport got free, the soldiers would gun him down before he got near Wolf.

The doctor turned to his machinery. "Okay. I'm ready."

"Give him the dose," Joyce ordered.

The doctor put out his hand to touch the machine and a powerful jolt thumped the exam chair underneath Wolf. He jostled against his straps, but he didn't wake up.

"What happened?" Joyce demanded. "Why didn't it work?"

"I didn't do anything!" the doctor cried. "I didn't even touch it! I never gave him the shock."

"Well, do it now!"

The doctor extended his hand again. He actually did touch the machine this time, but he didn't depress the switch to administer the shock.

Another thump banged Wolf's chair. The doctor spun backward to stare at the boy, and at that moment, three more deep crashes shook the floor directly under the chair.

Joyce and the medical people looked around them and then, without warning, an almighty boom rocked the lab.

The floor imploded and the whole section with the exam chair attached plunged through the crater. It dropped straight down with Wolf still strapped in place and out of his mind from the drug.

Joyce and the medical team reared back in alarm as Wolf vanished from sight. Dust, rubble, and shattered masonry billowed across the lab. When it cleared, everyone gaped at the vacuous hole in the floor where the chair used to be.

Joyce and the medical team moved forward. Admiral Joyce stuck his head over the whole and an XQ blast almost took his head off.

He lunged out of the way as more gunfire erupted through the breach. He spun away and bellowed at the guards. "Get down there! They're getting away!"

"What......?" one of the guards stammered.

"The Wide Patrol! They blew the floor and now they're stealing the prisoner! Get downstairs and stop them before they get off the ship!"

The guards charged to the door. They forgot all about restraining Davenport and the boys. The whole room cleared out in a second with Admiral Joyce caught in the confusion.

Davenport glanced over at the boys and caught Bandit's eye. Rodeo was frowning at the door and then the whole crew bolted for the exit.

They charged outside into a scene of unmitigated chaos. Dice stood in the corridor blocking the stairs the Wide Patrol used to bring the crew down here.

Davenport had never seen Dice like this and he hoped he never saw Dice like this again. Davenport had only heard stories about Adiks gone berserk. They doubled and even tripled their size when they got angry, but that must have been a massive understatement.

Dice towered over the Reserve Wing soldiers who ran out of the lab directly into his path. A few of the dumber ones actually had the balls to shoot at him, but as usual, their shots only bounced off his bulging muscles.

He clenched his fists and his gigantic body stretched and pulsated with muscle ripped with veins and striations. His horns had grown along with the rest of him and he wheeled his head sideways to smash them into the wall.

As soon as he tore them free, he stretched even taller and pounded his head into the ceiling. Plaster and gravel rained on top of him. Hitting his head against things seemed to satisfy some rage-fueled need and encouraged him to keep doing it.

He bared his fangs at the soldiers and stormed five steps closer to them. A few stood their ground, but many bolted in the other direction.

"Shoot him!" Admiral Joyce roared. "Kill him!"

He didn't notice Dice getting more furious by the second. One foolish bastard squeezed off another shot that deflected off Dice's bony eyebrow.

He roared to shake the whole world, stomped over to the shooter, and seized the guy gun and all. Dice crushed the unfortunate man in one massive fist. The soldier's XQ got caught in Dice's grip and he squeezed it into the guy's body.

The guy screamed, convulsed, and then flopped limp against Dice's swollen knuckles. Dice hauled back his arm and hurled the body straight at Admiral Joyce, but the admiral didn't seem to realize the gravity of the situation.

"Shoot him, I said!" he thundered. "Get him under control! What are you waiting for? We have to recapture that prisoner!"

Davenport stopped in the lab entrance viewing the mayhem unfolding in front of him. The boys collided with him and they all packed the doorway watching the scene disintegrate.

"Wow!" Axel breathed. "Remind me never to piss that guy off."

"Come on!" Davenport ordered. "There's only one way out of here."

He bolted forward. Hands tried to pull him back, but he was already breaking away. He yelled one last time, "Come on!" and charged straight for Dice.

Dice hunched his shoulders and swelled even more. His back hit the ceiling and he snarled in fury at the puny creatures in front of him. He couldn't get any bigger without destroying the whole ship.

Davenport tucked his head and sprinted past the soldiers. Guns went off behind him, but he kept picking up speed. Dice bellowed again and Davenport dove headfirst onto the floor. He rotated his legs forward and skidded past Dice's ankle to the corridor beyond.

Dice thundered even louder. He flung out one fist and punched through a wall to his right. The wall collapsed and he brought both fists down in a crushing smash on the floor.

Davenport pivoted to his feet. "Come on!" He waved the boys forward and Rodeo dashed down the corridor. That was the signal and all the boys broke into a run to catch up.

Several guards tried to intercept them and Dice saw them coming. He rushed them and smashed the guards out of the way with one mighty smack. He slapped them against the wall and flattened them before turning his rage on the admiral.

Admiral Joyce tried to stand his ground, but the next time Dice charged, Joyce bolted and vanished.

Dice lost it completely and went back to crashing his head into anything and everything. He charged the lab, doubled over, and impaled his skull through the wall.

He pulled it out and turned around to destroy the next room. He worked his way up the corridor and didn't look back at Davenport or the boys.

Davenport tugged Bandit into the stairwell and the whole party took off running, but Davenport went down and the boys went up.

They both ran back and bumped into each other. "We have to get Wolf!" Davenport panted.

"The Wide Patrol has him," Rodeo told him. "We have to get back to the *Artemis Rex.*"

"We can't leave without Dice."

The boys blinked up at Davenport in confusion. "How would we fit him inside the ship?" Coon asked.

"Okay, okay," Davenport gasped. "What about Emmett? Where is he?"

The boys looked at each other. "They took him away," Rodeo replied, "him and Dice both."

"And you don't know where they took him?"

The boys shook their heads.

"They must have taken him to the hold," Davenport decided. "Joyce said it was at the bottom of the ship."

Chapter 33

Davenport burst into the hold and scanned the cells around him. He went all the way to the far end, but every cell was empty.

Bodies littered the floor and the bars showed the unmistakable evidence that the Reserve Wing tried to hold Dice down here. Dozens of bars had been smashed in. Large sections of walls and bulkheads had been destroyed by some incredibly strong blunt force.

Davenport raced back to the boys. "Emmett isn't down there."

Rodeo cocked his head. "There's another holding section directly above us. I can hear voices up there."

Davenport led the way back into the stairwell and exited on the next deck above.

All the cells up here had people in them, but none of them was Emmett. Davenport was on his return trip back to the boys when he stopped by another cell. He frowned into it. "Well, Robberburn? So you're here at last, aren't you?"

Red and Robberburn rushed the bars. "You have to get us out of here, Davenport!"

"You don't want to do that. There's an Adik on the rampage upstairs."

"Oh." Red frowned. "That's not good."

"We can handle an Adik," Robberburn replied. "Let us out, Davenport. Please. Don't leave us here."

"You know I can't do that, man. I'm a sheriff and you're a criminal in custody. I wouldn't be doing my duty if I let you out."

"Aw, come on, Davenport," Red pleaded. "You wouldn't leave us here. You know what the Reserve Wing is like."

"Yeah. I sure do."

Rodeo touched Davenport's elbow. "The soldiers are coming down. They're searching for the Wide Patrol. The Patrol got away with Wolf and the soldiers think they're down here."

Davenport let the boys draw him away from the Mad Men's cell, but the crew didn't return to the same stairwell.

Rodeo guided everyone to the opposite end of the hold where they entered a different stairwell. They started climbing, but they hadn't passed more than three floors before they heard gunfire echoing down from above.

Bandit and Alla crowded close to Rodeo. "Can you hear anything?"

"Shut your hole!" Rodeo hissed. "I can't hear anything you can't hear."

"Stay here," Davenport murmured. "I'll go see what's...."

An XQ blast ricocheted down the stairwell followed by a bellow. It shook the stairs all the way down to Davenport's position.

The boys jumped and took off running as the Wide Patrol retreated down the stairs and overtook the *Artemis Rex* crew.

Davenport shoved the boys ahead of him. Bolander stumbled over Laub and whipped backward to fire up the stairs.

Treese and Yarborough tripped a few steps higher than Bolander. The two deputies supported Wolf between them while Deacon Pritchard defended them from gunshots farther up.

"Move!" Pritchard roared over his shoulder. "He's coming down fast!"

Davenport spun away and the whole crew took off at top speed. They jumped down three steps at a time, but Dice's furious roars kept getting louder. Gunshots pinged off the walls and railings.

Davenport veered to another door. "Here! In here!"

The whole crew dashed back into the prison hold with the Wide Patrol deputies right with them. Davenport froze on the threshold and almost got mowed over by the others trying to get through.

Davenport almost didn't believe what he was seeing. Beauty stood down the corridor right in front of the Mad Men's cell. Beauty was in the act of opening the barred door to let the Mad Men out.

The Mad Men stepped out of the cell. They were free. Robberburn grinned down at Beauty and then rubbed Beauty on top of the head. Beauty smiled back up at him, but it wasn't the rapturous smile Davenport remembered.

A flash of malice winked in Beauty's eyes and his teeth showed a little too much. Davenport's blood ran cold at that smile and then he heard it.

The stairwell rocked behind him and the next bellow boomed so loudly that it almost had no sound at all.

Davenport lunged for the deputies and shoved them out of the way. "Get down!"

He dove the other way and tackled four boys. The *Artemis Rex* crew almost didn't get out of the way fast enough before Dice exploded through the wall. He demolished the whole stairwell in one blow.

Dust and rubble clung to his horns along with some suspicious dark stains that might have been blood. His clothes hung off him in tatters and he snarled and roared more furiously than ever.

He took one look at the people in front of him. Nothing stood between him and the Mad Men.

Beauty retreated grinning and he didn't even try to hide his sadistic pleasure. Davenport's guts lurched. This was it. This was Beauty's revenge. He swore he would pay the Mad Men back for kidnapping him from his home planet.

Red, Robberburn, and the others turned to face Dice. Beauty shrank back against the bars and huddled behind the Mad Men where Dice couldn't see him.

Dice stormed into the hold shooting ferocious glares at all the prisoners and bellowing at the Mad Men. He pivoted sideways and his horns destroyed the bars of a cell on that side. The prisoners shrieked and retreated to the back wall, but Dice was already moving on to the next cell.

He smashed the floor with his fists and impaled his horns into a concrete pillar before attacking another set of bars.

The Mad Men backed away and then bolted for the far stairwell, but when they got there and tried to make a break for freedom, they found the door locked. They yanked at it and a few of the Mad Men screamed at Robberburn to stop messing around and open that door.

Beauty snickered softly to himself, but no one heard him over Dice's roars. Davenport's skin crawled watching this. Beauty trapped these men in the hold with Dice. Now they couldn't get away.

Dice let out an earth-shaking roar, doubled over to make himself as compact as possible, and charged. Five of the Mad Men screamed and tried to flatten themselves against the wall, but Robberburn and Red kept attacking the door right until the end.

Dice picked up speed, bent his chin against his chest, and ran full tilt into the door. His horns crashed straight through it and pulverized the Mad Men in one blow.

Dice ripped his head out, threw back his head, and bellowed even louder. He reared and smashed his horns into the Mad Men again just in case any of them survived the first strike.

Pritchard grabbed Laub and Alla. "Get to your ship! Take Wolf! We'll cover your escape!"

Laub and Bandit took Wolf from Treese and Yarborough. Bolander, De Rosa, and Pritchard swiveled in front of the boys as they dashed into the stairwell hauling Wolf between them.

Pritchard rotated into position and all four men leveled their weapons at Dice. "Get out of here, Davenport!" Pritchard ordered. "Go now!"

Davenport couldn't move. "I can't. He's part of my crew. I can't leave him."

"You're crazy!" Bolander yelled. "He'll kill you!"

"Go on!" Davenport called back. "Get the boys and yourselves away. I still have three people on this ship. I won't leave without them. Go on. You'll only make him madder if he sees you aiming guns at him."

The deputies muttered some more about Davenport's sanity, but he was never more certain of anything. He wouldn't leave without Dice and Beauty and he still had to find Emmett, too.

Dice tore his horns out of the wall for the second time, whipped around, and glared at Davenport in murderous fury. He stalked a few threatening steps nearer up the aisle.

Davenport drew in a deep breath. He was betting his life on this, but he'd come too far. He wouldn't leave one of his friends behind in Reserve Wing custody, especially with Admiral Joyce running loose on this ship.

Davenport strode forward and halted in the middle of the aisle. Sobs and screams came from the cells on both sides, but Davenport kept his eyes trained only on Dice.

Dice clomped a few more steps, roared at Davenport, and then punched his fists down hard on the floor.

Davenport tensed and then forced himself to relax. This was his friend. He never thought he'd say or even think that about Dice, but it was true. Davenport risked his life for Dice before and he would do it again.

Dice took a few more menacing steps and bellowed right in Davenport's face. Davenport couldn't stop himself from flinching. He didn't try to hide it, but he didn't leave, either.

Dice stalked right up to him, towered over him, and thundered right down in Davenport's eyes. Dice's hot breath blistered Davenport's skin. If Dice decided to kill him right now, Davenport wouldn't be able to stop him.

Dice stopped bellowing and glared down at Davenport. That was all the signal Davenport needed. "You okay there, buddy? Did they hurt you?"

Dice scowled at him and grunted something.

"If you come with me, the boys are waiting to get us out of this shithole. We can get you something to eat if you feel like it. I think the boys brought some Smoky Hotskin Duckwhats from Nyx Anonyma. I never could stand those things, but some people like 'em."

Davenport heard himself babbling about anything and nothing. He didn't care what he said as long as Dice heard his voice.

Dice scowled even more and grunted again, but he seemed to be shrinking even now.

Davenport prepared to launch into another nonsense speech when Beauty sidled around Dice's oversized form. Beauty met Davenport's eye for a split second and then turned to Dice.

Beauty smiled up at his big friend and pulled something from behind his back. Beauty unwrapped it with exaggerated care and held it out to Dice.

Davenport took a second to realize what it was. It was an unblemished, untouched block of pure Devilspawn, the paste of a seed pod found only in the Thala system.

Davenport's mouth started to water at his first sight of the block. This stuff was one of the most expensive and sought-after delicacies in the whole galaxy—way too expensive and rare for lowlife smugglers like the *Echo Omicron* crew to ever find, so how did Beauty get it?

A thread of adrenaline wormed into Davenport's guts. Beauty must have stolen this Devilspawn from the Reserve Wing. He might have stolen it from Admiral Joyce himself. Who else on the *Rambler* would be able to get their hands on this stuff?

Dice frowned at the block and blinked. Then he plucked it out of Beauty's scrawny fingers, turned it over once, and sniffed it.

Beauty grinned up at him and this was Beauty's old genuine smile. That first smell of the block made Dice shrink even more. Davenport could see Dice getting smaller with every passing moment.

Dice bit off a corner of the block and his features cleared. He imploded in a second and the swelling in his head and shoulders drained away. He returned to his usual form and a curious, concentrating expression came over his face as he chewed.

Beauty laughed and patted Dice's shoulder. "You like it, don't you?"

Dice chuckled. "It's not too bad."

Davenport laughed in pure relief. "Did you see where they took Emmett when they brought you in, big guy?"

"They took him to another hold—a lower security one." Dice took another bite. "I haven't had this stuff in years. It really is delicious." He held out the block to Davenport. "You want some?"

Davenport couldn't help but beam at him. "I think you better keep it. You earned it."

"I did?"

"Yeah. You sure did. Let's go get Emmett and get out of here."

Chapter 34

D ice, Davenport, and Beauty ran up the stairs. Pretty soon, they came to a section that Dice had completely destroyed. The friends had to cut through a different corridor lined with lab rooms to get to the opposite stairwell.

Dice paused inside and examined the walls. "I've been here before."

"Are you sure?" Davenport asked.

"This is the way we came when they brought me in. I know where Emmett is. Follow me."

He climbed two more floors, passed down a different corridor that looked a lot like the medical deck, and turned into a cell very similar to the one where the admiral used truth serum on Wolf.

Emmett hunched against one wall and sprang to his feet when the other three showed up. "What the hell is going on? I heard there was some monster on the loose."

"There is," Davenport replied. "Come on. We're getting out of here."

"The boys will be long gone by now," Dice replied.

"Then we'll have to steal another ship. Maybe the Wide Patrol will help us out."

Emmett stopped on a dime. "The Wide Patrol?"

"Yeah. They're here. They've been helping us."

Emmett shook his head fast and backed away. "Oh, no! Oh, no! I'm not going near those bastards again! No way."

"You know the Wide Patrol?" Davenport asked.

"Do I know them?" Emmett snorted. "You couldn't pay me to get in the same room with one of those assholes."

"Fine," Davenport hedged. "Just come on. We gotta get out of here."

Emmett balked again when it came time to leave the cell. He must not have thought to check if the door was locked. He looked back in confusion when the other three waltzed out with no trouble.

Emmett glanced over his shoulder. "Where are they?"

"Who—the monster?" Davenport asked.

"No, the Wide Patrol."

"I don't know. What's your problem with them, anyway?"

"Are you kidding?" Dice rumbled. "The Wide Patrol are notorious lawmen. They're unstoppable."

"Yeah? So?"

"They're sheriffs," Dice boomed, "and deputies."

"I'm a sheriff," Davenport pointed out.

Emmett snorted and Beauty gave Davenport a dirty look. "My point exactly," Dice growled.

Davenport didn't ask any more questions. Didn't De Rosa say the Wide Patrol knew more than they ever wanted to know about the *Echo Omicron* crew?

The *Echo Omicron* crew was a bunch of the worst smugglers and bounty hunters Davenport ever had the misfortune to deal with. No wonder they ran afoul of the Wide Patrol.

The Wide Patrol must have busted the *Echo Omicron* crew too many times to count ....and with spectacular results.

Davenport bit back a grin when he thought about checking the Sheriff's Service records and finding out what went down between those two crews. He probably wouldn't get a chance anytime soon, though.

Dice stopped a second time when they got a few more decks higher. He furrowed his brow in concentration. "I hear gunshots."

"It's coming from the hangar," Beauty added.

Davenport's resolve hardened. "Let's get up there."

"We don't have any weapons," Emmett argued. "How are we going to get to the ship if people are shooting at each other?"

The noise got louder as they climbed, but Davenport kept going. Going back was no longer an option.

The party slowed as the noise built to a steady thunder of gunfire. Crashes and smashes struck the walls and the whole stairwell vibrated.

Davenport couldn't talk to his friends over the racket. He motioned them to stay behind him as he snuck closer to the hangar door.

He peeked out of the stairwell. The door opened onto a catwalk high above the hangar floor.

The *Artemis Rex* hovered above the deck spraying Howitzer fire in all directions. Hundreds of soldiers crouched along catwalks and scaffolds all over the hangar. Some knelt right in front of Davenport.

The soldiers had their backs to the stairwell. They didn't see the friends sneaking up on them and Davenport didn't show himself. How the hell was he supposed to get down to the *Artemis Rex* with them in the way?

More ships wheeled past the hangar bay. They somersaulted around each other in the stars outside. They exchanged shots with a bunch of Reserve Wing Daggers flying just as fast. Davenport gritted his teeth when he saw the *Prometheus Vox* out there. Healey was still here.

The *Artemis Rex* pivoted a few more times spitting dozens of shots at the scaffolds. A second later, two Daggers fought their way through the battle and rocketed right up to the hangar bay.

They unloaded on the *Artemis Rex* from behind and Howitzer fire scattered into the hangar.

A cruel shot punched the *Artemis Rex's* back end. The Drifter skidded forward and would have crashed into the wall.

It whipped around to return fire, but the Daggers only crawled deeper into the hangar. The *Artemis Rex* couldn't escape, but at least it was closer to Davenport's position. "Let's go! We can get to the ship."

The friends launched out of their hiding place and charged the nearest soldiers. The soldiers were too busy pounding the *Artemis Rex* to notice until the four friends pounced on them from behind.

Davenport grabbed his victim's head and bounced the guy's face off the railing. The guy folded and Davenport snatched the XQ out of the guy's hands.

He turned the gun on the soldiers nearest him and all four friends started plowing their way to the stairs. Most of the soldiers didn't see the danger until it was too late.

Davenport sprang onto the first step wheeling his weapon up at more soldiers on the tiers. The order hadn't come down yet to target the intruders and the troops kept unloading on the ship.

The *Artemis Rex* had enough to worry about holding the Daggers at bay. Davenport still couldn't see how to get on board until the *Prometheus Vox* streaked past the hangar bay, cartwheeled sideways pummeling more Daggers, and came skating in behind the enemy.

The Nitrol bombarded the Daggers with guns blazing. Two more Drifters zoomed in behind the *Prometheus Vox* and defended the Nitrol from outside attack.

The *Prometheus Vox* pounded one of the Daggers and nailed it to the wall. It tried to rally and Healey pulled sideways just in time. The first Dagger slammed into the second one and both ships crashed hard on the opposite side.

The *Prometheus Vox* attacked with vicious ferocity and started thumping them both into the floor. The *Artemis Rex* saw the path to freedom clear.

The ship streaked past the stairs and Davenport looked right down through the cockpit cover at Bandit and Rodeo sitting in their cradles. Neither of them saw him trying to get to the ship.

The next instant, the *Artemis Rex* rocketed out of the *Rambler's* hangar and vanished into space.

"Son of a bitch!" Dice growled.

"Now what?" Emmett asked.

Davenport whipped backward. "Get back up there! Get back to the stairwell! Hurry!"

They retreated upstairs the way they came and Davenport paused to look back. The *Prometheus Vox* blasted one Dagger to smithereens before the other made its escape. The *Prometheus Vox* gave chase and disappeared into the stars.

The attack Drifters left, too. The whole hangar yawned empty and deserted. All of Davenport's allies were gone except these three men.

They gathered in the stairwell. The XQs in their hands hardly changed their miserable prospects.

"Got any more brilliant ideas?" Dice snarled.

"There is another hold," Beauty suggested. "It's full of ships, but they're all in storage. There's no way to get them out of the Stalwart."

"What good does that do us?" Dice boomed. "What good is a ship if we can't fly it?"

"These are all brand new—never used," Beauty told him. "I saw them when I was walking around on this Stalwart."

"If the Reserve Wing got so many ships into that hold, there must be a way to get them out," Davenport remarked. "Where is this hold?"

"It's just beneath this one. I'll show you." Beauty set off down the stairwell, but he didn't lead them to any other landing or any other door. He waved to a solid concrete wall. "The ships are behind here."

"This is stupid," Emmett spat. "Stop screwing around."

"It's no joke. They're in there."

"How can you be sure?" Dice asked. "If there's no way in or out, how did you find out the ships were there?"

Beauty squirmed and didn't answer.

"Tell me this," Dice boomed. "If this is the best we've got, how the hell are we supposed to get in there?"

Beauty grinned at him. "*You* can get in there easily, Dice."

Dice groaned. "Please tell me why I signed up for this."

"What do you have in mind?" Davenport asked Beauty.

"It's simple." He pulled something out of.... somewhere Davenport didn't want to think about. Davenport wouldn't mind living his whole life without ever finding out how Beauty was carrying this stuff around.

He held out a tiny package to Dice. "Take it."

"No!" Dice roared. "No damn way! No way in hell! Don't even think about it!"

"What is it?" Emmett asked.

"It's......" Beauty began.

"I said no!" Dice bellowed. "We're all holding XQs. We can blow the wall. We won't do *that*!"

"What is it?" Davenport held out his hand to Dice. "We'll blow the wall with our XQs. We won't use whatever it is. I just want to know. I'm curious."

Dice looked away and Davenport took the package from Beauty's hands. Davenport turned it over and read the label. It was a Maltese Chipmunk, one of the more popular kinds of candy from the famous Fengu markets.

Emmett read the label over Davenport's shoulder. "What's wrong with that? These things are great."

"Are we done here?" Dice hefted his XQ and turned to the wall. "Am I doing this by myself?"

Beauty plucked the Chipmunk out of Davenport's fingers, but Davenport didn't want to be done. Did Beauty's impish grin mean what Davenport thought it meant? Could something as delicious as Maltese Chipmunks be the secret superweapon to release Dice's inner monster?

The packet vanished somewhere behind Beauty. Emmett turned his weapon to the wall and took his place by Dice's side. That left Davenport and Beauty.

They came forward and all four aimed their weapons at the same spot. Dice opened fire and the other three joined in.

Their shots smashed the wall in and left a smoking hole in front of them. Emmett tiptoed forward, waved the dust cloud away, and peered through. "Well, I'll be damned! He was right!"

Davenport stuck his head through. Beauty wasn't lying. The breach opened into a vast hold full of brand-new ships—Drifters, Nitrols, Vagrants—everything.

"How do we get down there?" Dice asked.

"Like this." Beauty shoved his XQ into Davenport's grasp and clambered through the gap. He vanished into the darkness for a second.

"Great," Dice grumbled. "Now we're trusting this mud-slicker with our...."

Beauty stuck his head out again. "Come on. You can come through now."

Beauty took Davenport's and his own XQs back. Davenport supposed it was up to him to lead the others, so he stuck one leg through and then wedged his whole body into the hole.

Beauty guided him onto a metal ladder leading down to the hangar floor—except that this place wasn't a hangar. Beauty was right about one other thing. There was no way out of here.

Emmett came next. Then Dice nearly brought the whole Reserve Wing down on their heads by getting stuck in the hole that wasn't big enough for him.

He started bellowing again. "Be quiet!" Davenport warned. "Do you want them to come back and start shooting at you again?"

"Shoot me now!" Dice roared. "Just put me out of my god damn misery and be done with it!"

Davenport started climbing up there to take charge of the situation, but Beauty got there first. He turned his XQ backward and smashed the butt into the concrete next to Dice's big shoulders. The mortar gave way and Dice finally got through.

The four friends descended to the floor. "Which one should we take?" Emmett asked.

"How about one each?" Dice suggested. "You take a Bolt. I'll take a Dagger. Davenport can take a Skimmer to make up for the one he lost at Ultra Meridian, and Beauty can take...."

"Shut the hell up, jackass," Davenport snapped. "*You* take a Skimmer out into space and see how you like it."

Dice let out a big, raucous laugh and slammed Davenport hard on the back. "Take it easy, porkchop. You won't be happy without a Drifter, will you?"

"A Nitrol will be the only ship big enough for your fat head."

Dice laughed even louder, but a second later, they all fell silent and listened to a deep, powerful rumble shaking the walls to their left.

Davenport didn't know what was making that noise and he didn't like it. He looked around fast. "Here! This one!"

He dashed on board the nearest Drifter and charged to the cockpit. This Drifter wasn't much different from the *Artemis Rex*, but it lacked the boys' modifications that made the *Artemis Rex* so impressive.

Davenport pushed those thoughts out of his mind. The *Artemis Rex* wasn't here. It was long gone and he couldn't count on the boys to bail him out right now.

He slipped into the pilot's cradle where Bandit usually sat. He fired up the engines, the controls switched on, and he read the ship's identity profile. *Dryad Circe*. That was good enough for him.

Someone sat down in the tactical cradle. Davenport expected it to be Emmett. He had to check a second time when he saw Beauty powering up the tactical controls and working them with expert precision.

Another low boom rocked the hold. "What the hell is that?" Emmett asked from the back of the cockpit.

"You might want to buckle up!" Davenport called. "You and Dice get to the accessory cradles and be ready to fight us out of here!"

Emmett vanished and Beauty powered the tactical Howitzers. Davenport cycled up the engines and the howl of engine noise echoed through the hold. If this didn't bring the Reserve Wing running, nothing would.

He lifted off the deck and swiveled the ship toward the wall where the noise was coming from. The ship's instruments read the area around this hold.

That wall opened into space and a bunch of other ships were fighting out there. They were the same Daggers, Drifters, and Nitrols he'd seen fighting outside the hangar, but he couldn't identify any of them from in here.

He wheeled the *Dryad Circe* toward the wall. "Stand by to fire on my......"

A catastrophic explosion blasted the wall apart and piles of debris dropped from the hole. Davenport stared through it at a large ship hovering beyond the breach. It was the *Vindicator*, Deacon Pritchard's ship.

Pritchard stared back at Davenport from the ship's bridge. Pritchard was alone and five other Drifters guarded his tail while he blew the hold open.

He motioned Davenport forward and peeled the *Vindicator* out of the way. Daggers pelted across the gap trading shots with more attack Drifters. All their identity profiles belonged to the Wide Patrol.

Davenport hit the throttle and sprinted out of the *Rambler*. He flew straight into a blistering shower of fire from the Stalwart. A shitload of other Stalwarts moved in to pound the Wide Patrol to smithereens.

Four Daggers attacked the *Fortitude*. "Get off me, you jackasses!" Treese snarled.

"Hold tight, John!" Yarborough yelled. "These cocksuckers don't know what's good for 'em."

The *Conquest* zoomed in to defend Treese and the *Celestis* raced over to join the other two deputies. "I'll help you out," De Rosa added. "We'll learn 'em."

De Rosa and Yarborough charged to the *Fortitude's* aid, but two more Stalwarts hemmed them in. They hammered all three Drifters with heavy fire.

"We're pinned down!" Yarborough hollered.

"I'm on you!" Bolander wheeled around the first Stalwart, but one Drifter couldn't make a dent in even one of the big ships.

The *Prometheus Vox* tumbled out of nowhere and Healey added his fire to the battle. "Get the hell out of here, Sheriff!" Pritchard called to Davenport. "Get your ass clear! We'll hold them off!"

"Where's the *Artemis Rex*? Where are the rest of my people?"

"Don't worry about them," Healey replied. "They're on their way back to the Needle. I'll deal with them when I get there. I can hide them so the Reserve Wing never finds them."

"What about......?"

Another Stalwart ambushed the *Stormspike*. The *Fortitude*, the *Conquest*, and the *Celestis* all had to break off what they were doing to save Bolander from certain destruction.

"Go, Sheriff!" Pritchard yelled. "You won't get another chance."

Davenport pulled away. He tried to circle the battle and almost collided with another flock of Stalwarts moving in.

He wheeled back and had to carve his way through the battle to find a different path to freedom. Emmett, Dice, and Beauty all fired their Howitzers as fast as they could targeting Daggers on all sides.

The incoming Stalwarts circled the Wide Patrol with the *Prometheus Vox* trapped in the mix. Yells and orders echoed in Davenport's ears.

Davenport spotted an opening between the Stalwarts. Clear stars dotted the black sky over there. He could break away and leave these brave souls to take the fall.

He yanked the helm into reverse and sprinted for the nearest Stalwart. "Bring your cradles around to the starboard side and target the main generator"

"Are you stupid?" Dice bellowed. "That will blow the ship in our faces."

"Do it!" Davenport bent low over the controls and cut in hard near the Stalwart's hull. This Drifter didn't respond as tightly as the *Artemis Rex*. Then again, Davenport didn't have Bandit's flying skills. He only prayed it would be enough to finish the job.

He swooped low with Daggers hot on his heels. "Fire!" he ordered. "Hit it hard!"

Dice and Emmett opened up and Beauty joined in. Davenport couldn't shoot with them. Holding the helm steady took all his arm strength.

The Howitzers belched and their shots pounded the generator. It erupted in a plume of fire, but the *Dryad Circe* was moving too fast.

The inferno enveloped the pursuit Daggers and a deafening whoop went up from Dice's cradle. "Hell yeah! Eat my dust, you bastards!"

"Get us clear!" Beauty shrieked. "The Stalwart is going to blow!"

"Wide Patrol—get away from this Stalwart!" Davenport called to anyone who might be listening.

"No!" Pritchard countered. "Straight into it, boys! Full throttle! You, too, Marshall! It's the only way to lose them!"

The Wide Patrol wheeled hard and the deputies gunned their engines to the maximum. The *Prometheus Vox* hugged them close in a tight formation as the Stalwart shuddered and then detonated in a catastrophic boom.

The shockwave hit the *Dryad Circe* from the side and pelted the Drifter clear of the battle. The Wide Patrol blasted through the exploding wreckage with flames billowing around every ship.

"That's your cue, Sheriff!" Pritchard ordered. "Make tracks while you can."

"More Stalwarts coming in from Macron Calypso!" Treese announced. "Get your big boy pants on, folks."

"You heard me, Sheriff," Pritchard repeated. "Get your ass out of here now."

"Yes, Sir." Davenport turned away. He could already see too many Stalwarts advancing to join the battle. A dozen more still hung around the *Rambler* like a bad smell.

He would have liked to stick around and make sure Healey and the Wide Patrol made it out of here, but he had more important things to do.

The new ships formed a thick band of attack vessels across the sky. He couldn't go that way.

He pulled away in the only direction left to him and gunned his engines for Ultra Meridian. At least the planet was deserted with no other ships around.

He had to put plenty of distance between himself and the Reserve Wing. If he was lucky, he just might be able to locate the third component before Admiral Joyce caught up with him.

Chapter 35

Lyons wrinkled her nose at the controls. "Are we really coming back to this dust heap?"

"I don't see any ships in the atmosphere. Ultra Meridian is all clear."

"What does that tell us?" Lyons asked. "Why are we here?"

"To hide the Ithium. Let's contact the Armageddon Core."

Lyons laid a hand on Fiddler's arm. "Hold it. Not so fast."

"Why not? The Ithium will be safer with them than it will be anywhere else."

Lyons made a face. "You'll excuse me if I don't believe that. The Reserve Wing knows about the Armageddon Core."

"The Reserve Wing knows about the *Echo Omicron*, too. No one knows Ultra Meridian better than the Armageddon Core."

"Which is exactly why someone will target the Armageddon Core first if they want to find the Ithium."

"No one will target them because no one knows the Ithium is on this planet."

"I have a better idea." Lyons pointed at a chart on Fiddler's controls. "We can hide it there."

Fiddler's eyes popped staring at the spot. "That's the Vultus Wind Mines. We would have to be out of our minds to hide the Ithium there. It's Typhon Elexor territory."

"That's exactly why no one will expect us to hide it there. No one will look for it there, either."

Fiddler steered past the Ultra Meridian jail. The reconstructed jail and surrounding plane were completely deserted. The area didn't look right after so much recent activity here.

She flew over the hills and past the Khuntan Reserve. The reserve led into thousands of miles of dusty canyons carved into the planet's desert surface.

"This is nuts," Fiddler muttered. "You know that, right?"

"At least we'll be on a planet with your friends."

Fiddler sighed. "All right. If you're sure.... Here we go. We're crossing into Typhon Elexor country."

Lyons slipped her arms into her safety harness and grabbed the ship's laser cannons. Fiddler adjusted her grip so she controlled the helm with one hand and could shoot with the other. Two guns would be better than one considering the danger the two women were flying into.

The ship lifted over the canyon rim and Fiddler saw the Vultus Wind Mines ahead. Massive wind turbines rotated in the driving wind that scoured the planet. The windmills stuck up vertically on the plateaus and their fins revolved in a rapid whirl.

Masked aliens worked the mills and more of them manned giant laser cannons dotting the landscape. No other spacecraft flew around out here. Those cannons made sure no braindead intruders ventured anywhere near the Vultus Wind Mines.

"Hold on!" Fiddler hollered and dove the ship on a collision course for the windmills. The cannons erupted spouting huge lasers at the ship.

Fiddler angled her wings sideways and veered between the shots, but she only succeeded in flying into more cannon fire. The big guns swiveled into position all over the field.

Lasers winked past the cockpit. Fiddler had to maneuver every which way to stop the aliens from shooting the ship out of the sky.

She tilted dangerously close to one of the windmills. It dwarfed the ship by a hundred times. The mill towered to the sky and the fins almost sliced the ship in half.

She peeled off to starboard and almost smashed the ship into one of the cannons. The masked gunner on the seat lambasted her with dozens of shots. He never flinched or pulled his weapon away.

He smashed the cockpit in. Broken glass stung Fiddler in the face and a tempest wind slammed both women back in their seats. Lyons shrieked something that Fiddler didn't catch.

"Are you shooting or what?" Fiddler roared.

"I *am* shooting!" Lyons screamed back. "Are you trying to get us killed?"

Fiddler didn't have time to answer. More cannons wheeled in her direction, and a second later, a bunch of Vagrants launched from behind the mountains.

Fiddler didn't see where they came from before they all came shrieking in to attack her. Their lasers joined the general mayhem of cannon fire blasting from the surface.

Fiddler threw herself hard to port to dodge them and blinked in stupid shock at a massive windmill right in front of her. She dove straight for it with not a second to avoid it.

She ripped the controls back to starboard and banked. She dipped her wings vertically and skimmed between the giant fins. Lyons yelled something, but the whole maneuver lasted a split second.

The ship sprinted out the other side and the Vagrants piled in with a vengeance. "Please God tell me you didn't plan this!" Lyons bellowed.

"Something like this!" Fiddler returned. "Get in the back and arm up!"

"Don't you dare! I'll kill you myself!"

"Not if they don't kill us first! Find us some weapons, goggles, and masks. Hurry up! We don't have much time!"

Lyons muttered something else that Fiddler didn't hear. Fiddler turned back to her task and Lyons unbuckled her harness.

Fiddler tumbled between the windmills doing her best not to crash into them, the laser cannons, and the Vagrants hounding her everywhere. The Vagrants unloaded on her.

She pulled around another windmill and flew into a curtain of lasers coming from another cannon bank. Typhon Elexor wasn't taking any chances on defending this field.

Of course not. The Vultus Wind Mines were way too valuable. They were the foundation of Typhon Elexor's wealth, influence, and power.

Fiddler hardened herself for her finally assault, punched the engines, and flew straight into the cannon fire. The Vagrants closed the gap pounding her hull. She would have one chance at this. If these people destroyed her ship, the Ithium would be released right here at Ultra Meridian.

She locked her teeth and sprinted right into the enemy guns. They laid down a crushing barrage and the Vagrants howled in from behind.

She burned up within a few feet of the cannons. They couldn't hit her as well here, not without turning far enough toward the center that they risked hitting each other.

She threw all her weight to port and smashed the helm down hard. The ship screeched sideways and she crushed the throttle. She zoomed past the stunned cannoneers with all their lasers tracking her.

Three Vagrants flew into their own cannon fire and two of them blew. One incinerating fuselage cartwheeled into the cannons and another somersaulted away to smash into the nearest windmill.

The whole windmill exploded in a gargantuan column of fire. It licked the atmosphere and then a colossal boom blasted the whole understructure to smithereens.

Whole blocks of bedrock blew out of the plateau underneath the windmill. Debris and boulder-sized chunks hurtled into the nearby mills. They all started blowing in a domino chain down the plateau.

"What the hell are you doing?" Lyons shrieked. "Typhon Elexor will kill you for this!"

"Did you find the goggles and masks?" Fiddler hollered over her shoulder.

"Yes, but……"

"Strap in—now! Brace of impact!"

"Impact!" Lyons roared. "Are you crazy?"

"Just crazy enough to survive on this damn planet! This is your last warning!"

Lyons staggered back to the front and collapsed in her seat. She barely got her harness on before the Vagrants struck without mercy.

Fiddler rocketed away from the windmills and raced out over the maze of canyons. The Vagrants hounded her all the way and smashed her with dozens of lasers.

"Are you sure about this?" Lyons yelled.

"Yes! Here we go!"

Fiddler slammed the throttle all the way down, but she was already flying as fast as this ship would go. It streaked over the canyons leaving the windmills far behind, but not the Vagrants.

They crawled up on her no matter how fast she flew. Canyons twisted and twined below her. She could go down there and probably lose these Vagrants, but she didn't want that.

Another brutal smash struck the tail and the ship wheeled out of control. "Hey!" Lyons yelled.

Fiddler ignored her. She swerved to starboard and slalomed back to port. The Vagrants wavered for a second and then surrounded her. They hammered her with lasers until, inevitably, they struck the port engine.

The engine detonated with a brutal crash and the whole craft dipped violently to port. It started to plummet and all the Vagrants attacked in force.

They carved off the port wing and then a vicious strike caved in the cockpit. Scorching flames blasted in Fiddler's face. The impact tore her hands off the controls and smacked her head back hard in her seat.

She must have blacked out for a second because she came to being dragged across the floor. Lyons lugged Fiddler by the jacket, slid her across the compartment, and dumped her by the hatch.

Fiddler tried to look around. "What the......?"

"Stay down!" Lyons snapped. "You got us into this. Just lie down and cover your head."

Fiddler didn't understand until she laid down. Once she did, she got a glimpse through the cockpit window.

The ship was flying in a lightning streak through some random canyon. No one sat at the controls and the helm wobbled dangerously from side to side.

Lyons flopped down next to Fiddler and shoved something into Fiddler's hand. Fiddler looked down at a heavy cargo strap anchored to the bulkhead.

Fiddler glanced back at the cockpit window. The ship was plummeting nose first into a solid cliff wall.

"Now!" Lyons bellowed.

Fiddler hurled herself sideways. She rolled over and over to wrap the strap around as much of her body as she could. Lyons threw herself the opposite way and tangled herself in another strap on the compartment's opposite side.

Fiddler flung herself against the hull just in time. An earth-shaking impact yanked the strap tight around her. It crushed her bones as the ship hit the wall at full speed.

Fiddler screamed and threw her one free arm over her head. Random stuff pelted her from all over the compartment. The ship slammed down hard and everything went quiet.

Fiddler dared to open her eyes to find Lyons scrambling to untie herself. "Come on! Hurry! We have to go before they come back."

Fiddler got busy. She rolled the other way and kicked off the strap. She pounced on the mask and goggles lying near her, but Lyons was more concerned with the weapons locker.

She took down laser rifles and started handing them to Fiddler. "We need to be ready to fight."

"We need these more." Fiddler pulled on her goggles and then her mask.

"You're stupid," Lyons muttered and took down more rifles and a largish cannon. She paid no attention to the mask and goggles.

Fiddler took the weapons Lyons offered her and then Lyons cracked the rear hatch.

The two women darted outside aiming their weapons at the skies. They ran into a pelting, driving wind peppered with stinging sand.

It immediately started that familiar scouring sound on Fiddler's goggles. It bit through her clothes. Not even her leather jacket and mask could stop it from infiltrating every part of her body.

The Vagrants came shrieking back the instant the women got outside. Enemy craft wove up the canyons on a dead course for the crashed ship.

Fiddler snatched Lyons's arm. Lyons couldn't see anything in this wind and Fiddler didn't try to talk to her.

Fiddler yanked Lyons under the fuselage to hide from the Vagrants. The enemy ships screamed past, banked at the head of the canyon, and came bombing back.

Fiddler saw them coming. She'd seen far too much of this in her time at Ultra Meridian.

She ducked under the wreck towing Lyons with her. Fiddler burst out on the other side and took off running. She never lost her grip on Lyons and charged straight into the biting wind.

Lyons stumbled, but Fiddler didn't let her go. They escaped their hiding place just as the Vagrants unloaded on the ruined ship.

The whole vessel detonated in a hail of laser fire. Fiddler sprang sideways into a hollow carved out of the wall. She hid there for a split second while the Vagrants whizzed past and dove in for another pass.

Fiddler heard Lyons yelling at her, but Fiddler couldn't make out the words and didn't try. One of the two women knew how to survive at Ultra Meridian and it wasn't Lyons. Fiddler had to take over.

The Vagrants wheeled into the sky to make their third pass. Fiddler stuck her head out and spotted what she wanted. Another side chasm cut into the cliff up ahead. That was the best she could hope for.

She took a fresh grip on Lyons, dashed into the open, and sprinted for the gap. Lyons staggered again. She couldn't see with all the sand in her eyes.

Fiddler didn't stop until she cut into the chasm and shoved Lyons in front of her. "Go!" Fiddler hissed. "Keep going! Don't stop!"

Lyons stumbled up the incline climbing deeper into the chasm. The walls converged to a tight crack. Even Fiddler had to turn sideways to fit through it.

She kept prodding Lyons farther and farther up the slope. Lyons tried to turn around. "I don't hear them anymore...."

"Keep going!" Fiddler whispered. "And keep your voice down. They'll hear you!"

She herded Lyons up and up. The chasm twisted and wound for miles until it finally angled sideways into a shelf. Fiddler followed it and located a cave the wind had etched between this tiny pathway and the main canyon.

The two women collapsed inside and Lyons slumped. "Of all the places we could go to hide the Ithium, we had to come here."

"It was your idea," Fiddler pointed out. "It's a good thing we got away from them when we did. Look."

She flattened herself on her stomach at the far end of the cave. Lyons came over and crawled up next to her. This opening gave them a perfect vantage point to see the canyon floor for miles in both directions.

A whole pack of Vagrants landed not far away. Masked aliens emerged, surrounded the crashed ship, and advanced aiming weapons at it.

"If we were down there, they would have killed us," Fiddler murmured.

"They would only kill us because you attacked the Wind Mines. Did you HAVE to?"

"Yes, I had to. This is the best place to hide the Ithium."

Lyons snorted again. "I didn't mean you should crash the ship."

"I crashed the ship to make them think we were dead. They would never stop tracking us if they thought we survived."

Lyons flopped over on her back and folded her elbow under her head. "You were right. I should have taken a mask and goggles."

Fiddler sat up and studied her. "You know, Lyons, you aren't so bad for a smuggler."

"I wasn't trying to win your good opinion of me. Trust me."

Fiddler had to laugh. Then she took the second mask and set of goggles out of her pocket and handed them to Lyons. "Be glad you did. Here. You're gonna need them."

Lyons blinked at the mask and goggles and then she blinked at Fiddler with a very different look on her face. "Thanks. You didn't have to do that. I wouldn't have blamed you if you left them behind."

"We're crewmates now."

"We aren't crewmates of anything. I don't have a ship and you would never let me into the Armageddon Core. I'm too tall."

Fiddler laughed even harder. "Let's put it this way. You don't have the *Echo Omicron* and neither of us has the *Artemis Rex*, so maybe we'll just have to call ourselves Davenport's crew."

"I can go along with that—assuming we ever see Davenport again."

"I'm sure we will." Fiddler took the wrapped box out of her pocket. "We just have to figure out where to put this."

"What did you have in mind?"

"My idea was to hide it under one of the windmills."

Lyons only nodded. "I thought you'd say that. That means sneaking back up to the field and hiding it there without any of Typhon Elexor's people seeing us."

"We can do it at night." Fiddler set the box aside and stretched out against the bare rock. "We should get some sleep before then."

She rolled up her mask and put it under her head to act as a pillow. She wished now that she had some water, but that would have to wait. The first task was to hide the Ithium and get away from Typhon Elexor alive.

Lyons curled onto her side, pillowed her head on her arm, and shut her eyes. In a few minutes, her breathing lengthened, but Fiddler didn't fall asleep.

She studied Lyons for a long time. Everything that happened since Fiddler left Ultra Meridian changed what she thought she knew about herself and the people around her.

She trusted the *Echo Omicron* crew just as much as she trusted the Chorion Team. She trusted Lyons with her life, but in the end, they were all Davenport's crew.

Everything hinged on Davenport. When all was said and done, Davenport's influence told Fiddler what to do. She had to do what was best—not for Davenport himself, but for the mission.

His mission was to keep the Ithium out of the wrong hands. He would want her to do the same thing, no matter what.

She pushed herself off the ground and sat up. She watched Lyons sleeping for a long time. Whatever Fiddler was going to do, she better do it now.

She untied the fabric bag and opened the box. The Ithium cartridge lay inside. It was still intact.

She and Dice had been right about one thing. The fewer people who knew where the Ithium was, the safer it was. She and Dice did right to hide it on HTWV-983. She and Lyons only moved it because the Cannibals and Mexia's people were there and Mexia's people were looking for it.

The Ithium would have been safe on HTWV-983 otherwise. Now it was at Ultra Meridian. It was a whole lot more accessible here to a whole lot of people who wanted to get it.

She lifted out the cartridge, shut the box, and tied it up in the bag again. She left the box on the floor and got to her feet.

She strode down the cave tunnel and paused to look back. Lyons still lay curled on her side, sound asleep. Lyons hadn't moved.

Fiddler continued deeper into the tunnel. The wind had carved indentations in the walls. Different sized pockets dotted the tunnel's sides.

Fiddler halted halfway to the entrance and listened again. She could just hear Lyons's breathing over the steady whisper of the wind outside.

Fiddler walked over to the wall and located a small skull-sized pocket at her eye level. She set the Ithium cartridge inside and covered it with soft sand. No one could see it. No one except for her would ever know it was there. If she got killed, no one would ever find it, not even Davenport.

She went back to the cave and sat down in the same place. She stuffed the wrapped box in her pocket and leaned back to watch Lyons sleeping. Lyons's cheeks and lips sagged. She was out cold.

The comforting sound of the sand beating the canyon walls lulled Fiddler into a trance. She started to drift off and she didn't try to stay awake anymore. She was back home, back at Ultra Meridian where she knew everything and everyone. Only Davenport was missing.

Chapter 36

F iddler snapped awake to Lyons shaking her. "Wake up. It's dark."

Fiddler looked around at the dusty cave before she realized what Lyons was talking about.

The sun had gone down over the canyons outside. Stars twinkled beyond the cavern opening. They barely gave enough light for Fiddler to see.

"You have the Ithium, right?" Lyons asked.

"Uh.... yeah." Fiddler pulled the box out of her pocket and looked at it. Her brain clicked remembering everything that happened in the last few weeks.

"Do you know how to get back up to the Vultus Wind Mines? We won't be able to talk once we get up there. We need to decide on our strategy before we go."

"You're right." Fiddler got to her feet and put the box back in her pocket. "And yes, I know how to get there."

"Typhon Elexor will have guards stationed around the windmills. We'll need to neutralize them—silently. Once we clear the way, you can hide the Ithium."

Fiddler nodded. "Sounds good. Let's go."

"Aren't you going to argue with me? Are you just going to go along with this?"

"Why should I argue? I was going to suggest the same thing."

Lyons scowled at her in the dark.

"Do you want me to argue? I can come up with another strategy if you really want me to."

Lyons humphed and turned away. She started walking back up the tunnel toward the chasm where the two women entered this cave.

Fiddler pulled her goggles over her eyes and put on her mask before she got outside. Lyons forgot and had to stop at the entrance to put on her gear.

Fiddler snorted to herself, but she didn't say anything. Lyons would learn the ways of Ultra Meridian soon enough. No one spent much time on this planet without learning the hard way.

Fiddler suppressed laughter at Lyons's appearance. She didn't look nearly so stunning in her goggles and mask.

Fiddler walked away to hide her amusement and headed up the chasm winding deeper and deeper into the canyons. The two women walked for over an hour.

The path kept climbing and Lyons fell behind a few times. Fiddler had to stop and wait for her, but Fiddler didn't comment on that, either. Lyons wasn't a hardened desert rat. Fiddler couldn't expect her to become one overnight.

Even Lyons for company would be better than facing this project alone. No one survived alone at Ultra Meridian. Fiddler couldn't imagine how Davenport managed on his own for so many years, especially when the residents hated him as much as they did.

She finally climbed to the very top. The chasm got steeper at the end. She and Lyons had to clamber hand over hand to scale the last couple hundred feet.

Fiddler swung her leg over the rim and hauled herself onto the plateau. Then she crouched down and helped pull Lyons up.

The two women panted there for several minutes searching the darkness while they caught their breath.

Impenetrable night blanketed the planet. Not a wink of light interrupted the blackness except for one hilltop in the distance.

Searchlights swept the desert in all directions. The windmills kept rotating and spinning around the clock.

Masked people moved between the windmills and the guards all carried weapons. Fiddler bumped Lyons's shoulder and silently set off to cross the plateau. They couldn't even talk to each other to pass the time.

They walked for two more hours before they got to the Vultus Wind Mines. Fiddler dodged sideways and hunkered in a side chasm that dropped into the plateau. She plastered herself against the walls and peeked out.

"This is it," she whispered to Lyons. "We'll split up here. Make sure you stay out of the light. Get onto the field as quick as you can and eliminate as many guards and cannon gunners as you can."

Lyons nodded, but she didn't answer. They both knew what they had to do.

Fiddler waited until the searchlight swiveled past her hiding place. As soon as it passed her, she sprinted into the darkness moving fast. She skimmed the ground and darted behind one of the windmills.

The masked alien guards patrolled everywhere. She couldn't even see what species they were.

She held her breath watching and counting down the seconds. One of them marched past her hiding place and she struck without warning.

She waited until the guard walked past her. Then she sprang out behind him, grabbed him by the head, and snapped his neck.

She guided his limp body to the ground and dragged him into the shadows behind the windmill. She squatted there trying to hear over the pounding of her heart. She didn't have a moment to wait before another guard came toward her from the other direction.

She skimmed around the windmill's other side and had to cower out of sight when the next searchlight pivoted in her direction.

She followed it all the way around the windmill and found the second guard bending over his dead friend.

Fiddler pounced on him. She couldn't let him raise the alarm. She broke his neck, too, and left him lying on top of her first victim. Maybe this growing pile of bodies was the best bait to catch the rest of them.

She stole a peek out from behind the windmill. The searchlights wheeled toward the cannons and Fiddler spotted a black shape sailing through the darkness. It whizzed from one cannon to the next.

The gunners dropped from their seats and vanished into the gloom. They wouldn't be shooting anything tonight.

The sight gave Fiddler new energy. Breaking necks from hidden locations was taking too long.

She set off across the field on a beeline for the nearest guard. She didn't even try to stop him from seeing her.

He rotated his weapon to his shoulder and his chest expanded preparing to demand what she was doing there. She couldn't let him call out.

She stormed up to him, grabbed his weapon, and slammed it back into his face. It cracked his goggles and his skull snapped back. She rushed him the rest of the way and twisted his head violently to the right.

She didn't have time to hide the body before a gunshot went off right behind her. The shot brushed her hair and gunshots rang out all over the field.

She bolted for the nearest windmill as dozens of guards flooded the area. This wasn't the way she planned to take the mines, but what difference did it make in the end?

She dashed around another windmill. Guards converged from all over the field. They all headed for where the shots broke out.

She used that to her advantage, snuck around her windmill, and crept up behind them.

She straightened up behind two of them, cracked their heads together, and snapped the neck of a third guard who came near her hiding place.

She was just starting to enjoy herself when more shots erupted in the darkness. Fiddler braced herself to run for her life when she spotted Lyons storming across the field from the gun placements.

Lyons didn't try to hide and she had completely abandoned the plan to keep quiet. She pivoted an XQ at the guards. The weapon looked an awful lot like the ones the guards carried.

Lyons blasted three guards away and advanced aiming at the others. Ten men stood against her.

Fiddler reacted without thinking. She jumped on the nearest guard from behind, snapped his neck, and darted down the line attacking at top speed.

Lyons unloaded on the others, and in half a second, the two women had brought down everyone who might try to stop them.

Lyons pulled off her mask and goggles to say something and instantly changed her mind when the wind hit her in the face. "Damn it!"

Fiddler searched the area while Lyons got her gear back on. No one came. The two women had the Vultus Wind Mines to themselves.

Lyons jammed her weapon to her shoulder and pivoted with her back to Fiddler. "Do it! Hide the goods now. I'll cover you."

Fiddler took a second to make sure the field was clear. She stumbled over to the nearest windmill and yanked the bagged box from her pocket.

She rotated it in her fingers for a second. The cloth bag covering the box had become dirty, frayed, and misshapen since the *Artemis Rex* crew took it to Sacron Enigma.

Lyons backed up a few more steps and checked over her shoulder to see what Fiddler was doing. She watched Fiddler squat down by the windmill's understructure and dig out a hollow in the sand.

The windmill rested on a giant reinforced steel frame rooted in the bedrock. Thirty giant girders plunged into the rock. The windmill's understructure anchored to the girders by enormous bolts sunk in the thick steel.

Fiddler hollowed out the sand and stashed the bundle in the gap between the anchor plates and the rock beneath. She buried everything in sand and covered it up. No one could see it from the surface.

Lyons kept her back to Fiddler, but Lyons kept glancing behind her to watch the procedure. She knew exactly where Fiddler hid that bag with the box inside it.

Fiddler stood up and hoisted an XQ out of one of the dead guards' arms. She and Lyons collected as many weapons as they could carry.

"You ready to go?" Lyons asked.

Fiddler nodded. She had no more reason to stay here. She and Lyons headed south across the plateau. They made it to the first chasm and Fiddler paused to look back.

The wind was already erasing the footprints leading to where she stashed the box. By the time she and Lyons got to the canyon bottom, all trace of their visit would have vanished entirely. Only the guards' bodies would remain to show that she and Lyons had ever been here.

The two women dropped down into a different chasm. The downward slope led back to the canyon floor. The wind wasn't as bad here, but Fiddler kept her goggles and mask on no matter what.

They walked in silence as the sun rose over the desert. Fiddler went in front and Lyons fell in behind her on the long trek back to Ultra Meridian. The two women had many miles to cover before they saw a friendly face again.

End of Book 2.

Keep Reading.....

Keep Reading

Ultra Meridian Series: Book 3: Armageddon Core

Nothing is what it seems in the battle to keep a deadly weapon of annihilation away from countless criminal elements who want to unleash it and wipe out the galaxy. Too bad some of these criminal elements are hiding right inside the Confederate Reserve Wing.

Sheriff Mace Davenport and his friends get scattered across known space fighting for their lives and battling deadly alien creatures for the fate of the world. The most dangerous enemies are their own people and they're all after Davenport's crew. The problem just got a whole lot more complicated when the crew discovers that the weapon consists of not just one catastrophic element but three of them.

The line between friend and enemy continues to blur as the crew hurtles toward the ultimate confrontation that will leave the billions of lives in jeopardy.

You can find it at your favorite book retailer.

Sign Up Once--Get all Theo Mann's free books including brand new releases

S ign Up Once--Get all Theo Mann's free books including brand new releases

Humanity on the brink of annihilation.

A mysterious package, a corrupt officer, and a conspiracy that goes all the way to the top? What could possibly go wrong?

When a routine mission goes horribly wrong, Warrant Officer Ewing Archer and a handful of faithful friends get trapped in a battle to save the last survivors of Earth.

The human race has abandoned the ecological disaster of Earth. Now all that remains is a network of interconnected ships, stations, and satellites surrounding the planet.

But when war breaks out, Archer becomes a firebrand that could destroy it all....or save it.

Sign up at www.theomann.com to read it for free

About Theo Mann

I write 70 books per year—and yes, before you ask, all these books are my original creative work. Nothing written under my name is AI-generated or ghostwritten because I write better than AI and any ghostwriter out there.

People don't read fiction for entertainment or to escape from reality. People read fiction to see their humanity reflected in another person's character and story.

This is my promise to you. When you read my books, you'll see your own humanity reflected in the characters and stories. I take this commitment to my readers very seriously. My books are an intimate form of communication between us. I would never disrespect my readers by turning that over to a machine or another writer. This is my bond between me and you as my reader.

I write 20,000 words per day as my daily work output. If anyone with a public platform would like to challenge me to prove this in a controlled environment, feel free to contact me on this website's contact page.

I worked as a professional ghostwriter for fifteen years. Now I'm on a mission to set a Guinness World Record by writing 700 books over the next ten years and 1400 books over the next twenty years, all originally written by me. See my website for the full book list.

I'm also the author of *Proof for the Existence of God* and the *Crimes Against Fiction* blog. You can find all my nonfiction work at www.crimes-against-fiction.com.

If you have a story idea, or if you would like me to explore a series in more depth, or if you'd like me to explore a character by writing a spinoff series about that character or world, leave me a message on my website's contact page. I answer all reader emails, so ask me anything, tell me what you liked and didn't like, and let me know where you'd like your favorite series to go. I would love to hear your ideas and find out what you'd like to read next.

Find out more at www.theomann.com.

Also by Theo Mann (so far)

www.ingramcontent.com/pod-product-compliance
Lightning Source LLC
Chambersburg PA
CBHW070511030726
47503CB00004B/1238